The Case of the Dead Dowager

(Michaela McPherson Book 2)

Books by Judith Lucci

Michaela McPherson Mysteries
The Case of Dr. Dude
The Case of the Dead Dowager
The Case of the Man Overboard
The Case of the Very Dead Lawyer
The Case of the Missing Parts

Alex Destephano Novels
Chaos at Crescent City Medical Center
The Imposter
Viral Intent
Toxic New Year
Evil: Finding St. Germaine
RUN For Your Life
Demons Among Us – Coming 2020

Dr. Sonia Amon Medical Thrillers
Shatter Proof
Delusion Proof
Fool Proof
Tamper Proof – Coming 2020

Artzy Chicks Mysteries
The Most Wonderful Crime of the Year
The Most Awfullest Crime of the Year
The Most Glittery Crime of the Year
The Most Slippery Crime of the Year

Other Books
Beach Traffic: The Ocean Can Be Deadly
Ebola: What You Must Know to Stay Safe
Meandering, Musing & Inspiration for the Soul

The Case of the Dead Dowager

A Michaela McPherson Mystery

A NOVEL BY

Judith Lucci

Bluestone Valley Publishing

Harrisonburg, Virginia

ISBN-13: 978-1539822318

ACKNOWLEDGEMENTS

Thank you for supporting my writing through the years. It's because of you that I write!

Chapter 1

"Perfecto, this stuff looks flawless," Boris said in his thickly accented voice as he held a test tube to the light. The Russian smiled broadly, his thin lips stretched across his decayed teeth and skeletal face. The light from the window outlined his permanently crushed, but healed frontal skull that gave him the appearance of the monster he was. He agitated the test tube between his fingers and reexamined its contents. It was a masterpiece. "There's enough here to kill everybody in Yankee Stadium and all the cops in Richmond," he predicted from his tall, though stooped height of six feet, five inches. He reached for a small glass container and transferred a portion of the five gallons to a laboratory beaker. He held the larger quantity up to the window and examined the liquid. "And look, there's no residue in the bottom and the fluid is clear." He turned to his friend and gushed, "Perfecto, tovarich, perfecto!"

Snake laughed and clapped his partner on the back. "Way to go, tall guy. Good deal. You know we gotta maximize our efforts. Neither one of us wants to work hard or take extra chances, especially now since they're lookin' for me anyway." Snake moved closer to the glass carboy and smiled as he saw the colorless, odorless and tasteless five gallon drum of liquid. "Man that looks good. Does it smell?"

Boris bent his shiny, bald head forward and sniffed deeply. "No, not that I can tell. I can't smell anything, but I haven't got a good nose anyway. You give it a sniff and see what you think," he said as he gestured towards the liquid.

Snake moved next to the large glass container and noticed other small beakers and test tubes of fluid sitting to the side. Each container was labeled and numbered. "You must've been a hell of a chemist back in the day," he remarked as he finger-combed his greasy black hair off his face. Sometimes he wore it in a ponytail, but he hadn't pulled it back today. He bent over and sniffed the carboy. "Nah. Nothing." He shook his head and said, "I can't smell nuthin' either. Good job, my man," he said enthusiastically, a slow smile spreading across his swarthy, pockmarked face. "You're a real scientist."

Boris lit a cigarette, coughed and said, "Man, you have no idea of the stuff I can do. You ain't seen nothing. I got more killing recipes than Carter's got little liver pills." He smiled ominously and showed his rotten teeth. Snake felt a tingle run up his spine. *This guy even looked like the monster his reputation claimed he was.* He decided to watch himself carefully around Boris and never give him the upper hand.

Snake nodded, "Yeah. Well, I got plenty of chances to see your talents this week!" Once again, he checked out his partner and sized him up. He was a dangerous, unpredictable, scary dude.

"Yeah, but I'm never tellin' you much," Boris assured him. "There'll most likely be one day I'll wanna kill you," he admitted, the broad grin again slicing through his pale, skeletal face. *This guy's serious. He is crazy.*

Snake ignored him and brushed invisible lint off the front of his blue scrubs. "Shut-up, man. No need for talk like that." He knew Boris was a madman, a wacko. His handlers had told him to be careful. Money had been the motivator and he knew he could take good care of himself. His reputation spoke for him. He had no idea who his bosses were and he knew little about the Russian scientist. Rumor suggested he'd long been a mortal enemy of the United States and other stories suggested he was a murderer. Snake didn't want to push the point. He picked up the container of fluid and placed it in front of him, his face a mask of evil.

"You know what, Boris old man, I'm thinking we can wipe out an army… or at least a police force with this stuff. Whaddaya think?" He gave him a half smile.

Boris stared at him, his cold gray eyes, bony face and crushed skull glistened in the light from the barred windows. His eyes roamed the room to the large aquarium that housed all kinds of prickly fish and marine life. The huge tank glowed eerily in the fading light. Boris stared at his fish fondly, gave Snake a strange look and said in a quiet voice, "Of course we can. I already said that. What do you think the plan is?"

Chapter 2

"Dottie, where did you get that marvelous Italian leather bag? I'd die for one like that," Camilla Rothrock gushed in her drawn out Alabama accent. "I've just gotta have one."

Dottie held up her newest leather pocketbook so all of her best friends could ooh and ah over it. "I had it made especially for me in Italy," she bragged. The bag was beautiful, soft and buttery between her fingers. "I love it. It has a special gun pocket stitched in so I can carry my Glock," she said proudly as she pulled her holstered gun out of her purse and swiftly returned it before anyone noticed.

Margaret Massie glared from across the table. "Oh for heaven's sake, Dottie! Give it a rest! Whatever do you need to carry a gun around for? We're a bunch of old women. No one is gonna mess with us," she admonished as she rolled her eyes and batted her false eyelashes at her best friend of many years. "We're hardly ever left on our own."

"Margaret Massie, how can you possibly be so short-sighted?" The Countess Dorothy Borghase exclaimed, disgust obvious on her aging, but still lovely face. She flipped her head and a long piece of silver-white hair escaped from her elegant chignon. "After all you've been through?" She stared at her friend in disbelief and continued, "That's precisely the reason we need to pack some heat. Because we are old, weak, and can't run as fast. We're sitting ducks for most of the bad guys out there."

Margaret squinted her eyes and frowned at her. "Pack some heat? Really? You sound like you're in a..." Margaret paused for a moment and looked at her friends, "what do they call it, a gang? What is it? Gangsta talk, or however you say it?" she added sarcastically. The wife of one of the wealthiest men in Virginia and a blueblood from birth, Margaret didn't know much about gangs or crime. "But still, Dottie..., a handmade purse... from Italy, nonetheless, especially designed for your gun? Puh-leeze. That's ridiculous, a bit over-the-top, wouldn't you agree, Kathryn?" Margaret asked as she glanced over at Kathryn Lee who watched her friends with an amused look on her face.

Kathryn Lee of Wyndley Farm in Hanover County laughed, her blue eyes crinkling in the corners as she smiled over her water goblet at her friends of many years. Kathryn was the wife of law and order politician Adam Patrick Lee of Virginia and she clearly had an opinion. She was an excellent target shooter and could shoot better than most men. She opened her mouth to respond when Dottie interrupted her.

Dottie rearranged one of the intricate wire combs holding her classic updo in place. Her silver hair gleamed under the brass and crystal chandelier in the elegant restaurant at Richmond's historical Hotel Madison. "I didn't design it just for my gun," she said defensively. "I designed it for my cell phone, my makeup, for the color of the leather, the intricate stitching, the design, and beyond that, the label," she replied in a snarky voice. Dottie paused for a moment and added, "Besides Vitrio Lanbrucci has been designing fine leather for the Borghase family for over a hundred years."

Margaret rolled her eyes and turned to Kathryn. "So, Kathryn, what do you think? I know you'd tried to answer my question a few minutes ago," she said pointedly as she turned to stare at Dottie, "but the countess forgot her manners. Don't you think Dottie's gun purse is a little over the top?" she asked, a smirk on her face.

Kathryn opened her mouth to answer when Dottie interrupted again, her vivid blue eyes wide with concern. She stared at Camilla who looked strange, frightened, actually. Her pupils were wide and she seemed unable to speak.

"Camilla, whatever is the matter with you? Your face is flushed and your eyes are enormous. Are you ill?" Dottie asked as she rose from her seat.

Kathryn was alarmed as well since Camilla was unable to respond. Her eyes stared wildly at them and she opened her mouth, but no words came out. Suddenly, she fell forward, and her head lolled on the table.

"Kathryn, call 911 on your phone. She must've had a stroke or something," Dottie commanded as her heart raced with fear. *It could be my head lying on the table and not Camilla's.* Life seemed very precious to Dottie at that second. *I sure don't wanna die in Lamaire Restaurant in the Hotel Madison. What a spectacle that would be!* Of course, she knew Camilla didn't want to die there either. As she stood by her friend, tears popped into her eyes. *I'll have to call General Rothrock and tell him something dreadful has happened to his mother.*

Kathryn flagged a waiter, moved closer to Camilla's chair and checked her pulse. She could barely feel it; it was weak and irregular. Kathryn looked into Camilla's eyes. Her pupils were large pools of fluid. Her face was flushed and red.

A moment later, a young waitress carrying a serving tray staggered forward and fell to the floor, spilling food, water and wine on the oriental carpet. She lay prone and unresponsive.

"Make that two ambulances," Dottie motioned to the maître d' who was on his way over.

Chapter 3

"What's wrong with this young woman?" the emergency medical technician student asked the paramedic working with her. "I've never seen anything like this," she added as she stared at the unconscious young waitress. The patient's face was bright red in color and her heart rate was over 150 beats per minute. Her mouth and lips were dry and her pupils were fixed and dilated. "She looks like she's gonna die or something. Is she?" Fear etched the student's face.

The paramedic scratched his head. "Don't know, but she can't feel anything. I think she's paralyzed. Watch this," he said as he scratched a pin across the waitress's foot. "See, she has no response so she must have some kind of paralysis," he added.

The student gawked and nodded. "Yeah, if you ran that pin across my foot, I'd be kicking you by now. But, what's wrong? Look at her pupils. They're huge, and they don't react to light," the student said as she used her penlight to check the young woman's pupil response. "I thought that meant brain injury or something."

The paramedic shined his penlight into the girls eyes, "Yeah, they are. She's must have some neurological involvement. The restaurant staff said she'd had a massive seizure so that could have caused some brain damage. What did the maître d' tell you?"

"He said she lost her balance and fell carrying a tray loaded with food. That's about it," she said with a shrug of her shoulders.

"If that's the case, she must have hit her head on the floor. What's our ETA?" the paramedic asked the driver.

"We're five minutes out," the driver said. "Here, talk to the emergency doctor. He's on the line now," he said as he passed the phone back to the paramedic.

Chapter 4

"How is she, how's Camilla doing? Is she better?" Margaret wailed into her cell phone. Do they know what's wrong with her?"

"I don't know, Margaret. Now, will you stop calling me so I can talk with the doctor?" Dottie snapped, her patience at the breaking point. "Do *not* call me again and tie up my phone. I'm trying to reach Michaela," she hissed into the phone.

"Humph. Now, Dottie, don't get all 'countess' with me. I know that frosty, hoity toity, aristocratic voice. It won't work," Margaret declared. "Just don't even try it."

Dottie gritted her teeth and pressed the red disconnect button on her iPhone. She looked over at Kathryn and moaned, "She's driving me nuts. I'm glad she didn't come with us to the hospital, aren't you?"

Kathryn patted Dottie on the shoulder. They'd been friends for years. "Well," she said slowly, "it probably is making you crazy. She's still excitable and has been since all that happened to Allison. It was a good decision not to bring her," she commented as she looked at Dottie. Dottie's face was flushed. Kathryn's heart flip-flopped. "Are you feeling okay, Dottie? I don't want anything to happen to you," Kathryn added as she surveyed her friend critically.

Dottie sat on one of the couches in the Medical College of Virginia's emergency room waiting area. She fingered the soft, buttery feel of her new leather purse. The bulk of her gun comforted her. She reached inside and touched the cool metal. She felt her heart slow down. She didn't like it when it felt like her heart would jump out of her chest.

"Yes, sure, I'm fine. Just a little excited, that's all. I want to find Michaela. She's been out of town, but she's due back this afternoon." She smiled broadly, "It's Tuesday and she's never gone longer than three or four days. She never misses going to Biddy's for more'n four nights. Besides, tonight is police night and all the cops will be there for reduced-priced Guinness. Especially, the Irish ones," she added with a smile.

Kathryn laughed. "Well, good for them. They need it based on what they do. It's a great restaurant, great décor, and great food. Adam and I had dinner there a couple of weeks ago. We were in Richmond on a Thursday evening. I had the Shepherd's pie and it was the best I've ever eaten," Kathryn added. "We're taking some friends there soon."

Dottie smiled, "Great. I'll tell Mic. How is the congressman?" Dottie had a secret crush on Congressman Adam Patrick Lee, the senior legislator from Virginia. She liked his looks and his sense of humor. She always had a grand time when he was around. But she knew that Adam only had eyes for his "bride" of fifty years.

Kathryn rolled her eyes. "Same as always. Works all the time. In D.C. half of the time. Hasn't slowed up a bit… although, I do see he manages to be at home more now that Alex is around," she added with a broad smile. "That man does love his granddaughter."

Dottie nodded. "I'm sure. I'm delighted that Michaela and Alex have become friends."

"Me too," Kathryn agreed. "They're good for each other. Both are single, accomplished, beautiful and perhaps a little too daring," she said with a smile. Kathryn was proud of her granddaughter, Alexandra Destephano, who was currently in Virginia on leave from her job as an attorney for Crescent City Medical Center in New Orleans. "Oh, look, Dottie. Here comes the doctor." The two older women clasped each other's hand and stood up.

"He looks grim," Dottie said in a low voice, almost a whisper. "I don't see a smile hiding anywhere on his face. I hope he doesn't have bad news."

The two old friends tightened their grip on each other as they watched the young physician's long strides as he moved quickly to them.

The young man smiled with his eyes. "Are you here for Mrs. Camilla Rothrock?" he asked as he looked at the two older, fashionably dressed women over his half glasses, his gray eyes filled with concern.

"Yes, yes, we are," Dottie said fearing the worst. "I'm Countess Dorothy Borghase and this is Mrs. Kathryn Lee. Camilla is our close friend."

"How is she?" Kathryn interrupted.

The emergency room physician looked grave. "I'm Dr. Spencer. I'm one of the ED doctors here at MCVH."

"How is our friend?" Dottie asked in a brusque voice. She didn't give a damn what his name was. She wanted information.

Dr. Spencer shook his head slightly. "Not well. I'm afraid she's very ill. She's suffered a heart attack and she's not conscious. She was confused when she came in but gradually became lethargic and slipped into unconsciousness," he said as he surveyed the women who were definitely part of Richmond's aristocratic, blueblood society.

"Whatever do you mean?" Dottie asked angrily. "You slip on the floor and fall down. How on earth do you 'slip' into unconsciousness?"

Kathryn placed her hand over Dottie's well-manicured nails to quiet her. She knew Dottie Borghase well enough to know she was a nano-second away from adopting her hoity-toity countess voice and that would get them nowhere. At least nowhere in the United States and most likely nowhere anywhere else in the world. "You'll have to excuse my friend. She's quite upset," Kathryn admitted to the emergency room doctor. "Can you tell us what happened to her so that we can understand?"

The physician examined the two women over his glasses, shrugged his shoulders and said, "Frankly, we don't know."

Kathryn felt Dottie bristle next to her as she said, "Surely, you have some idea?" *What's wrong with this man? Is he an idiot? Medical College of Virginia usually had great emergency doctors.*

Dr. Spencer ignored the sarcasm in Dottie's voice. "Can you ladies tell me exactly what happened? I understand you were out having lunch, correct?"

Dottie nodded, "Yes, we were eating at the Hotel Madison. Camilla was fine and contributing to the conversation. In my opinion she was having fun," she said as she glanced over at Kathryn for affirmation.

Kathryn nodded. "I agree. Camilla was just fine. There was nothing wrong with her at all. But suddenly, I looked over at her and her pupils were wide and she had a flush on her face and she couldn't answer my question. She tried to talk, but she couldn't. We kept asking her what was wrong and she wasn't able to talk with us."

Dottie noticed the furrow deepen on the physician's face.

"Then she fell over on the table and we called 911," Kathryn finished.

"So," Dottie began again as she attempted to hold her temper in check. "Now, what do you think happened to her? Why's she so sick?" Dottie's ice blue eyes flashed her impatience, as her aristocratic heritage demanded an answer. She impatiently smoothed her updo with her hand and rearranged a comb to make sure she looked perfect, or as perfect as she could for someone eighty-two years of age.

The physician shrugged his shoulders and said, "Ladies, I don't know. She's had a rather severe heart attack. There's no question about that. We've done a panel of blood work and so far, nothing seems unusual based on her age and state of health. We've sent other samples away for further testing."

“Was she poisoned?” Dottie asked abruptly.

Dr. Spencer raised his eyebrows, “I don’t know. We’re considering that. Do you think she was?”

“I don’t know. You’re the doctor,” Dottie responded flippantly, a hint of anger in her voice.

“But why would you ask such a question?” the physician asked as he stared at Dottie. "What did she have for lunch? Did she say anything about her lunch? Maybe it tasted bad or something?"

Kathryn shook her head. "No. She had the Chesapeake crab cake sandwich with fresh fruit and coleslaw and she said she loved it. I had the same thing and it tasted fine."

The doctor turned his attention to Kathryn. "So you feel absolutely fine, correct?"

"I feel great. There's absolutely nothing wrong with me. I promise you. And the lunch was good, very good in fact."

The physician nodded. “Good.”

"So when will you get the results of the blood work?" Kathryn asked.

"I'm not sure to be honest. Hopefully by this evening. We put a rush on it. And shortly, we'll move her to the critical care unit so she can be constantly monitored."

"She'll make it, won't she? Dottie asked, her eyes brimming with tears, as her anger dissipated. Dottie looked at Kathryn and Kathryn saw fear in her eyes.

Dr. Spencer locked eyes with the Dottie and said, "I honestly don't know. She's critically ill. She has other medical issues that aren't working in her favor and by that I mean her heart and vascular disease."

"But," Dottie began, as she looked over at Kathryn for support.

The doctor checked his iPhone and said, "I've got to go. Does Mrs. Rothrock have any relatives close by?"

Dottie shook her head and said, "No. Her son is a retired army general and he lives in Florida. Does he need to come up here?" she asked, as a shadow passed over her face.

The physician nodded, "I think that's the best thing. She's quite ill. Here's my phone number. Please have him call me ASAP."

"Should we stay here?" Kathryn asked him. "Or do you think we would just be taking up space in the waiting room?"

Dr. Spencer shook his head. "Honestly, there's nothing you can do here. We'll move her shortly to the ICU and you can call the nurse caring for her directly for updated reports. I think it's best if you leave and go somewhere more comfortable but that's up to you," he offered.

"Please, please take care of our friend, Doctor. We've been friends for sixty years and there's just a few of us left," Dottie said. "Camilla's in great shape, she's a triathlete.

Dr. Spencer nodded. "I promise I will. Take care of yourselves, ladies. The best thing you can do is be strong and healthy for your friend," he said as he headed back to the patient care area.

Kathryn and Dottie sat on the hard plastic chairs, each caught in their own thoughts. Finally, Kathryn broke the silence and said, "I wonder what happened to the waitress who passed out there as well?"

Dottie shook her head. "I don't know. I intend to find out. Something here's just not right."

Kathryn nodded and stood, "I think you're on to something, Dottie. Let's go."

"I'm calling Mic as soon as I get in the car. We'll get to the bottom of this nonsense," she declared, as she stuck her nose up and assumed her countess ramrod posture.

Kathryn gave her a bright smile and said, "Let's have at it." She smiled to herself. There was no one in her world like the Countess Dorothy Borghase. She was sure of that.

Chapter 5

Retired Richmond homicide detective-turned-private-investigator Michaela McPherson fiddled with the sound dial on her Sirius radio as she appreciated the astounding views of the Blue Ridge Parkway and the mountains of Virginia. She'd spent a long weekend holiday with college friends at Massanutten Resort. They'd had a wonderful time, visited some local wineries and enjoyed a taste of Virginia's growing craft-brew industry without the stress of crowds. She'd had a great time. There was nothing more fun than a girl weekend with your old-time best friends. Her cell phone rang and startled her from her daydream. Dottie's cell number flashed across her console digital display. Mic answered immediately. Dottie was her dearest friend in the world but could also be a huge pain in the tail.

"Dottie, what's up? How's it going?"

"Oh, Michaela. The worst thing has happened. Margaret, Kathryn, Camilla, and I were having lunch at the Madison and for some reason Camilla keeled over at the table. The paramedics had to come and take her to MCV. They don't know what happened to her, but they aren't sure she's even going to live." Dottie ended with a strangled sob.

Mic felt a knot form in her stomach. "Oh my, Dottie I'm so sorry to hear this! What exactly happened?"

Dottie hesitated before she answered. "I... I don't know. She was talking and then suddenly she looked flushed and her pupils got big and she fell into her plate." Dottie hesitated for a second and added, "It was awful."

Mic listened and asked, "Anything else? Is anyone else sick?"

"No, no. All of us are okay. The doctor didn't know what had happened, but he did tell us that she'd had a heart attack."

"Wow, I'm so sorry, Dottie. Did you call General Rothrock in Florida?" Camilla's son was an American hero and Camilla had always been so proud of him. Besides, the general was a nice guy and Mic had worked with him in the past.

"Yeah, Kathryn gave him a call. He's coming as soon as he can. His plane should land at Richmond International this evening."

"Had Camilla been sick or anything?"

"Nope. She's been fine. She goes to the gym with me four days a week. She's as fit as I am," Dottie responded proudly. "She's a tough bird, you know."

Mic laughed. "Yeah. You ladies are pretty amazing, no question."

Dottie paused for a second and said. "I just don't know about this, Mic. It doesn't feel right to me. She was fine and we were having such a good time. There wasn't even an inkling she didn't feel well and then... Next thing you know, she's lying in crab cake and fresh fruit."

Michaela was silent for a moment and said, "I'm gonna pull over at this overlook and take a picture of these views from Afton Mountain. Give me a sec and I'll be back with you, I promise." Dottie was silent, probably mad that Mic had put her on hold. Michaela continued, "You know there's never a really clear view here." Secretly Mic hoped she didn't arouse the countess's anger as she often did when putting Dottie on hold or asking her to wait for something. "Are you there?"

"Yep, hurry up. I'm not feeling right about this," Dottie said frostily. *Honestly, she's taking pictures and Camilla could be dying.* Dottie drummed her fingers on her dashboard, her impatience and anger building.

Mic turned her SUV into a parking spot at the overlook and clicked a few pictures. The May sunlight on the mountains was stunning and it made her feel warm and happy.

"Dottie, I'm back. I let Angel out to pee too," hoping that would decrease some of Dottie's wrath. "Did the ER doc think something else was going on other than a heart attack?"

"Nope," she said sharply. "I asked him if he thought she'd been poisoned and he didn't say anything. He asked what she'd eaten for lunch and that was it... crab cake and fruit."

"So, what makes you think she was poisoned?" Mic was curious.

“I don’t know. Just a hunch, I guess. I’ve heard about people getting sick very quickly and dying from poisoning, that’s all.”

Mic detected a note of impatience in Dottie’s voice. “Okay... And, what else?"

“Well, Kathryn piped up and said she had the same thing for lunch so that kind of killed my theory of poisoning," Dottie responded, a note of irritation in her voice.

Mic pulled her car back out onto the highway and answered, "Yeah, it pretty much does or at least most likely does. Is there anything Camilla ate that Kathryn didn’t?”

Dottie visualized the lunch plate and said, “No, I don’t think so.”

“Okay, anything else I need to know?"

Dottie thought a moment and said, "No, not about Camilla, but I’d forgotten all about this until right now."

"Forgot what?" Mic asked.

Dottie remained silent pondering thoughts.

“Dottie, what are you doing? Are you still on the line?" Mic was getting impatient. She wanted to enjoy the view of the Blue Ridge Mountains on her way home and not talk to a dead cell phone.

"Hold your water, Michaela," Dottie said sharply. "I'm thinking. And yeah, there's something else."

Mic could only imagine the iciness in Dottie's vivid blue eyes. It caused her an involuntary shiver. "Yeah, what's that?" Mic rolled her eyes aware she was in trouble with the aristocratic Countess Borghase.

"A waitress with a platter of food went down and hit the floor a few seconds later, seconds after Camilla fell on the table," Dottie announced. "Now, what do you think of them apples?"

Mic hesitated before she responded. "Humph. That makes it dicey," she added. "I'll be back in RVA in a couple of hours. Keep me posted, Countess," Mic joked.

"You bet. I think something's rotten and we've got ourselves a case."

"Yeah, maybe. We'll see," Mic said, her voice noncommittal. "I'll see you later," she promised. "But don't go gettin' us committed to anything."

"Yeah, yeah, yeah," Dottie promised never intending to honor it. She disconnected her cell and turned her big white Cadillac on to Richmond's historical Monument Avenue, oblivious to the honking of horns and cries of outraged motorists. She looked at her clock on the dash. *It's not even rush hour. What are all of them yelling about?* She wondered as she steered her mammoth vehicle down the middle of the road.

Chapter 6

“Adam, is that you? What are you doing?” Kathryn asked impatiently from her car phone. She’d left Dottie at the hospital and decided to call her husband to tell him about Camilla before she began the drive home. Kathryn’s home, Wyndley Farm, was about forty-five minutes northwest of Richmond.

"Kathryn, Kathryn is that you? I'm in traffic near the Capitol. Let me call you back," her husband said quickly. "I can’t hear a stinkin' thing you're saying."

"Okay, but make it snappy. It’s important." Kathryn said sharply. "I need your help.”

Congressman Adam Patrick Lee turned to his driver and said, "Frankie, find a quiet place and pull over so I can talk to Kathryn. She's barking up my butt about something and you know what that means," he said as his driver laughed loudly.

"Yo, Congress Man. I getcha somewhere ASAP. Doan want Miz Kathryn mad at me," he said as he made an illegal turn and headed for a quiet street in Georgetown.

Adam shook his head. "Yeah, man, you know what it's like when I'm in the dog house with her. Life just isn't the same," Adam lamented. In truth, he was worried. Kathryn never called him at work and whatever she needed must be important or an emergency. He hoped nothing had happened at the farm or with Alex. Surely if something had happened at Wyndley Farm, the Secret Service would've contacted him.

Frankie pulled Congressman Lee's spacious Mercedes into a private driveway. "Here you go, suh. 'Dis here's a safe place. My buddy works for da man in 'dat house and they be at work."

Adam nodded and quickly pushed the redial button on his iPhone.

Kathryn answered immediately. "Adam, will you secure a military transport for General Jefferson Rothrock? He needs to get to Richmond ASAP."

Adam was a little confused and said, "Sure I can, but so can he. Stuart Rothrock is a retired army general. He can get anything military he wants. Why me?"

Kathryn shook her head. *Men. What was it about them that always made them argumentative? Why couldn't he just make the arrangements without raising a ruckus?* She took a breath and explained, "I was having lunch with his mother today at the Madison and she's very ill. She's in the ICU at MCV and he needs to get here as soon as he can. I just thought that with your influence..."

Adam's heart did a flip-flop. He was fond of Camilla Rothrock and thought her son was one of the most courageous and admirable men in America. He'd move

Heaven and earth for both of them if he needed to. "Consider it done. Anything else I need to know?"

Kathryn stared into space as she reviewed the events in her mind. She hesitated and said, "No. It was just very strange. We'd been eating lunch and everyone was fine. All of a sudden, Camilla was unable to communicate. Her face was flushed and her pupils were large. I'm not sure she knew we were talking to her... she passed out. It was scary to say the least," she finished.

Adam was silent for a moment and said, "It sounds weird. Was it a stroke?"

"They said no," Kathryn replied. "To tell the truth, I don't think they know."

"Tell you what," Adam pondered. "I'll get the general to D.C. and then will drive by the farm, pick you up and go back to the hospital. Probably be early this evening."

Thanks, Congressman. I love you," she said as she signed off.

"Love you too, Kathryn." Adam Lee wondered if Kathryn would ever know how much he loved her. He seriously doubted it. She was the love of his life.

Chapter 7

Adam and Kathryn Lee met Beau and Margaret Massie in the foyer of MCV hospitals.

“We’re to go to the private family waiting room on the ICU floor,” Beau informed them. “It’s also called the VIP waiting room,” he added. “The general is already up there.”

General Rothrock looked every bit like a career military man. He was tall, lean and in great physical shape. He greeted them in full dress uniform. He literally shone with bronze, silver and gold medals. He kissed Kathryn and Margaret on the cheek and asked, "Whatever has happened? The doctor I spoke with was vague, almost evasive about what happened to Mother."

Margaret nodded and touched the general’s hand, "I'm very sorry, Stu. I honestly don't think they know what happened. We were out to lunch today, and by 'we' I mean Kathryn, Dottie, Camilla, and I. Everything was going great. We’d had a great lunch and all of a sudden, your mother seemed unable to speak."

The general shook his head. "I don't understand. Did she have a stroke? Did she have a dizzy spell? Why can't they tell me what's wrong with her… and what happened?"

Margaret shrugged her shoulders and said helplessly, "I simply don't know. However, it seems to me that by now they’d have a good answer, don't you think so, Beau?"

Beau Massie was one of the wealthiest men on the East Coast, an avid University of Virginia alum and mover and shaker in RVA. He was most decidedly a Virginia blueblood, just like the Rothrock family was in the great state of Alabama. Tall and impressive in his late seventies, Beau still pretty much ran Richmond from his downtown office. While his eyes showed concern for the general's mother, his face was flushed with anger. Beau was not known for his patience. "Beats the hell out of me. In my opinion, they should've known everything single thing that happened to your mother a few minutes after it happened. If we don't get the answers we want now, I'm gonna make sure we get them, even if we have to go to the Chief of Medicine."

Margaret touched his hand and said softly, "Don't get all upset, Beau. We're gonna find out what's going on with Camilla."

General Rothrock stood, his posture straight. His salt and pepper hair was short, his nails neatly groomed and his shoes spit-shined. "I'm going over there and ring for that doctor again. I've been traveling most of the day and I'd like answers."

Margaret stood and said, "I'll walk with you. They did tell you, didn't they, that she'd had a heart attack?"

The general nodded. "I knew that. Also that her lungs were failing and she was in heart failure. What I don't know is what happened to her. I'm a bit suspicious because no one seems to be able to tell me."

"Well," Beau blustered, "that's just unacceptable. Let's go find out," he said as he jumped from his chair, always ready for a good fight or battle. Beau Massie was a man of action. If he didn't have the answers, he'd travel the food chain to get them and bully his way to the top. He'd never been one to sit around and wait.

The group left the waiting room headed towards the ICU when they met a tall physician dressed in blue scrubs. The doctor was young and handsome, probably in his early forties. He had dark brown eyes and wavy brown hair. He looked at the well-dressed couple and the man in military uniform. His eyes studied General Rothrock as he said, "I'm Dr. Vancouver. You must be Mrs. Rothrock's son, General Rothrock."

General Rothrock nodded. "I am. I believe we spoke on the phone." He turned towards Beau and Margaret and said, "These are my mother's lifelong friends, Beau and Margaret Massie."

Dr. Vancouver smiled at Beau and Margaret. "Weren't you with Mrs. Rothrock at lunch today, Mrs. Massie?"

Margaret nodded and said, "Yes, I was."

"I know you've been asked this a dozen times, but will you tell me once again exactly what happened?"

Margaret exchanged glances with Beau and the general and said, "Yes, we were having lunch at downtown. We'd just finished eating and were talking when suddenly it seemed as though Camilla couldn't focus and couldn't speak. Then her eyes got big and her head fell forward. That's about it," she finished as she surveyed the tall, young doctor. Dr. Vancouver nodded and glanced at Camilla's medical record. "Let's go back into the waiting room so we can talk privately."

A feeling of dread swept over Margaret and she glanced at Beau out of the corner of her eye. It may have been her imagination, but she could swear that General Rothrock stood taller than he had a moment before. The group returned to the waiting room and sat at a round table as General Rothrock introduced Adam and Kathryn. Five fearful but expectant faces stared at Dr. Vancouver.

"What's wrong with my mother?" General Rothrock blurted. "I'm unable to get any answers and I think the time has come to demand them," he said as his voice ended on a harsh note.

Margaret saw a flicker of something pass over Dr. Vancouver's face. She wasn't sure whether it was anger, impatience, or some emotion she just couldn't identify.

The doctor nodded and said, "I understand your frustration. To be straightforward with you General Rothrock, we're not exactly sure what happened to your mother. She was in and out of consciousness when she came in to the emergency department. Now she's in a coma. She has stabilized from her heart attack but from a neurological standpoint, it's unclear where she'll go from here."

"So... what exactly caused her to have that vacant look and stare on her face? What happened to her in the restaurant? And why did her pupils get so big?" Margaret asked. "It was totally scary. It was like Camilla wasn't in there anymore."

The doctor sighed deeply and said, "We're not ruling out the possibility that she could have been poisoned or, less likely, had an allergic reaction to something she'd eaten for lunch. We have no idea how or what, but we have contacted poison control and are checking every possibility."

"Poisoned! What the hell?" Beau blurted. "Who the hell would poison Camilla Rothrock? She's just a nice lady out for lunch. I doubt she's ever hurt anyone in her entire life. I can't imagine someone would poison her."

Margaret watched General Rothrock quietly acknowledge this information and pale beneath his deep Florida tan.

"Stuart. Do you think someone would try to poison your mother?" Margaret asked.

Stuart's voice was calm. "Deliberately? No. Absolutely not. That's not even a possibility," the general assured her.

He turned to Dr. Vancouver and asked, “You're thinking food poisoning, correct?”

The physician stood to leave. "You're correct, General. We suspect food poisoning. But, we're not ruling out any kind of poison. It’s a guess at this point, but there’s nothing else we've uncovered that can better explain her condition.” He looked at the folks sitting around the table, two of the most prominent men in Virginia. “I'll keep you posted on her condition. Thank you for your time," he said as he disappeared in a flash of blue.

Beau looked down, examined his fingernails and mused, "Poisoned? What the hell?"

Chapter 8

Dottie left the hospital shortly after Kathryn. She pushed the redial button to call Mic's phone for the fifth time in a row. It made her angry when she couldn't reach Michaela exactly when she wanted. Of course, it wasn't just Mic. It made her mad when she couldn't reach anyone when she wanted them. She'd seen a therapist once about her impatience and he'd pretty much diagnosed her as a brat or, specifically a "rich bitch." Then he'd said she was spoiled and impatient so she'd fired him and gone out and bought some new clothes. Dottie wasn't sure she believed in all that "psychobabble crap" anyway. If things weren't going her way, she'd always gone out and bought herself something new. Retail therapy. She was a believer in retail therapy. *I'm old school and damned if I'm gonna change.* Dottie just wanted what she wanted when she wanted it. It was just that simple. She looked at her watch. It was after seven o'clock in the evening. *Where's Mic? She should've been home hours ago. How dare she come home and not call her, especially when they had a potential case and her best friend was fighting for her life in the hospital.*

Dottie jumped out of her skin when her cell phone rang. It was Margaret. Margaret had told her that she and Beau were meeting General Rothrock and Adam and Kathryn Lee at the hospital. Margaret probably had an update.

Dottie picked up the phone and asked abruptly, "How's Camilla. What's goin' on?"

We're here in the waiting room and just talked to the ICU doctor. He still doesn't know much."

Anger shot thru Dottie's body. "Doesn't know much? Why, for God's sake?" she retorted angrily. "He's the doctor. They're supposed to know everything."

"Don't blast me, Dottie, blast him," Margaret said sharply. "I'm just the messenger."

Dottie knew Margaret was furious with her. She needed to make nice to get the rest of the info she needed. She took a deep breath, "I'm sorry, Margaret. I'm just worried about Camilla and I can't find Michaela."

Margaret sniffed and continued, "I understand that, Dorothy, but you don't need to eat me for lunch," she whined.

Dottie seethed in anger. She didn't have time for Margaret's antics. "I said, I was sorry. Now, what else is happening?"

"Tell me you won't be abrupt or ugly to me again," Margaret wheedled. "I'm tired of you jumping up my butt with your impatient self."

Dottie rolled her eyes. If Margaret were close to her, she'd shake her. "I promise. I won't. Now, how's Camilla?"

Margaret seemed placated with Dottie's groveling. She answered, her voice low, so low Dottie could hardly hear her and Dottie had excellent hearing for an eighty-two-year-old.

"She's no better. In fact, she's worse. And you know what else, Dottie?" Margaret said as her voice trailed off to a whisper, "They think she may have been poisoned."

"What, what did you say?" Dottie nearly screamed into the phone.

"They think she may have been poisoned. They think someone, somehow, maybe managed to poison her."

Poisoned? Dottie's heart skipped a beat. That'd been her theory all along. *Camilla didn't have any enemies. Who would poison Camilla? Somebody would probably poison Margaret, or me, but not Camilla. She's always nice and polite.* "Are you sure, Margaret? Who'd poison Camilla? She's nice. Kind even. Now, people are standing in line to poison us, but not Camilla," Dottie said, her voice confidant.

"Speak for yourself, Countess," Margaret said icily. "They'd probably want to poison your aristocratic ass, but I've spent my life doing good deeds. No one is after me," Margaret assured her.

Dottie sighed deeply and replied in a bored tone. "Okay, whatever you say. I don't care, but for the record, I totally disagree. I can remember a hundred times when you've been less than kind... but drop it. What else did the doctor say?"

"Not much, but Beau and Adam were talking about some group - possibly terrorists - retaliating against the general. He's been a lot of places and angered a lot of powerful people in foreign countries... Who knows, he could've pissed off ISIS or something."

"Humph." Dottie considered this. "I don't know, Margaret... kill his mother? To get payback? That's a bit out there, don't you think? We've all got a coupla years on us. Seems like they'd go for one of the general's kids or grandchildren." Dottie speculated for a moment and added, "I just don't think so. My gut says no."

"Well," Margaret huffed, "That's what I overheard Adam telling Beau. And Adam would know. He's part of the National Security Agency or something like that." She paused for a breath. "He does all kinds of stuff with the military and CIA. Spy stuff. You remember that don't you, Dottie?"

Dottie shook her head. "My gut still says no. I don't think Camilla was poisoned because of her son," Dottie said stubbornly.

"To hell with your gut, Dottie," Margaret added with frustration in her voice. "General Stuart Rothrock is an American war hero and he was with the NSA and everything. I even think he was one of the Joint Chiefs of

Staff. Beau said he led all kinds of operations and commands in the Middle East and Eastern Europe."

Dottie mused this over. "Humph. What does Kathryn think? Did you talk to her about this?" Kathryn Lee was a victim of a terrorist organization because of her husband's position in Congress and his work against the terrorist groups in the Middle East. Dottie would love Kathryn's opinion on this.

"No, I was eavesdropping on Beau and Adam. I heard them out in the hall on my way back from the ladies room," Margaret admitted, her voice barely a whisper.

Dottie snorted. "Oh, you were eavesdropping. Good, kind, honest, caring, dependable you without a bad bone in your body... would eavesdrop? You, possibly the only woman in the world without an enemy?" Cynicism dripped from Dottie's mouth as she grinned into the phone. She loved getting Margaret back.

"Shut up, you old bag, I'm about sick of you. I'm hanging up," Margaret retorted angrily.

"Keep me in the loop, Margaret. I'm passing this on to Mic and we'll probably come around and see the general."

"Okay, gotta go. Don't call me back," Margaret ordered as she clicked off.

Dottie sat and stared through the French doors into her lovely, manicured courtyard. The rhododendron, azaleas, and irises were in full bloom and the roses had huge buds.

They'd be open in a day or so. *Thank goodness for Henry. He keeps things perfect around here.* Dottie enjoyed the view for another moment and tried Mic's number again.

Poisoned? It was a possibility. But why? Did some foreign terrorist poison her friend to retaliate against her son? It could make sense.

Chapter 9

Michaela pulled her SUV into her parking space in front of her home in Richmond's historic fan district. She opened Angel's door and the massive German Shepherd jumped down from his seat. He whimpered a little as his back leg hit the pavement. Mic reached down and scratched his ears as she checked her watch.

"It's time for your medicine, old boy, and besides, you're probably stiff from the ride," she said to her best friend in the world. She grabbed his lead and they walked a little way down the block so Angel could stretch his legs. "You had a big time in the mountains. All those walks in the George Washington National Forest. You're probably tired from that," she said as Angel stopped at every tree, sniffed, and lifted his leg.

Michaela stopped and waved at Mrs. Merkel, an elderly spinster who lived at the corner of the block and was working in her front yard. Mrs. Merkel lived at the opposite corner of Mic's block. As soon as Mrs. Merkel saw Michaela, she put down her pruning shears and scurried over. Mic told herself to be patient. Mrs. Merkel was a pretty good neighbor, but she gossiped about everything and everyone in the neighborhood.

"Hello, Mrs. Merkel, beautiful day don't you think?" Michaela commented.

Mrs. Merkel pushed her gray hair behind her ears and said, "Yes. A beautiful day. We've waited a long time for spring."

Mic nodded and said, "Indeed we have. Your azaleas look beautiful."

"Yes, thank you, Detective. It pays to feed them in the fall. Makes them bloom a lot longer and I honestly think the blooms are bigger," she said as she glanced over at the two-foot-tall azaleas that lined her front porch." She took a breath and said, "I was just listening to the early news and I'm wondering what you think about all those people getting sick and dropping like flies at those restaurants?"

Mic looked confused. "What do you mean 'people dropping like flies'? Honestly, I've been out of town and I've just gotten in so I don't know what's going on." Mic felt the slow thud of her heartbeat as her anxiety increased. Angel whimpered and looked up at his mistress. He picked up on her emotional distress.

Mrs. Merkel stood a little straighter because she was one up on Detective Michaela McPherson. "Well, today two women passed out or fell down or something at the Hotel Madison during brunch. Then, an hour ago, three other ladies got sick at a restaurant. They took them to St. Mary's Hospital in ambulances."

Michaela shook her head and her heart rate jumped above a hundred and said, "This is horrible. It can't be a coincidence. Not with five people sickened in just one day… all in restaurants."

"Humph, that's what I thought," Mrs. Merkel said. "I'm not a detective, like you, but I thought it sounded fishy too. Just too big of a coincidence, isn't it?" She paused and added, "It'll be a long time before I go out and eat."

Mic gave her neighbor a tight smile and said, "Don't think like that, Mrs. Merkel. Lunch and dinner out is a treat. You need to remember that I'm no longer a detective and I now own a restaurant. I retired last year from the RPD. I'm just a private citizen just like you."

Mrs. Merkel snorted and gave a short laugh, "You're still a detective, Mic. You just do it on your own now, right?" Mrs. Merkel gave her a broad grin and added, "You'll always be a detective. Always have been."

Mic nodded and said, "I guess I still am, sort of. Thanks for the update. I need to give Angel a little bit more exercise. He's had a long drive in the car and his arthritis is acting up."

"They're just like us, aren't they, Mic?" Mrs. Merkel opined. "They've got the same problems in old age that we do."

Mic smiled and said, "They're like us. There's no difference. Keep in touch," she added as she and Angel continued their walk down the street. "Keep everyone in the neighborhood straight, will you," she grinned as she moved away.

"I'll do my best, but these people… I just don't know," she said as she shook her head and returned to her front border to scalp her trees and pull weeds out of her border. "Have a good day, Detective."

Mic shook her head and continued her walk with Angel. *That lady would never learn.* Angel looked up at her and gave her his doggie smile. He knew exactly what was goin' on.

Chapter 10

Adam Patrick Lee sat in the corner booth of the Medical College of Virginia's cafeteria with General Stuart Rothrock. The two men had each ordered the meatloaf Blue Plate special for dinner. Stuart Rothrock picked at his meal and pushed the green peas around his plate.

"What's up, Stu? You don't like the hospital food?" Adam asked. "I think it's kinda tasty," he said as he shoveled creamed potatoes and gravy down his throat.

The general shrugged his shoulders. "I guess it's okay. I've eaten worse." He sighed deeply and asked, "What do you think is goin' on here, Adam?"

Adam sat back in his chair and studied the general. "I'm not sure. We got feelers out. We can't rule out any personal retaliation towards your mother, especially if she's been poisoned."

Rothrock nodded. "Yeah, I know."

"Have you all gotten any threats lately? And by 'you all,' I mean anyone in your family... your wife, the kids, anybody? Poisoning sounds more like the Russians than the Jihadists, but it's hard to tell them apart now."

Stuart shook his head. "Nada. Nothing, not a thing. I was beginning to enjoy life as a retired military man," he said with a short laugh. Adam gave him a shrewd look and said, "Remember, Stuart, you're not retired. The work you're doing, the project you're running is critical to national security. If anyone finds out you're in charge of it the reactions would be heinous."

The general's erect posture relaxed a bit as he nodded. "Yeah, I know, but I'm not gonna be bullied into abandoning my work. Not now, not ever. Not by anybody and I do mean that."

Adam nodded. There were very few Stuart Rothrock's around anymore. He'd do anything he could to protect this American hero and keep him working for national security.

Stuart grasped his coffee cup tightly. "I don't think my work and this business with my mother are related. I can't imagine anyone going after an old lady. I think it's something else, if indeed she was poisoned. At her age it could be most anything."

Adam nodded. "You could be right, but let's not rule it out quite yet. The nasty arm of terrorism stretches around the world and the degree of evil is beyond our ability to expect or plan for."

The general nodded and said brusquely, "I hear you, Congressman. Now shut up and eat your meatloaf," he said with a grin.

Adam laughed and returned his attention to his Blue Plate special dinner. He thought he might have some cherry pie for dessert.

Chapter 11

It was men's night at the Starlight Titty Bar in the seedy part of old South Richmond. Lap dances were half price. Snake looked around at the five or so women pole dancing, who were humping each other and the wall. All were in various stages of undress and none of them were hot. Their faces were vacant, stoned most likely. He was bored beyond belief.

He glanced over at Boris who had a dancer in his lap and asked, "Hey, man, how'd we do today? How many did we get?"

Boris didn't respond, caught up in the moment as the young dancer ground into his pelvis. Snake stared closely at the woman and decided that she was uglier than a mud fence. She was just about as ugly as Boris only her head wasn't half caved in. No wonder she was half price. She was a cake face because she had on so much makeup and one false eyelash hung half off her eyelid. He could see acne scars under her thick makeup.

"Boris, answer me, man? How'd we do today?" Snake asked again as anger flooded him. "I've been waiting all day to find out how things went."

Boris remained silent as the young redhead continued to grunt and grind to give Boris the full lap dance at half price. She was obviously hoping for a big tip. Her eyes were closed and her brightly painted lips were slightly open. Snake glared at Boris with disgust. *You could get screwed any time.* The Russian stared at the ceiling, his jaw slack. Spittle gathered in the corner of his mouth.

Snake couldn't stand it any longer so he stood up and moved to the side of the couch. In a flash, he grabbed the young woman by the back of her bra and jerked her off Boris's lap. He threw her forcefully on the floor where she stumbled and fell, a mass of white flesh, dyed red hair, splayed legs and boobs. A few seconds later she rose, whimpered and limped off to the back of the bar.

"Are you crazy? What'd you do that for?" Boris roared, charging towards Snake as angry as any man could be. "It was just getting good. What is wrong with you?" he asked his face red and his eyes blazing. "I ought to kill you," he threatened as he reached for Snake's neck.

"Man, I was talking to you. It was business. There's business and then there's booty. But business always comes first," Snake snarled as he dodged the angry man.

Boris continued to come at him until the bar's two bouncers, both built like sumo wrestlers, came toward them and ordered them to leave. Boris punched one of the bouncers before Snake wrestled him to the floor. He held him there in a chokehold until he quieted down.

"You okay, man? Are you gonna hit me if I let you up?" Snake asked Boris. The two bouncers looked down at him.

Boris panted from exertion but was silent. He stared at Snake, eyes filled with hate and anger.

"I ain't gonna let you up until you promise to quiet down," Snake assured him. "And then we gotta talk 'bout today." He glanced at the bouncers and added, “Somewhere else.”

In an incredible moment of strength, Boris stood, pushed Snake and the two men away from him and left the bar, slamming the door behind him.

Snake shrugged his shoulders, watched him leave and wondered when he’d hear from him. They had so much work to do. But, truth was, Boris was a strange, crazy, dude and Snake didn't know what to expect.

He guessed he’d find out. He finished his beer, paid the check and left.

Chapter 12

The shrill ringing of her house phone pounded in Michaela's ears as she toweled dry her short dark hair still wet from her shower. It was Dottie. Mic shook her head and reached for the phone.

"Hello, Dottie. You've hardly given me a chance to get home. Where's the fire? I've just gotten out of the shower," Mic said, a note of irritation in her voice.

"Michaela, Michaela, why didn't you call me? I need to talk to you," Dottie said sharply.

Mic sighed. "Dottie, I just got home, I stopped at the grocery store, took Angel for a walk and hopped in the shower. Have a little patience," Michaela admonished. She heard Dottie sigh angrily on the other end of the phone. Mic smiled to herself and added, "Patience, Dottie patience. Patience is a virtue. Even for the aristocracy. People like you need to practice patience."

"Humph. Well, let me tell you one thing, Michaela McPherson, we'll just see how much patience you have at the age of eighty-two. I don't have that much time left and I'm certainly not gonna waste part of it by developing patience now."

Mic rolled her eyes and said, "Okay, Dottie. I get it. Tell me what's up. Any news about Camilla?"

"Yes, yes, there is." Dottie's voice was hushed. "The general is here with Adam and Kathryn at the hospital. She's not any better and Margaret's pretty upset about that. But the news is they think she was poisoned! What do you think of those apples, Michaela?"

"What do you mean they 'think' she was poisoned? Either she was poisoned or she wasn't."

Dottie cursed under her breath and frowned into the phone. "I don't know. I'm just telling you what I heard. I guess all the blood tests aren't back. The general was pretty upset about it. Margaret eavesdropped and heard him and Congressman Lee talking about retaliation of some kind against General Rothrock."

Michaela was quiet for a moment as she processed this information. "I thought Stuart Rothrock was retired and living quietly in Florida," she mused.

"That's what we've all been *led* to believe," Dottie said in a conspiratorial voice. "Perhaps he's not retired at all. Perhaps he's engaged in some secret mission and the bad guys are trying to stop him by killing his mother. Maybe it's a message and his wife is next and then his kids," she added in a hushed tone. "You know as well as I do that terrorists do all kinds of crap like this."

Mic laughed briefly. "That's a bit far-fetched, Dottie. I see you have your royal imagination in overdrive. I'd rather believe this is just food poisoning or some underlying medical condition that Camilla has that was undiagnosed."

Dottie could be on to something. She said early this afternoon that she thought Camilla had been poisoned.

Dottie sighed heavily and impatiently said, "I told you, Mic, they think she could've been poisoned. I'm thinkin' real poison. Not bad crabmeat. I've never heard of people having poisoning as an underlying medical condition anyway or whatever you call it," she sniffed.

Mic was quiet for a moment. "My neighbor just told me three people became very ill in a restaurant downtown this afternoon. You heard anything about that?"

"Umm… No. Nothing. But, if that's true, what other kind of proof do you need, Mic? There are too many coincidences."

Mic didn't respond. She was thinking.

"Michaela, whatever are you doing? We've gotta get on this! People are dropping like flies in Richmond's best restaurants," Dottie lamented. "This could be very bad. After all, you own a restaurant," Dottie reminded her, like Mic didn't remember her restaurant and pub, Biddy McPherson's in Shockoe Bottom.

"You're right. I'll make some calls," she promised.

"Call me back, Mic. Don't try to bypass me on this one or you'll be *very* sorry," Dottie threatened.

Mic could smell her dinner in the oven and said, "I gotta go. My dinner's burning. Keep me in the loop because I truly want to know how Camilla is doing."

"Okay, will do, but don't say I didn't tell you so." Dottie snapped. "Hold on," she said and paused for a moment to check her call waiting and said, "That's Margaret calling me on my other line. I'll get back with you later."

"Later," Mic agreed as she clicked off. "Call me if you need me. I should be home."

Mic moved into her kitchen and removed her mushroom casserole from the oven. The possibility of murder continued to play over and over in her mind. *Crap, this could be bad. People poisoning people in restaurants. What a nightmare.* She reached for her cell and called Lieutenant Steve Stoddard, her old boss from the RPD. He'd know what was up.

Chapter 13

"What do you mean she died? You just told us a little while ago that she was doing okay," Margaret cried, her voice becoming louder and louder. "You're the Medical College of Virginia, right, Beau?"' she said as she reached for her husband's hand. "You perform miracles and now you're telling me my friend is dead."

Beau reached for Margaret and hugged her, stroking her back in an attempt to comfort her. Offering comfort and emotional support is not Beau Massey's strong point so he looked over at Kathryn Lee with wild eyes that screamed "help me."

Kathryn moved next to Margaret, looked into her eyes and said, "Let's go get some coffee, Margaret, and let the doctor talk with Stuart and Adam about the next steps. I'd like a piece of that apple pie I saw earlier downstairs in the bakery on the first floor."

Margaret nodded through her tears and Kathryn walked her slowly, like a child, to the elevator. As the elevator door closed, Margaret said in a defiant voice, "There's something wrong with all of this, Kathryn. I think someone hurt her on purpose," she blurted.

Kathryn nodded and said slowly, "Well, if they did, I can promise you we'll get to the bottom of it. You know how Adam is – he'll put every single resource the government has on it until he gets the answer."

"Good," Margaret said. "And, if there's anything Adam can’t do, I'm sure Beau can," she added. "Camilla has been our friend for years and we're really going to miss her," she said softly as she wiped a tear from her eye.

Kathryn put her arm around Margaret as the elevator descended to the first floor. “Yes, we’ll miss her beyond words. She was a dear and the best Bridge partner I ever had.”

Chapter 14

Lieutenant Steve Stoddard, a veteran cop of twenty-five years commanded the Richmond downtown precinct. Stoddard possessed a steely, no nonsense attitude, played by the book most of the time and had a well-honed gut based on many years of pretty impressive police work. The lieutenant was checking paperwork and arrest reports when his personal cell phone rang. He recognized the number in the digital display. It was Mic. "Mic, what's up? It's not Friday night, is it? I'm not late to Happy Hour am I?" he grinned into the phone.

Mic smiled to herself. The boys in blue never missed happy hour at Biddy's on Friday night. Biddy McPherson's had quickly become the local watering hole for the Richmond Police Department and hundreds of downtown yuppies and patrons who loved Irish stout, Irish whiskey, and great food. "Nope, you've got a couple of days and I'm sure I'll see you there. Never known you to miss a Friday happy hour," she quipped.

"And I never will. I haven't missed a happy hour since I turned twenty-one and that's getting to be a long time ago," Stoddard said with a chuckle. "Going to happy hour is in my marriage contract, I had Sadie sign the paper before we ever saw the parish priest." He paused for a moment and asked, "What's up, Michaela? You never call just to check up on me," he guffawed.

"Come on, Steve. I'm always checking up on you. You know that. I'm always watching out for you too," she laughed.

"Yeah, sure. What do you want, Mic? Get to the point. I got a ton of paperwork to do and you know how much I like that," he added sarcastically.

"Okay, so that accounts for your bad mood. And yes, I do want something. Today, around lunchtime, Camilla Rothrock was questionably poisoned at the Hotel Madison. My neighbor told me a little while ago that there'd been three other potential cases of poisoning from other restaurants in the downtown area. Is there any truth in this?"

Stoddard sighed deeply and said, "Yeah. There was also a young waitress that went down at the Madison the same time as Rothrock. The other cases are three thirty-something ladies whose late lunch turned into an early unhappy hour. All of them are in the hospital and all are unconscious."

Mic was quiet for a moment. "What's the poison? Have they identified the poison yet?"

"Nope." Stoddard played with his pencil and doodled on his legal pad. "They haven't said for sure that it is poison. That's proving to be more difficult than they thought. The FBI is involved and they're sending down their poison team. I guess it takes time to get the blood work back."

"Man, this could be really bad," Mic muttered more to herself than Stoddard. "Any idea about suspects?" She had a sick feeling in her stomach.

"We got nothing, but we're workin' on it. Can't find any evidence where this has happened anywhere else. So far, it looks like Richmond's on its own with this kind of crime."

"Camilla's in critical condition and they called her son, General Rothrock, up from Florida. Do you know the condition of the other women?"

Stoddard sighed and said, "Two of them are listed in grave condition and the third is critical. Three of them are over at St. Mary's Hospital and the waitress from the Madison is still unconscious at MCV."

"Great, a serial poisoner. Just what we need. Anything I can do to help?" Mic felt her heart thud deeply in her chest as she considered the ramifications.

"Just keep this person or persons away from Biddy's. I don't want anybody screwing around with the Guinness taps over there. It would be the end of me if someone poisoned my beer," he said with a short laugh. "No, not yet, but I'll keep you in the loop. Slade'll be up to his eyeballs in it soon. You'll probably hear from him."

Mic's heart rate picked up at the mention of Detective Slade McKane. They'd been partners some years ago and sort of had a romance going on, but it was really weird. They shared a love for Angel who'd also been their partner when they'd been partners. Slade loved the big German Shepherd as much as Mic loved him. "I promise you I'm gonna take care of the beer and the restaurant," Mic assured him. "I'm going down there now and talk to the staff about this. Make sure they're extra vigilant about everything."

"Good idea, Mic. Slade gets home from Cleveland in an hour or so. He's flying into Richmond International. He'll be in charge of this investigation since he's moved to the position in major crimes."

Mic nodded, "Good. I'll talk to him. Is poison control working on this?"

"Yeah. Local poison control and the Feds' poison people will be on it soon. Check with them about some safety precautions you can take at Biddy's. If you ask, they'll probably go down to the restaurant and do an assessment for you.

"Thanks, Lieutenant. Keep me in the loop will you?"

"Yeah. Stay safe, Mic, but most of all, keep my beer untainted!"

Mic laughed as Stoddard clicked off.

Mic's heart hammered in her chest. *Damn, this could be bad. If anybody gets to my beer tanks, they could easily poison several hundred people in one night, not to mention the thirty or forty Richmond police officers who hang out there all the time.*

Angel looked up at Mic and whimpered. He knew she was upset. She reached down to rub his ears and he licked her hand. The love between Michaela and Angel was nothing short of amazing and the pair was inseparable. There was no question that Michaela would lie down and die for Angel at any given moment, and he'd do the same and he almost had several times.

"Come on, buddy. We've gotta get down to the bar and make sure everything is safe. Go get your leash and we'll get in the car," she said as Angel headed to the kitchen for his leash and she went into the hall to pick up her keys.

Chapter 15

Mic had just pulled her SUV into her parking spot behind Biddy's pub when the call came in from Dottie. The clock on her dash flashed a little after eight in the evening.

"Dottie, what's up? Are you at home?" Mic asked.

There was no response.

"Dottie, are you there? Can you speak up?" Mic asked as a tinge of alarm sounded in her mind. She heard a deep sigh and a stifled sob and Dottie began to speak, then choked up and stopped.

"What's wrong, what's wrong, Dottie. Are you okay?" Mic asked as fear permeated her body. She looked over at Angel who was alert in his harness in the front seat. Mic and Angel locked eyes for a moment and Mic reached over with her right hand and scratched his ear, in an attempt to settle his anxiety.

"It's Camilla. She's dead," Dottie blurted out bluntly. "Margaret just called me… said she was dead. Just like that. Here today, gone tomorrow." Mic knew the diffidence in Dottie's voice covered her pain.

Mic's heart raced. *What the hell had happened?* "Oh my, Dottie. I'm so sorry. I didn't expect this. Is Cookie with you?"

"I don't need Cookie, I'm fine," she snapped at Michaela. Cookie was Dottie's long term, long-suffering, live-in housekeeper that kept her eye on the countess for Michaela. Cookie's husband, Henry, was also in Dottie's employ and kept the automobiles, gardens, and pool in pristine shape. He was also a chauffeur for Dottie although she seldom let him drive her. Dottie was hardheaded and stubborn about her driving and would risk the lives of others before she'd let Henry drive her. "What do you expect Cookie to do? Bring Camilla back to life?" she asked sarcastically.

"What I need to do is find the SOB who poisoned her," Dottie said fiercely in an unusual burst of profanity. "That's what I need to do," she ended, a little short of breath.

"I'd just like Cookie to be close by in case you need something," Mic said softly as she continued to scratch Angel's ear. "Do you know what happened?"

"No, I don't. She just up and died," Dottie said harshly. "Most likely a side effect from the poisoning, I guess."

"How'd you find out? Have they said poisoning for sure?"

"Margaret called me. She was screaming and crying so much I could hardly understand what she was saying," Dottie said with a note of disgust in her voice. "Finally she put Beau on the phone and he told me Camilla had died. Don't know whether she had another heart attack or what, but she died. And that's that," Dottie said, a note of anger in her voice.

Mic was quiet for a moment and said, "I'm very sorry. I know you all have been friends for years and it has to be hard for you and for Margaret and Kathryn," she said truthfully.

"That's true. We had a lot of great times and it shouldn't have happened like this. Camilla was in great shape. She had some more good years in front of her and I'm pissed that this happened to her. I promise you, with your help probably, I'm gonna find out who did this to my friend," Dottie said a note of finality in her voice.

"Yes, I'll help you Dottie and we will find out who did this," Michaela assured her. "Wait, a minute, my other line is ringing and it looks like it's General Rothrock. Hang on, Dottie, I'll be right back. Still better, I'll call you back."

"You'd better," Dottie threatened, "or I'll be on your doorstep in thirty minutes."

Mic shook her head, smiled to herself and clicked over to General Rothrock. "Good evening, sir, I just learned of your mother's death and I'm sorry," she began.

"Thank you, Detective McPherson. That's exactly why I'm calling you," the general said in a formal voice. "Can we meet a little later and talk about things?"

"Of course, would you like to come to my home in the fan district? I should be home in about an hour and a half."

"I'll see you then, Detective. Thank you," he said and hung up the phone.

Chapter 16

Boris sat in his dark, gloomy "office" deep in the subbasement tunnel of the old MCV Hospital. Most of the tunnels were closed off years ago when they built the "new" Main Hospital. Recently the Critical Care Hospital had been built and renovations of the Cancer Center and Pediatric Hospitals had pretty much destroyed MCV's extensive underground transport system. His deep subterranean office was safe and isolated. He doubted anyone knew it was down there. There was only one way in and he had to take two flights of stairs to get all the way down. He always laughed when he passed stretchers he knew had been in the tunnel for over twenty-five years. One stretcher had the skeletal remains of a patient who'd been waiting in the tunnel for thirty years too long. He guessed no one had missed the guy.

Boris loved his subterranean world. Sometimes he stayed there for days on end, leaving only to grab a sandwich from one of the fast food restaurants in the hospital's atrium. He had an old hospital bed, a television, a little refrigerator and microwave for when he worked late. But far more important, he had his fully equipped lab next door where he concocted all kinds of bad stuff. Boris experimented with antifreeze, cyanide, and plant poisons. They were his favorites. If he ever needed laboratory supplies, he went upstairs to the huge, fully accredited pathology lab and helped himself to anything he needed. Of course, this wasn't his *main* lab. That wasn't on the hospital premises. This was just a lab where he worked at night after his "day" job as a laboratory assistant. His main lab was in town where he kept his reptiles and aquarium.

He moved over to his workbench to the poison he'd be working on. This time he'd made it even stronger. He'd dissolved ten milligrams of poison in a hundred milliliters, or a little over three ounces of water. On a good day that ratio of poison to water could easily kill a thousand adults and probably twice that many children. He rubbed his hands in anticipation. He had a whole new scheme figured out and locked in his mind. He wasn't sharing it with Snake. He was angry with his partner who, to quote the Americans, was much too "big for his britches." He dreamed of the day he could kill "The Snake," a man he'd first heard of years ago.

The loud ringing of his cell phone jerked him out of his daydream. He checked the digital display and saw it was Snake. He turned the phone off and decided to take a nap. The seventy-year-old iron hospital bed with the yellowing sheets looked inviting so he hopped in. That's what he loved about his subterranean hideaway. Nobody would ever find him. Screw Snake. He'd deal with him later.

Chapter 17

Michaela hung up her cell phone and entered the bar through the back door. She dropped her purse in her office and smiled as she entered the main taproom of the pub named for her mother. The original Biddy McPherson's pub was in Dublin, Michaela's hometown. It had been built by her father years and years ago, shortly after he'd married her mother. The pub was a local watering hole for seafaring men and locals. The bar was no longer owned by her family, but the new owners had kept her mother's name. Michaela's bar was almost an exact replica of the one in Ireland. She'd spent three years with contractors and builders, and her life savings to get it right.

Sean, her drop-dead gorgeous restaurant and bar manager, was working behind the bar. Business was brisk, especially for Wednesday night, so she joined him, pulled a few taps using the perfect Guinness pour to help him catch up. He flashed his brilliant smile at her as his dark eyes approved her appearance. "Hi, thanks for the help. You look good. You must've gotten some rest on your trip. We've been fairly steady tonight. Business is good for mid-week."

"Well, it is hump day so that's good to hear," she said as she flashed him a smile. "Can you meet me in my office? I've got something I want to talk to you about. Gather some of the waitstaff too, as many as you can without slowing down service."

A shadow crossed Sean's handsome face and he nodded. Something was up and it wasn't good. "Sure, let me check the kitchen, gather a few folks and we'll be right in.

Michaela stopped at a few tables and greeted her guests as she and Angel made their way around the bar and back to her office. She waved to several tables of Richmond police enjoying some Irish Red and Guinness in their favorite corner. The bar had a lot of local traffic and happy hour was always busy during the week. And Wednesday, well it was almost the weekend, so the weekend had begun. Biddy McPherson's wide assortment of Irish beer and whiskey made Mic's bar one of Richmond's favorite nightspots.

Sean met her in her office. He had gathered the maître d', several waiters, waitresses, and bus boys.

Mic greeted them warmly and said, "I don't know if you've heard about the questionable restaurant poisonings today at the Hotel Madison and one of the restaurants down the street but—"

"Poisonings? That's horrible, but how?" a young waitress interrupted, her young face filled with fear.

Michaela nodded, "Yeah, the police are thinking someone poisoned either food or beverage at these restaurants and so far, one lady has died and four others are hospitalized and they sound very sick."

"Have they identified the poison? How'd they do it?" Sean asked as his eyes scanned the restaurant patrons outside of Mic's office.

Mic shook her head. "We don't know. The poison hasn't been identified, but I'm confident it will be soon. The Poison Control experts are involved, they've called in the FBI forensic experts and they're analyzing data now. In the meantime, they've closed the kitchens at the Hotel Madison and Fred's down the street. Both places have forensics techs climbing out of the woodwork… checking every floor board and pot in the place." Mic read fear and concern on the faces of her employees.

Sean nodded. "What do you want us to do? We'll do anything and everything to prevent this," he promised, his handsome face darkened by anger and resolve.

"Oh my God, this is terrifying," a young waitress cried. "Poisoning people in a bar. That's criminal, just horrible," she wailed as she flashed frightened eyes at Michaela.

Michaela nodded. "Yeah, it is," Mic agreed, "but we're not gonna let it happen here at Biddy's," she said convincingly as she touched the young woman's shoulder.

"How, how can we stop it? This place is big." The waitress asked as her teeth started to chatter. She hugged herself to stop shaking.

"We're gonna talk about that right now," Mic said. "If you're scared or uncomfortable, you can take a few days off until all of this is over. It'll be fine," Michaela offered. "No problem."

The young woman stuck out her lower lip and said, "No. I'm stayin'. We'll fight this together," she said stubbornly. "I'm in."

Mic checked the faces of her staff. "Any of you are welcome to a short vacation. I'll understand if you take time off. I never considered anything like this would ever happen when I hired you," she ended with a weak smile.

"No, no. Hell no. We're in," Sean said. "We love this place right, gang?"

Mic looked appreciably at her restaurant crew as they all nodded. "Thanks, guys, really appreciate it.

A waiter nodded and asked, "Now, what do we do?"

Mic was quiet for a few seconds and said, "I think we're vulnerable because of the high number of police, and law enforcement guys who come here. The best thing we can do is be vigilant, check for anyone who looks suspicious or tries to access non-public areas."

"We should limit access to the keg room and refrigerated areas to you, me, and one other staff member," Sean suggested. "If we have someone poison or tamper with a keg, we're dead in the water."

Fear jumped up Mic's spine at that thought. She fought for control as she considered a poisoned keg of beer. "Yeah, absolutely. I cringe at the thought," she admitted as she rubbed chill bumps from her arms and fought the hysteria that was creeping through her body. "I'd also like to install several more bolt locks on those areas… both on the doors and windows… make them as secure and as hard to enter as possible. Maybe even a keypad lock with the combination known only to two or three people."

Sean nodded. "That's easy. What about the kitchen? We can't lock that off."

Mic considered this and said, "Let's assign a waiter to that area. Just to watch people who come and go. I'd suggest someone who knows all of the waitstaff and can easily identify anyone who isn't."

Sean nodded. "Sure. We can do that." He looked over at Jerry and said, "You're on, man. When you're off, I'll cover for you. We can easily get a bartender."

Jerry nodded and Mic said, "Thanks, Jerry. I'm gonna hire off-duty police officers, hopefully ones who know most of you. I'm going to go over," she pointed to the RPD booth, "and ask them for recommendations."

"So, you'd keep police officers in the kitchen 24/7? Is that the plan?" Sean asked.

Michaela nodded. "Yeah. That's the best plan I have for right now. I'm open for suggestions from any of you."

Sean checked out the staff and said, "I think we're okay for now, Mic. I'll keep you posted. How much longer will you be here tonight?"

She looked at her watch and said, "Only a few more minutes. I have another meeting I need to get to but call me at home or on my cell."

Sean nodded, "Done, what else?"

"Just communicate this to the day staff. I'll be in by lunch, but if you could get the communication flow going, I'd appreciate it."

"Will do," Sean assured her. He looked around the group, "I'll get the bolts and take care of the locks now. Anyone have any questions?"

The waitstaff shook their heads.

"Thank you all," Mic said to the group as they began to file out of her office, most of them stopping to pat or play with Angel on their way out. "I appreciate your work and your vigilance."

Her restaurant staff assured her things would be fine and Mic hoped they would be. *Boy, I've hired some great folks and I am so lucky to have Sean.*

Mic called to Angel and, along with Sean, they toured the keg room and the kitchen. She frowned as she looked at the four windows in the commercial kitchen. Even though the kitchen and tap room windows were barred, she knew a determined criminal could easily get in. She and Angel left by the back entrance and she called Lieutenant Stoddard and asked him for recommendations for security. *Damn the world we live in.* She and Angel got home only ten minutes before General Rothrock was due to arrive. *This is no different from terrorism. In fact, it is terrorism, domestic terrorism.* She shook her head and cursed softly.

Chapter 18

Snake sat in the front seat of his old Chevy Suburban near Boris's rundown rooming house on Floyd Avenue. He'd been waiting almost five hours and wondered where Boris was. In the past few months since they'd been working together, he'd disappear for days at a time. Sometimes he wondered if crazy Boris had a woman tucked away somewhere. *What else would keep him occupied for so long?* But then, what kind of woman would hang out with that scary, ugly, skinny bastard.

Snake thought back to the ruckus at the titty bar. He knew Boris was unstable and volatile. He knew he shouldn't have attacked him but that was history. Snake hadn't ever had a partner that wouldn't let him in on the details of the mission. The mission had already started and he had no idea of the next step. He was used to being boss, not taking orders from some deranged, cracked skull bastard. He knew he'd have to get back into Boris's good graces. But it was possible the crazy Russian would kill him as soon as he saw him again. Just in case that happened, Snake had placed his gun on the seat beside him. He bent over and reached down to touch the cool stainless blade of the knife tucked in his boot. His assault rifle was in the back covered with a tarp.

The sunlight filtered through the trees and Snake's eyes became heavy. He shut them for a few minutes for a quick nap. After all, he'd just worked a shift at the hospital and he was pretty tired. A few minutes later, he was jerked from his car and slammed against the side of van. Boris stood over him, his thin lips sliced across his decayed teeth and his eyes blazing. His putrid breath permeated Snake's senses.

Boris hissed at him. "Who the hell do you think you were playing with back there at the bar? I'm gonna kill you for that," the Russian growled as his strong fingers closed tightly around Snake's neck.

Snake could feel himself getting dizzy. He looked up and down the street hoping someone would intervene, but the streets were quiet. *Oh well, I figured I'd die young at the hand of someone else.* He looked up into Boris's face and noted the Russian's raw determination to squeeze the last breath of air out of him. Rage empowered Snake. In a last-ditch effort to save his skin, he kicked Boris as hard as he could in the groin. The Russian fell backwards screaming in pain on the pavement as he clutched his genitals. He looked up at Snake and cursed. "I'm gonna kill you, you fool. You just got lucky this time. You won't know when, you won't know how, but you'll know why when it happens." He screamed through a mass of anger, tears and pain.

Snake walked over and put his foot on Boris's chest. He looked down at him and said, "This is about business. There is a time to play and a time to work. After we work, we can play. Right now, we've got a lot of work to do, just like we did at the titty bar so let's get the hell in there and do it.

Boris looked up at him, turned his head and spat on Snake's shoe.

Snake kicked him hard in the ribs but didn't break them. He needed this man's expertise. He didn't know anything about poison or what the plan was to use it. He had been hired to "assist" Boris who he gathered was some hotshot Russian. Snake wanted to finish the job so he could get paid and move on.

Boris cried in pain and stared up at Snake, his eyes dark and evil. "I'll get you," he hissed. "You just wait and see," he threatened as he rubbed his right side.

Snake looked at the man writhing in pain and said, "Shut up and get up. We can kill each other and cut each other into pieces once we finish the job. Get your ass up and inside and get cleaned up because we've got work to do."

Boris struggled off the ground and pulled himself up using the fender of the car to steady himself. As he came to an upright position, he stared at Snake and said nothing. He limped into his house with a new respect for his partner.

Chapter 19

It had been years since Michaela had seen General Stuart Rothrock and then it'd been at a formal dinner in his mother's home. She hardly knew the general, but knew of him and his outstanding military career. She'd also heard it rumored he'd been involved at the highest levels of national security. She was surprised that he was accompanied by Congressman Adam Patrick Lee.

She opened her front door with Angel at her side and smiled, "General Rothrock, Congressman Lee, I'm so glad to see you." She leaned over, gave Stuart Rothrock a hug and whispered, "I'm so sorry about Camilla. She was such an outstanding woman and I admired her greatly."

"Thank you, Michaela," he said softly. "And please call me Stu."

"You're welcome, Stu. And Adam, it's always great to see you." Michaela added as she flashed the powerful congressman a warm, flirtatious smile. "What can I offer you gentlemen to drink?"

"Well, I kinda like that Irish whiskey you got down at Biddy's," Adam admitted. "You got any of that here?"

"I sure do, wouldn't be an Irish household without it," she grinned at him. "General, oops I mean Stu, what can I offer you?"

"That sounds great to me. Adam here usually knows his booze. I always take his suggestions and he's never steered me wrong yet."

Mic laughed as Adam spoke. "No question 'bout that, but don't say it in front of Kathryn or I'll be in the doghouse or the horse barn for sure."

Stu grinned. "I'd live in your horse barn anytime." He turned to Mic, "You ever see that place? It's nicer than my place in Florida."

Mic shook her head. "No, I haven't seen the new barn but honestly, the last one was five stars."

"You gotta come out, Mic. It's been a while and you know Alex is home, well, sort of home. She's in NOLA now but will be back in a few weeks."

"Just say when and I'll be there. You guys want to come back to the kitchen? That's where I hide the whiskey," she taunted them.

"Yup. Sure, after you," Adam said gallantly with a sweep of his hand.

"This is one fine looking dog," Stu said, as he roughed up Angel's ears. "Where'd you get him?"

"Oh you haven't met Angel? He's the love of my life," Michaela said as she headed towards the back of the house to the kitchen. "He was my partner at the RPD. Matter of fact, he's the best partner I've ever had," she laughed as she handed Angel a piece of jerky. The dog accepted the treat politely and moved over to his bed by the kitchen hearth to savor it.

"Way I heard it," Adam Lee interrupted, "this here dog saved your life once or twice."

"Yep, that he did," Michaela agreed. "He took a bullet for me a few years ago, saved my life, and they retired him so he came to live with me." Mic gave her dog an adoring look. "We've been together since then and he pretty much goes everywhere I go." She paused for a moment and smiled, "You know how it goes, right? Love me, love my dog."

General Rothrock nodded, "That's quite a story, Michaela. In my opinion, there's no better friend than a well-trained police, military, or medical working dog. There's no argument they save lives, thousands of lives each year."

"Yeah, no argument here," Mic agreed as she took the whiskey bottle, three crystal glasses and a small container of ice over to the table and invited the men to join her. "Do you mind if we sit in here? It's cool outside and the kitchen is warm."

"This is a mighty fine kitchen, you've got here, Michaela. You must do a lot of cooking," Adam observed. "What's that I smell? Is something in the oven?"

Mic walked over to her oven. "Yes, I threw together a few snacks for us. I didn't know if you had found time for dinner. It's just a snack."

"That's kind of you, Michaela. To be honest we didn't have time to eat much although Adam did consume an ungodly amount of questionable meatloaf. We met with the doctor shortly afterwards and then my mother passed away. Anyway, this smells great," Stu said as he smiled gratefully.

Adam poured each of them two fingers of Irish whiskey and said, "This is good for starters. It's been a long day hasn't it, Stu?"

Stu nodded. "Yeah, it has and this whiskey is just what my bones need after that ride in the military transport you arranged for me, Adam. I'm getting old, next time could you send a better ride?" he joked.

Mic laughed and the three clinked glasses as Adam looked at Stu and said, "Really, General, you didn't give me much time but at least it got you here, didn't it? You didn't have to stand in line at security either."

"Yep, I gotta say that's true. Thank you, buddy," Stuart said as a smile faded from his face. He turned to Michaela and said, "I'm wondering if I can hire you to look into my mother's death. The physicians at MCV think there is poison involved although they haven't been able to isolate what kind."

Michaela nodded. "Sure. I’m happy to do this for you, General, but I need to know everything they've told you."

General Rothrock nodded. "Of course, I understand that, but there's not much," he said as he sipped his whiskey and reached for the Boursin and a cracker. "Basically, they said she was poisoned, most likely from something she ingested at Hotel Madison. The doctor suggested her advanced age might have contributed to her death. She didn't have the stamina to fight against the poison that a younger person would have." He looked at Adam and asked, "Did I miss anything or forget to tell Michaela anything, Adam?"

Adam shook his head. "Nope, that's what I heard. He did say that they weren't sure if the poison caused her heart attack, but they could possibly determine that on autopsy."

Michaela nodded, "That would make sense to me. Did the physician mention anything about the waitress from the Madison that passed out at about the same time your mother became ill?"

General Rothrock nodded. "He said the young woman was still unconscious. They're running the same tests on her that they ran on my mother. I think the cases are related and I believe he does too. I think he said she had a neurological disorder of some type."

"Hell yes! They've gotta be related," Adam sputtered as he slammed his glass on Michaela's oak table. "How could they not be?"

Mic nodded. "I imagine they're both victims of some foul play. We've just got to figure out what they ate to become ill. That's key." Michaela picked up her glass of whiskey and looked steadily from General Rothrock to Congressman Lee and asked, "Are you both confident the attack on Mrs. Rothrock was random?"

Adam gave Michaela a funny look and asked, "What exactly do you mean, Mic?"

"Do you think the general's mother was targeted by someone, perhaps for some reason I wouldn't know about... like in retaliation for something he did in the military or for the government?" she asked.

Adam smiled slightly, and gave Michaela a shrewd look. He took a sip of his whiskey and responded, "Of course we have to consider that and we are. Stuart's military career – and his current work - is one that ruffles and pisses off bunches of people." He looked at Stu and grinned, "Who could it be, man? The Arabs, the Israelis, the French, or the Russians?"

Stuart raised his eyebrows, gave Adam a quizzical look and said, "Well, now, don't forget the Mexican cartel. They're standing in line, Adam. You pick," he said with a broad smile.

Adam didn't return the smile. "No one knows any more than me the effects of terrorism directed against Americans and their families." He turned to Mic and repeated, "But honestly, we don't know." He gave Stuart a surreptitious look. He knew his friend was heartsick over the death of his mother. He admired the brave front he'd maintained all day.

Mic nodded. "I know you know about the terrorism, Congressman," she said softly. "No one could possibly know any better than you," she admitted as she remembered the attack against Adam's home and family just over a year ago.

"I think this poisoning is random," Stuart said. "It's true, I have quite a battle record and I probably have thousands of people who'd like to do me in, but I think the attack against my mother is something that just happened. I don't think she's ever been on anyone's radar."

Michaela nodded as Adam broke in and said, "You may be right, General, but I'm not convinced."

"We've got the Secret Service and the intelligence agencies looking for a terror link, but would like for you to check things out locally and coordinate with the Feds. Just see what you can find out for us," Rothrock said.

Mic nodded, "I'll be happy to do that. I've already been in contact with Lieutenant Steve Stoddard and I have the police files to review." She paused for a moment and said, "I don't know if you gentlemen are aware, but there were three other women who were poisoned this afternoon at a downtown restaurant after lunch. The cases may be related so I'm looking into that as well."

"Holy shit," Adam exploded. "This is bad. Three more women? Poisoned?"

Michaela nodded, "That's where the evidence is leading us. Their symptoms are very much like your mother's. So far all remain unconscious and one is in critical condition."

General Rothrock shook his head and examined the whiskey in his glass, "If you've got a serial poisoner on your hands, you've got your work cut out for you."

Michaela nodded. "I hope you're wrong about that," she said.

Stuart Rothrock stared into her eyes and said, "Me too. We tailed a serial poisoner in the Middle East for months. He killed thousands of people before we caught him. He was one of the worst criminals I've ever known of. He made Hitler look like a nice guy."

Mic felt nausea pit in her stomach. *This was gonna be bad.* She could feel it.

Chapter 20

The day dawned dark and rainy. Neither Mic nor Angel was eager to get up. Mic peered over at Angel who was fast asleep with his eyes open in his orthopedic bed in front of the bay window in her bedroom. She spoke his name softly and he struggled out of bed. She leaned down and scratched his ears. "It looks like a good day for ducks, old boy. Are you gonna want to come with me today?"

Angel looked into her eyes and gave a slight nod of his head.

"Okay, then, let me get up and get us ready. We're gonna work on this poisoning business so it's gonna be a long day," she said as she ruffled his fur. She jumped as her cell phone rang. It was Slade McKane. She smiled to herself. Her heart raced. She loved hearing from him.

"Good morning, Slade. It's so early. Why are you calling me so early?" Mic complained sleepiness obvious in her voice.

"Get up, lazybones. It's after nine o'clock. I took the red eye home from Cleveland. I want to hear about your trip to the Blue Ridge and catch you up on a few things, so get the coffee pot perking and I'll be over in an hour or so." Mic shivered a bit at the sound of his deep voice. She could see him sitting in his office downtown.

"Yeah, well, it's too early," she teased him. "Besides, it's raining and a benefit of retirement is not working in the rain, or snow for that matter."

He ignored her. "Get ready, I'll be there in an hour. We've got work to do," he promised her.

Mic picked up the tenseness in his voice and chill bumps popped out on her arms. "Okay, I'll try to be ready. You bring the doughnuts," she bargained.

"Just be sure the coffee is fresh," he said. "My ulcer already hurts from drinking this precinct swill."

"I'll be ready," she promised as she hopped out of bed. Angel reluctantly followed her downstairs. She let him out in the backyard and reached for her French coffee press. She smiled to herself. Slade loved her coffee.

Chapter 21

Boris sat outside on the bench and watched the school bus full of children run and skip into Busy Burger for an early lunch and milkshakes. He knew they'd just ended their class trip down to the State Capitol. The weather had cleared and it was warm. He removed his heavy flannel shirt and let the sun beat down on his back. He lit a cigarette as he watched a young fast food worker walk out of the side door and light up a cigarette. He looked like a dumb teenager. It was time to make friends.

Boris stood, stretched his long legs and walked over to the young man who was sitting on the curb frantically texting on his phone. "Hey, dude, bet you had to get away from all those kids. It has to be crazy in there."

The young man had a bad case of acne, gauges in both ears, bleached blond hair and a little eye makeup. He smiled up at Boris and said, "Yeah. It's loud in there. I had to get out. Take a break," he said as he returned to his phone.

Boris sat beside the guy and asked, "What do all those kids eat? They have a set lunch or something?"

The teenager kept texting and said, "Yeah. They get either a cheeseburger or a chicken sandwich. Everybody gets a chocolate shake. I've got to get my ass back in there and start making the shakes," he said as he hit send on his phone. He stared at his phone, hoping for a quick return message.

Boris fingered the whiskers on his chin and said amicably. “Tell you what, dude. How 'bout I work for you for about an hour? I've been thinking about applying to Busy Burger anyway so I’ll just give it a trial run."

The teenager's eyes lit up, "Man, that'd be great. I'm having a fight with my girlfriend and I need to text her back."

"You ain't gonna win, you know that, right? You don't never win a fight with a woman," Boris said, a note of impatience in his tone.

The teenager sighed deeply and said, "You're probably right. But I gotta give her a chance.”

Boris stood up and said, "Okay, just gimme your shirt and I’ll take your place for about an hour. Or maybe shorter if somebody pisses me off."

Once again, the teenager stared at Boris. "You sure, man? Those kids are gonna drive you crazy. It's going to be loud in there, louder than you can possibly imagine."

Boris gave him a wide grin and said, "Nah, it won't be that bad. At least not for long," he promised as he slipped the guy’s shirt on. "The chocolate milkshakes are served from the machine, right?"

"Yeah, they're all gettin' chocolate and everything you need is in the stainless refrigerator under the machine," the teen said as Boris entered through the back door. The kid never looked up from his phone. He was texting non-stop and oblivious to everything around.

Chapter 22

Michaela opened the door before the second knock, Angel at her side, his tail wagging furiously. Angel loved Slade McKane and Slade loved the dog. What Michaela didn't know was what to do with Slade. They'd been an item a few years ago, but Mic wasn't sure she wanted to travel that long road again. *Of course, we are older and more settled now…* Mic's heart fluttered a bit as she looked into Slade's gray eyes that held so much promise and asked, "What brings you out so bright and early?"

Mic looked beautiful. She wore a loose-fitting greenish-blue linen pantsuit and a pair of silver sandals, silver jewelry and a clunky, silver and turquoise necklace. All in all, she looked ready for a day in town. "Is the coffee ready?" he asked as he focused on business.

Michaela nodded as the pair made their way back into the kitchen. She'd made fresh coffee and the smell made his mouth water. One thing Slade loved about Mic was her ability to cook just about anything – and he always made himself a willing participant to taste anything Michaela cooked.

Slade waited eagerly as Michaela poured him a cup of coffee and placed coffee cake on a white luncheon plate. "Yum, that looks and smells wonderful," he said as he accepted the plate, his eyes shining in anticipation. "I guess we're not gonna eat the doughnuts I bought?"

Mic shook her head. "Let's sit at the table. You look like you've got a lot to say and that's a big file in your arms."

Slade nodded, "Yeah, unfortunately I do and not much of it is good."

Mic's stomach did another flip-flop. "Uh oh. Is this about the poisonings?"

Slade nodded as a dark shadow crossed his face. "Word on the street is that General Stuart Rothrock hired you to look into his mother's death. Is the rumor mill correct?"

Mic shook her head and smiled. "Yeah, it is, as always. I talked with him and Congressman Lee last night. General Rothrock is sure his mother was poisoned. Apparently, MCV hasn't gotten all the lab tests back, but they're leading him in that direction."

Slade put down his coffee cup and said, "You make a great cup of coffee, Mic, no question." He paused a moment as if savoring the taste in his mouth and added, "I think General Rothrock is right. Unfortunately, one of the three women poisoned at lunch died this morning and the other two are in critical condition. St. Mary doctors think she was poisoned as well."

Mic's mouth formed an "O" as the knot in her stomach hardened. "Oh my, Slade, that's two murders."

Slade looked into her eyes and said "Yeah and my guess is there'll be more. Most likely the other two ladies that were poisoned yesterday will die, I'm afraid," he said in a low voice.

Michaela stared into her empty coffee cup and rubbed Angel's neck. Angel knew his mistress was upset and had come over and sat next to her. He knew Michaela like a book, better than she knew herself. He licked her hand to comfort her and she spoke to him softly, taking comfort in rubbing his back.

She looked up at Slade and said, "Well, it looks more and more like a local killer. I think the general and the congressman were ruling out some sort of act of international terrorism directed at General Rothrock."

Slade shook his head and said, "You never know. It could be an international terrorist threat. It wouldn't be unusual for a terror group to retaliate by killing others."

Mic nodded and said, "Yeah, I've thought about that. But still, we can't rule out terrorism against Rothrock, at least not yet."

"That's right," Slade agreed. "Terrorists are diabolical and organized and these crimes are planned and orchestrated well."

"Yeah," Mic agreed. "No question. Last night I went down to Biddy's and we secured the taproom, the kitchen, and storage areas as best we could. We doubled security and I hired several RPD officers to be on duty twenty-four-seven. I have them stationed between the kitchen and storage room. I just can't be too careful."

Slade nodded his approval. "Good. You can't be too careful. You don't need this crap happening at Biddy's. It's probably more vulnerable because it's a police hangout."

Mic shrugged her shoulders. "Yeah. I thought about that. We also installed a keypad on the taproom door and only three people can enter to change the taps or refill beer kegs. That's pretty much all I know to do," she finished wistfully. "Do you have any more ideas on how I can secure the kitchen and storage areas?"

Slade considered this for a moment and said, "You've got good security camera surveillance everywhere, right?"

"I do, but I could use a few more in the back of the restaurant. If anyone comes and tries something, they'll most likely come through the back, don't you agree?"

Slade looked uncertain. "Well, you'd think so but who knows. Still, you should get your security company over there ASAP. Can you access your camera feed from your phone and computer?"

Michaela nodded. "I can and I look at it a lot. I always like to stay at least three feet in front of the Virginia Alcohol Control Board laws."

Slade laughed, "Yeah, there're some tough guys over there. You never want to get on their bad side because from what I hear, they never let you alone."

Mic nodded. “Yeah. That's what I hear too. So, are you headed out to meet with the poison investigative team, or whatever they’re called? The combination of local poison people and the Feds’ poison team?"

"Yeah. The FBI has sent their poison forensic team. You are welcome to come with me. It’s this afternoon. I’m sure the general or Congressman Lee can get you a seat at the table. I'll share what we’ve got with you now, which isn't much." Slade stopped and picked up his phone that signaled a text. His face paled, "Oh my God, Michaela. We've got a class full of elementary school students passed out at the Busy Burger downtown near the Capitol. They’re on a class trip and stopped for an early lunch."

Mic jumped up from the table. "Kids, oh no.” A look of dismay and fear flashed across her face. “We're dealing with a serial poisoner, a maniac. Come on, Slade, let's get over there.”

"I'll drive. Angel can ride in the back," Slade said as he grabbed a pastry to go. He looked at Michaela who grabbed her purse and sunglasses and said, "Set your security system and all the bells and whistles you pay for each month."

Mic nodded, "I'll be out in a minute. Oh, my God, a school bus full of kids. This guy is pure evil.”

Slade gestured to the door. “Hurry up.”

Michaela nodded. “Take Angel and start the car. I’ll be right there as soon as I arm my system."

Chapter 23

Snake was in a foul mood, the kind of mood when he liked to hurt people. He'd been looking for Boris since yesterday afternoon and the Russian hadn't returned to his rooming house last night. He had no clue where he was. As he drove his battered vehicle around places where Boris was likely to hang, he became angrier and angrier. *Screw him, we had a deal, a plan and now we're behind. My boss's gonna be furious with us. I've got a reputation to protect.* Even though he was a low life criminal and capable of committing the worst of crimes, Snake was proud of his work record. In a sense, he had a code of ethics and was proud of his unblemished reputation.

Where the hell was Boris? He crossed the Lee Bridge and drove over the James River into south Richmond. He knew a friend of Boris's from the old country lived on Porter. Fedor was an old guy, and there was a strong bond between the two men. Once, during a heavy bout of drinking, Snake tried to force Fedor into telling him why Boris left Russia. It was useless. There was no way Fedor was telling tales on Boris and Snake wasn't sure he wanted to know. Fedor was sitting on his front porch, a bottle of vodka next to him. Snake slid his vehicle into a parking place right in front of the house, slammed the door and looked around the neighborhood.

Fedor wasn't happy to see him as Snake bounded up the steps two at a time. Fedor stood, the bottle of vodka in his hand. "Wuz up, Snake? Wasn't suspectin' to see you anytime soon. Pretty sure I don't want to see you," he said as he studied him through half-closed eyes. Snake was trouble.

Snake examined Fedor closely noting the broken veins and telltale flush of too much alcohol etched into his face. "Man, you look like you been hitting it hard. What's up?"

"Ain't nothing up," Fedor said crossly. "What do you want?"

Snake gave Fedor a half-smile. "I'm looking for our friend. You know where he is?"

Fedor shook his head. "Nope ain't seen him. Don't know nothing either. Boris ain't been around here for weeks."

"Come on, man," Snake persisted. "Aren't you going to offer an old buddy a drink? It's hot out here."

Fedor shoved the bottle of cheap vodka towards Snake. "I'm telling you the truth. I don't know where Boris is. And truth is, if he doesn't want you to find him, you won't. He's good at being missing."

Snake sat on an old rusted metal chair on Fedor's front porch. "Nice porch you got here," he said sarcastically as he looked around. "Neighborhood still sucks, though," he remarked. "Now, where's Boris?"

Fedor eyed him suspiciously. "I dunno nuthin 'cept that I think you and Boris are killing those ladies and kids. He's been foolin' around with the poison for years." His eyes glistened with anger. "Somebody's going to take both of you out one day and I hope I'm here to see it."

Snake jumped up, the rusted chair clattering against the porch and hollered, "Kids, what the hell you talking about, man? Who's killing kids?"

"Someone, my guess Boris, killed a bunch of school kids at that fast food place. Put some kinda poison in the chocolate milkshake machine. Or at least that's what the news said a little bit ago," Fedor growled and gave Snake a disgusted look. "You make me sick, like I wanna puke," he added as he returned to his vodka bottle.

What the hell? Has Boris gone rogue on me and killed a bunch of kids? That ain't gonna work at all. He walked up and grabbed Fedor by the collar. "I'm askin' you for the last time. Where is Boris?"

Fedor snarled as him. "Told you, I ain't seen Boris for weeks, you damned child killer."

"I didn't do anything to school children," Snake snarled as he grabbed his phone and looked for news reports on school kids being poisoned. There was, he saw it. *Two dead.*

"Two kids are dead already," he said, a smile replacing the scowl on his face.

Fedor shook his head. "You found it? Bad, isn't it? Like I said, you make me wanna puke," he added with disgust. "Only chickens prey on children and that's what you and Boris are, Chickenshits. Pick on someone your own age," he said, as revulsion and anger darkened his face. "Anybody can kill kids. You disgust me."

"Shut up, old man, before I shut you up forever," Snake scowled.

"Screw you," Fedor spat and before he could move, Snake came at him.

Fedor winced as Snake grabbed his arm and squeezed it as hard as he could. The tattoo on Snake's hand whitened with pressure. The evil eyes of the tattooed reptile stared at him. Fedor was paralyzed by the pain and remained quiet.

"Now, for the last time, where is Boris?" Snake's voice was a hiss and Fedor felt fear in the pit of his stomach. He knew Snake would kill him and think nothing of it.

Fedor shrugged his shoulders. "Dunno. You can kill me if you want to, but I don't know where he is."

Snake stared into Fedor's eyes and realized he didn't know where Boris was. He threw him roughly against the metal glider on his porch. Fedor howled in pain as his hip scraped on the rusty frame. He cursed Snake in Russian.

"If you see him, tell him I'm looking for him, old man," Snake growled as he walked down the steps towards his van.

Fedor watched him drive away. *Good riddance.* He'd never tell Snake a thing. Never. He'd die before he helped that killer out. He hated both of them and he was disappointed in Boris. A real man would never hurt a kid. Boris had shown so much promise in his younger years, but now he was a criminal, just like his father. He had half a mind to call the Richmond police about them.

Chapter 24

Michaela and Slade pulled into the Busy Burger parking lot amid a dozen ambulances from Richmond, Henrico and Chesterfield. There were at least eight police cars. Mic watched as paramedics rolled a stretcher from the restaurant, a blanket covering the small body.

"Oh my God, Slade, how many of these children are dead? I was hoping they'd just be sick for a few days," she said, her eyes big as saucers. Angel stood by her side, the bristles of his fur sticking out. He knew something was seriously wrong. He sniffed the stretcher as it went by and growled.

Slade McKane was angry. His face had turned to stone. *Who the hell poisons children? What kind of monster is this?* He put his arm around Michaela and said, "I don't know, but there's Stoddard, and there's the chief. The big brass is out. That'll slow us down for sure," he predicted and rolled his eyes. "We'll never get anything done with the chief here. He'll watch us like a hawk."

"Yeah, no question," Mic agreed as she noticed the group of brass from the Richmond Police Department. "The mayor too. How'd these people get here so fast?"

"Come on, let's go find out how bad this is," he said as he urged her forward.

Stoddard's face was red with anger and filled with grief as he saw Slade and Mic approach Command Center. Mic knew he saw his grandchildren in the bodies of the children. He shook his head. "This is bad, really bad. We've got three dead kids and I don't how many others critically ill. The ambulances just keep coming."

Slade met Stoddard's eyes and said, "Lieutenant, we'll get these SOBs. I promise you we will. Tell me what's going on. How many kids are down and how'd it happen?"

Stoddard looked at Slade and said, "Detective McKane, you know Chief Herndon, right?" Stoddard said as he looked at the two men.

Slade saluted the chief. "Yes, sir. Good afternoon, sir. This is tragic."

The chief nodded and said, "Nothing good about this afternoon and yeah, it's as bad as it gets. A new Richmond monster at work." He turned his head to greet Michaela. "Ms. McPherson, what brings you out today?" he asked pleasantly, pleased to see Michaela. He bent down and patted Angel. "Ah, our hero canine. He looks good," he said as he grinned at Mic.

Mic smiled at Chief Herndon, an avid lover of Welsh rarebit, Guinness, Celtic music, and Biddy's pub. Herndon was in his late fifties, fit as a fiddle with a full head of white hair and a tanned, lined face. He played a lot of golf. He was well respected by his men but had enemies, as any police chief, would be in this day and age. Mic and the chief knew each other from way back. They'd worked homicide together when Mic was a newly promoted detective. She reached down and patted Angel, "Yeah, he's doin' great. Still has a little arthritis in his hip that bothers him in bad weather, but other than that, he's as good as he ever was," she admitted as she squatted and looked into Angel's eyes. The dog literally smiled at her. "How'r things with you, sir?"

"Well," he said as he looked around. "They were going well until this broke. What a maniac," he explained as anger flashed across his face.

Michaela stood up and looked into Herndon's eyes. "Yeah, this is bad, sir," she agreed.

"I heard you were investigating the death of General Rothrock's mother. That true?" the Police Chief asked as he squinted into the sun.

Michaela whistled. "Wow, word gets around. Yeah. I just got the job last night," she said as she flashed him her million-watt smile.

The chief laughed. "Of course I know. Heard first thing this morning. Congressman Lee called me almost before I got outta bed. He was on his way back to D.C. and I was first on his list, I guess. He wanted to make sure I gave you everything you needed," he said with a short laugh.

Mic nodded and laughed. "Yeah, I heard he gets a lot done early now since they assigned him a driver. Kathryn says he spends the two-hour commute on his cell phone hassling folks and ordering people around."

"Yeah, well I do believe that," the chief said with a smile. "I do the same thing. We call it efficiency."

Slade shuffled from one foot to another and felt like an outsider. *The least they could do is include me in the conversation.* But he controlled himself. He knew Mic and Herndon had a special relationship.

"You got anything?" the chief asked.

She shook her head. "Nah, gonna see the ME this morning to get results of the post. Then I'm going to see Dr. Peggy Grey for lunch. Later, I'm goin' to meet with a group of Feds working on the case. Congressman got me an invite to that meeting," she grinned.

Chief Herndon scratched his head. "Yeah. Peggy Grey. Hadn't thought about her. She's probably the best we've got. We'll all be meeting with the Federal forensic team. I'll see you there," Chief Herndon informed her. "This is now a federal case," he said as he gestured widely with his arms. "The fibbies have invited a couple of profilers from Quantico."

Mic nodded, "Yeah, so I heard. That's fine with me. We've got to get this guy soon. If they can profile him, I'm all about it."

The chief turned to Slade and said sharply, "What about you, McKane, you willing to work with the Feds?"

Slade nodded, "Yes, sir. I'm ready to do anything I can to stop these crimes."

The chief smiled and said, "Carry on, then. Get this creep. I gotta get downtown for a press conference. Can't wait," he added sarcastically as he signaled for his driver. He turned to Lieutenant Stoddard and said, "Keep me posted, Steve. I want to know everything." Moments later, his entourage surrounded him and he was in his car backing out of the Busy Burger's parking lot.

Stoddard pointed to the ambulances. He turned to Slade and Michaela and said, "Let's go get an update."

Slade was flushed. "Let me get Mic's permission since the chief loves her," he said, a caustic edge to his voice as he glared at her. Mic knew he was mad about what he perceived as a slight from the Richmond Chief of Police.

Mic gave him a reproachful look and said, "The chief and I go back years. Years before you ever came to Virginia so give it a rest. Chief Herndon was my partner when I came to homicide." She smiled at him and added, "Don't be so touchy. You're supposed to be a tough Cajun cop."

Stoddard relaxed as they walked over. "It's about time you got here, Mic. We've got a busload of elementary school kids who were visiting the state capital. Most are from

Southside Virginia. A couple are from North Carolina but attend school on the Virginia side of Lake Gaston."

"Yeah," Mic said, "So, now it's a federal crime. That's what the chief told us."

Stoddard rolled his eyes. He hated working with the Feds. "Crimes like this would be a federal crime anyway. But to answer your question, we've got two states and the FBI is involved. They're sending their profiling unit down," he announced, "and honestly, we need all the help we can get." Stoddard's eyes blazed and the muscles in his face were frozen over gritted teeth.

"What happened?" Michaela asked. "Does it look like poison - like Camilla and the others?"

Stoddard nodded. His eyes were dark with anger. "It seems so. There's a poison forensics team here. They're going over the restaurant with a fine tooth comb and sampling everything. So far, they think the poison was in the chocolate milkshakes. The kids had different meals, but they all had chocolate milkshakes."

"So the chocolate milkshake is the common denominator. How many are dead so far?" Slade asked.

Stoddard's gaze moved over to the ambulances. "Right now, there are three, two girls and a boy. I think there are others who might not make it, though. The paramedics said a couple had stopped breathing."

Mic felt sick as she watched first responders from the last ambulance load up the last few kids and head to the hospital. The restaurant's parking lot was packed with news trucks, reporters, parents and oglers. She reached down to pat Angel when she felt his fur bristle. He had alerted. *He must see something*. Mic scanned the area quickly.

"Slade, Lieutenant, look at Angel. He senses something. I wonder if the perp is standing around somewhere watching all of this – the results of his handiwork - and gloating," Michaela wondered aloud as she peered through the crowd.

She was interrupted by a young male officer in blue who ran over to them "Lieutenant, get over here. We've got a lead," the breathless young officer gasped. "There's a kid who lent his shirt to some guy who offered to work for him for a few hours."

"You got a description?" Stoddard asked quickly.

"Yes, sir. Come over here," the young officer pointed.

Slade and Mic walked with the officer into the Busy Burger where police sat with a teenager who was scared out of his mind. The kid had dirty blond hair and stuttered. He had tears rolling down his acne-covered face. Mic's heart went out to him.

The young man saw sympathy in Michaela's eyes. "It's all my fault, lady. It's all my fault those kids are dead or sick."

"Tell us what you know, son," Mic said in a soft voice as she rubbed Angel's neck. Angel's tale was bristled and he was panting. She knew Angel sensed something. She turned to McKane, "Take him outside and give him his lead. I think our guy is out there somewhere close."

Slade nodded and took Angel's lead. "Yeah, and loving all the chaos and attention," he said as he spoke to Angel. "Come on, boy, you're in charge," he ordered the dog.

Chapter 25

Dottie paced her Monument Avenue mansion huffing and puffing every step of the way. Where is Margaret? Where is Michaela? *Every time I need to talk to them, they're not available. That's not the case with me. I'm always available for my friends. Damn them,* she thought as she cursed her friends.

"Countess, want to sit and have a bite of lunch? I made you a tuna sandwich on whole wheat with mayonnaise. It's your favorite," Cookie said as she looked at the flushed, angry face of her aristocratic boss.

"Has anyone called me on the house phone? I can't reach Michaela or Margaret and I need to know if plans have been made for Camilla's funeral. I also want to know what the real deal is on how she died," Dottie said impatiently.

Cookie shook her head. "No one has called the house phone." Sadness flashed across Cookie's face. "I think I know where Michaela may be," she offered.

"Where? Where is she?" Dottie snapped. *How come Cookie knew where Mic was and she didn't?*

"Sit down, I'll put your lunch on a TV tray and I'll turn the television on for you. Something horrible has happened over at the fast food restaurant on Bank Street. It looks like the poisoner is back to work. This time he's killing children," she added her voice choked up.

Dottie dropped into her chair, her mouth wide with amazement. "Killing children, you have to be a monster to kill children," she said, her eyes were large with disbelief. Dottie didn't know much about children, nor did she particularly like them, but she knew only a monster would hurt them.

Cookie nodded as she set up Dottie's TV tray. "That's precisely correct, Countess. There's a monster on the loose here in Richmond," she assured her as she flicked on the TV. "Here's the remote, see for yourself. It's horrible and it's upsetting."

Dottie watched the Channel 6 News and her vivid blue eyes never left the TV screen. She saw numerous police cars and ambulances. The reporter confirmed the death of two children and said others were in critical condition. She shook her head and looked up into Cookie's eyes. "I've got to find Mic. We've got to get this guy before he kills anybody else."

Cookie opened her mouth to speak, but Dottie silenced her with a wave of her hand. "Don't start, Cookie. I'm perfectly able to take care of myself and help Michaela catch this killer."

Cookie shook her head and said, "Just promise me you'll be careful and not do anything rash or stupid," she said as she glared at Dottie.

"I promise, Cookie." Dottie said dutifully, but her eyes never left the TV screen. She did not intend to honor her promise and she knew Cookie knew it. Those words just had to be said.

Cookie shook her head as she left the room. She knew Countess Borghase was going to do exactly what she pleased and no one would be able to stop her.

Dottie watched Cookie leave the room and as soon as Cookie was out of sight, Dottie picked up her cell phone and texted Mic putting 911 in front of her message. *That'll get her attention,* she said smugly to herself. Dottie took a bite of her sandwich and had an idea as she watched the same soundbites repeatedly on the news. There was a way she could help. She knew just the person to help them. She picked up her phone again and speed dialed Madame Toulescent and asked for an emergency appointment. Dottie was gonna get stuff done. She pushed her plate aside, grabbed her purse with her Glock snugly nestled in its compartment and went into the kitchen to get her car keys. Cookie was at the sink scrubbing the already gleaming porcelain.

"Cookie, I'm going out for a while. Would you ask Henry to pull my Cadillac around front, please?" she instructed her housekeeper. Dottie no longer backed her Cadillac out of the garage because she'd hit the wall several times. They'd made a deal that Henry, even if she wouldn't let him drive her, would always park her car and bring her car to the circular drive.

"Of course, Countess. Perhaps he can drive you where you need to go?" Cookie suggested.

Dottie shook her head firmly. "No, I'll be just fine. I should be home in the late afternoon. If not, I'll call you," she promised.

Cookie shook her head and went out to search for her husband. *I wonder what she's up to. Whatever it is, it's not good. I can tell by the gleam in her eyes.*

Chapter 26

Mic, Slade, and an FBI agent from the local office sat in a booth with the teenager in the Busy Burger. The young man was scared to death. He'd told his story three times, but Slade asked him to tell them once more.

"I don't know what else to tell you," the boy said tearfully. "This man came over to me during my break and saw me texting to my girlfriend. He asked me what it was like working here. I told him it was okay. Then he stood there and watched me text my girlfriend. He said something about my texting and I told him my girlfriend and I were having a fight."

"And then what happened?" Michaela asked.

"The guy offered to take over for me for an hour or so. He said he had been thinking about working at Busy Burger anyway and this way he could... well... test the water so to speak. See if he really wanted to. I said 'sure, you can take my shift' because I was having this fight with my girlfriend and I wanted to settle things."

"Why were you so anxious to have another break?" The FBI agent asked.

The young man turned red and said, "I was having a fight with my girlfriend and we were texting back and forth. I really didn't want to leave and go back to work in the middle of the fight so when this guy offered to take my shift for an hour, well... it was perfect. It gave me time to straighten out things with my girlfriend. I wanted to make up with her."

"Then what happened?" Slade asked.

"It's just like I said earlier. I gave the guy my Busy Burger work shirt and I went over and sat on that picnic bench under the tree. I didn't know nuthin was happenin' 'til the first police car rolled into the parking lot." The boy stopped for a minute and added, big tears filling his eyes. "I'm telling you the truth. That's exactly what happened."

"Okay," Slade said impatiently. "Now tell me again, what did this man look like?"

The boys shrugged his shoulders. "He didn't look like anybody in particular. He certainly didn't look like he was going to kill a bunch of kids. He seemed like a nice enough guy. He was pretty tall, maybe six feet and he had short, really short, blond hair or maybe he was mostly bald, I don't remember."

"Did he have any scars or tattoos or anything else that would make him stand out?" Slade asked as he looked into the teenager's eyes. "Son, you're the only lead we've got on a mass murderer. Please think and go back in your mind and see if there's anything else you can tell us."

The young man thought back and said, "Well, he had some sort of an accent. And, the top of his head was sort of caved in. You know, sort of like someone had hit him with a hammer. I don't know what kind of accent. He just didn't talk like an American."

"Was he fair-skinned or was he dark? What color were his eyes?" Mic asked.

"I'm, I'm not sure. I think they might've been pale blue," the boy said, "but I couldn't swear to it. He was pretty white, his skin that is," the kid added.

"Tell me a little more about this 'caved' in head. Where specifically was it caved in?" Slade asked.

The boy pointed to his forehead. "It was sort of caved in on the right side. About here," he said as he touched his forehead. "Like I said, it looked like someone hit him with a hammer right here," the teen said as he pointed to his forehead.

"Don't you think it was a little strange that some guy offered to cover your shift at Busy Burger when a bunch of noisy kids were there so you could text on your cell phone?" the FBI agent asked sarcastically.

The young man was quiet and didn't say anything.

The FBI agent persisted, "Don't you think that was weird? Answer my question."

The young man stared at the floor and said, "Yeah, I guess it was kinda strange. But to tell the truth, I didn't think about it then. I just wanted to make up with my girlfriend. That's all," he said, as more tears filled his eyes and oozed down his face.

Slade slipped the young man his card and said, "We'll be calling you to come downtown to answer more questions later today. I also want you to look at some pictures, mugshots, and try to identify the guy. Can you be there?"

The young man nodded. "Yes, sir. Can I bring my mother?"

"Of course you can," Michaela assured him. "We actually prefer you bring her," she added as she touched the distraught teen on the shoulder.

The boy gave Slade a fearful look and asked, "Am I going to be arrested? I'm trying to get into college and I think that would hurt my chances."

"No, no," Mic assured him as she gave Slade a dirty look and answered for him. "We just need to know every single thing you can remember, no matter how insignificant or unimportant it seems. You're our only link to a murderer and anything you say or remember can help us."

"I know and I understand. Okay, can I leave now? I need to go home and tell my parents." The teen gave them a woeful look.

"Yeah, but come downtown to the police station around three this afternoon. Take some time to decompress and see if you can remember anything else," Slade said. "If you do remember something, write it down. Anything you can think of may be the lead we need to get this guy, okay?"

"Yeah. I'll be there," he said as he stood. Mic hadn't noticed how tall the young man was. He was close to six feet himself and skinny as a rail.

"This officer will take you home," Slade said as he motioned to a uniformed officer standing to his right. "Where do you live, son?" Slade asked.

"Um, I live in the Northside. Over in Ginter Park. On Seminary Avenue, sir," the teen mumbled as he gathered his backpack.

Slade nodded, "Okay, think about everything that's happened and please write anything down, the smallest detail may be important," Slade reminded him.

The kid nodded and left. "That's a good neighborhood," he said as he looked at Mic. "He seems like a pretty good kid."

"Yeah, he does. Maybe he'll remember something," Mic said. "I hope so. Let's line him up with a police sketch artist. Maybe we can get a composite... especially with the battered up head. We've gotta get this maniac."

Chapter 27

Boris stood across the street from the Busy Burger and watched the chaos from behind a large oak tree. He was so happy he had butterflies in his stomach. There was nothing he liked better than to watch law enforcement in action. It was funny in his mind. Hilarious, in fact. They were so inept, bumbling and scared of their shadow. He loved the way the uniformed cops ran around talking to each other about their "best theory." He'd been particularly happy when he saw the RPD Chief and the Richmond Mayor show up. He knew he had caused a stir when people like that appeared. He found a park bench and took a seat, oblivious to those around him.

"Do you know what's happened over there?" a female voice asked. The woman's voice was light and soft. Boris hated it. It plucked his nerves. He detested women. They reminded him of his mother who'd left him alone with his older sister who'd teased him unmercifully.

Boris remained silent and pretended he hadn't heard her. A moment or two went by and the woman asked him again, her voice louder, "Sir, what's going on across the street? At the Busy Burger? Do you know?" The woman stared at him and it made Boris uncomfortable. He didn't like anyone to look at him.

Boris glanced at her. She was a thin woman about forty years old and she was walking her dog, a frilly little poodle with bows on its ears and a huge rhinestone collar. He could feel anger spread through him. He looked up at her and said, "No, I've no idea. I'm just trying to enjoy the quiet."

The woman laughed and said, "There's no quiet here. Listen to all of those police sirens. Whatever it is, it must be serious because of all the ambulances."

The frilly dog started to yap and Boris wanted to grab the woman and strangle the dog. He stared at her, shook his head and walked away. *I'd like to kill her and that dog for messing up my good time.* He gritted his teeth as he moved to another bench about twenty yards away where his view wasn't nearly as good. That's when he noticed the dark-haired woman with the big dog talking to the police chief. *I know that woman, but I can't remember who she is.* He stared at Michaela. A bad feeling came over him and he knew he needed to figure out who she was and get rid of her. Somehow, they were connected and connected in a bad way. He racked his brain to remember her. He pulled his iPhone out of his pocket and snapped pics of Michaela and the dog. He also snapped a few of the policemen with her. He guessed it was time to talk with Snake. He'd heard Snake was good at taking care of problems and he was sure the woman was one of them.

He stood up and watched the paramedics roll another stretcher out of the Busy Burger. He smiled to himself and gloated over the horrific scene, thoughts of the woman and dog gone from his mind. *This is the best yet. I gotta figure out where to kill next.*

Chapter 28

Michaela and Angel sat in her SUV outside of the fast food restaurant, the air conditioning blasting in their faces. Mic couldn't rid the air of the stench of death and the air current helped. She searched her phone for texts and messages and noticed two from Dottie. She groaned to herself but knew she had to call her back. She speed dialed Dottie's home phone and Cookie answered.

"Hey, Cookie, it's Michaela. How are you?"

Cookie smiled at the sound of Mic's voice. She loved this spunky, ethical, generous friend of Dottie's. In fact, Michaela was her friend as well and they constantly conferred on ways to handle the eighty-two-year-old increasingly querulous countess who believed she was thirty-five. "I'm good, Michaela. That's bad business over there at the burger place. Whoever kills children needs to be strung up, no trial, and no justice. Just strung up."

"Yeah. No question about that, Cookie. I couldn't agree more," Mic said as she watched the final ambulance pull away.

"Any idea who's doing this?"

Mic sighed heavily into the phone. "We don't have any good leads, but I promise you, we will get him, them or whomever just as soon as we possibly can."

"I guess it's the same person who killed Camilla?"

"Yeah, it looks that way, but we won't know for sure until the actual forensic tests are done and back from the lab." Michaela paused for a moment and asked, "Is the countess around?"

Cookie sighed heavily and said, "Nope. She tried to reach you, couldn't and took off in the Caddy. No idea where she went." She paused and added, "Of course I asked, but she wouldn't tell me," she said in a frustrated voice.

"No surprise there. It's par for the course." Michaela said brightly. "Let me call her on her cell and I'll try to catch up with her. I'll let you know when I find her, I promise."

"Okay, Mic. That sounds great. And by the way, I've several big bones I've been saving for Angel. I asked Dottie to bring them to you, but she didn't want to put them in her purse. I suggested wrapping them in plastic bags, actually several layers of plastic bags, but she wouldn't have anything to do with it. I'll send Henry over with them later. Is it okay if he uses your hidden key and puts them in the fridge?"

Michaela couldn't stop laughing. "She wouldn't put them in her purse or take them in wrapped plastic bags? Boy, she is getting prissy in her old age. I've seen her pick up human bone fragments and put them in an evidence bag and I've seen her wallow in blood and brain matter." Mic shook her head and looked at Angel. "Angel would love the bones. Sure, have Henry come anytime. Tell him to disarm the security system. I put it on before I left. I'm headed downtown for a meeting and then I'm gonna try to catch up with Dottie so I'll be in and out."

"Sounds like a plan. Thanks, Michaela. Stay safe," Cookie cautioned.

"Always," Michaela assured her. "Talk later," she said as she clicked off her cell.

Chapter 29

Dottie steered her white Cadillac across the Lee Bridge headed for South Richmond. She glanced down at the water of the James River rushing beneath her. A feeling of panic overwhelmed her and she gripped the steering wheel tightly. She hated driving on bridges and over water. Generally, if there was water involved in any leg of her journey, she'd let Henry drive her. Her fear dated back many years when she'd driven over a narrow bridge in Amsterdam. The car in front of her ran off the bridge and crashed into the dark, inky water beneath her. She'd had a terror of bridges ever since that time.

This bridge always made her nervous because she thought it should be wider and, as far as she was concerned, the bridge was built too high over the river. As she sped across the bridge, she remembered the silver Fiat convertible she and Count Borghase had driven all over Italy and France fifty years ago. They'd visited every vineyard in Italy, the Alsace, and the Lorraine Valley. That was when she'd developed her taste for fine wines and her love of vineyards. Dottie saw herself as a young aristocratic woman with long dark hair coiled under a huge straw sun hat with a silk scarf around the brim. She changed the silk scarf to match her outfit every time she and the count drove the convertible. She could picture Count Borghase sitting next to her, impeccably dressed in a pinstriped suit. Bogy had been the love of her life. *Those were the days,* she remembered as a tear splashed down her cheek. She jumped when her cell phone rang and Michaela's number popped up on her digital dash display. She pushed the button and said in an irritated voice, "Where have you been, Michaela? We need to find this nut job that keeps poisoning people."

Mic grinned and ruffled the fur on Angel's back. He thumped his tail against the seat as he heard Dottie's voice. "And, hello to you too, Countess. Where are you headed?"

Dottie ignored her. "What's new on the poisoner? How many children are dead? Is it the same people who poisoned Camilla and the others?"

"Stop firing questions and let me answer. Yeah, it looks like the same perp or perps. I think three children have died, but I'm not positive. There were some rumors that they revived another child. The FBI is involved and they sent their poison forensics team to the scene. They're collecting and analyzing data as we speak. I'm on my way to meet with my old friend Peggy Grey, a retired medical examiner who works part-time for the medical examiner's office. She's going over Camilla's medical record and another autopsy report that's been completed. I think one of the federal poison experts will be there as well."

Dottie mulled this over in her mind and said icily, "I know Dr. Grey. Remember? I am connected. Otherwise, what you are doing sounds right. Let me know what you find out."

"Thanks, Dottie, for your permission to do this," Michaela joked. "Did I tell you General Rothrock hired me to look into his mother's death?"

"Humph," Dottie's sniffed. "Hiring you means hiring us and you know that. We're a team, don't you remember?"

Mic sighed. "Yes, I suppose it does," she said grudgingly. "Anyway, that's where I'm headed. What about you? Where're you goin'?"

"I've got a plan," Dottie said coyly. "I think it'll pay off. Can we plan a meet up later this afternoon or early this evening to compare notes and see where we are, you know, discuss the case?" she said in a frosty tone.

Mic ignored her attitude. "Yeah, I guess so. I'm going to Biddy's and make sure everything down there's okay. The last thing I need is someone poisoning my Guinness keg.

Mic could hear the sharp intake of Dottie's breath on her end of the phone. "Oh my, I forgot about Biddy's. Yeah, you're vulnerable. It'd be awful if the killer struck there. They could kill several policemen there." Dottie considered the seriousness of the threat as she drove quickly through the countryside.

"No question about that," Mic said through gritted teeth. "You're not going anywhere dangerous are you? I don't want any SOS call from you when I'm busy," she said with a laugh.

There was a long silence before Dottie replied. "Pardon me, but who saved whose life last time?" she shot back. "I'll be just fine, Michaela. You need not worry," she said, her voice as frosty as the winter's snow.

"Come on, Dottie, don't pull the aristocratic stuff on me. It doesn't work," Michaela said, her voice irritated. "I don't have time for these games."

There was no response. Dottie had hung up.

"I could just kill her," Mic hissed to Angel who looked at her with his soft brown eyes and then smiled his favorite doggie smile.

Chapter 30

Mic and Angel drove to her old friend, Dr. Peggy Grey's home off Pump House Road in the Carillon area of Richmond. Peggy had purchased one of the few condos built there in the late 1980s and had lived there since. Mic loved the condos with the huge windows and the sweeping views of the river. Retired from full-time practice at the state medical examiner's office on disability, Peggy now spent her time doing expert consulting on medical cases.

Michaela and Angel walked quickly up the handicapped ramp to Peggy's condo and rang the bell. Mic could hear the chimes echoing throughout the house. Then she heard the click, click, click of Peggy's crutches, as she got closer to the door and opened it, a huge smile on her face and a dog biscuit for Angel. She reached forward and gave Michaela a huge hug.

"I'm so happy to see you, Mic," Peggy exclaimed happily. "It's been at least six months and I've missed you!"

Michaela studied her friend with a critical eye. "I've missed you too, Peggy. How are you feeling?" she asked as she looked at the crutches. "Are these your best friends now?"

Peggy laughed and said, "No, not my best friends. As a matter of fact they're more like my nemesis, but sometimes I need them." She paused for a moment and watched Angel methodically chew his treat and look up for more. She reached down and scratched his ear. "I've had a relapse from the MS so I've been on steroids, but I'm feeling better."

A look of concern flashed across Michaela's face. Peggy didn't deserve this. She'd been diagnosed with multiple sclerosis twenty years ago, when she was about thirty-five years old. It had affected her hands so badly that she'd given up doing autopsies and the clinical practice of medicine at the office of the medical examiner in Richmond. Currently, she worked as an analyst in a consulting capacity. She'd trained other physicians at the School of Medicine in the "science of speaking for the dead" as she called forensic medicine. A few years ago, she had taken an early retirement and had set up a consulting practice from her home.

"How long since the last steroids?" Mic asked casually, concerned for her friend. Peggy was an excellent medical examiner, one of the best known on the East Coast.

"Honestly, it's been about four months and after the first round of steroids, I was so much better I didn't need any help." Peggy paused for a moment and added, "Michaela, I know you're busy, but I promise if I ever need your help I will call. Agreed?"

Mic nodded. That was Peggy's way of saying she wanted to change the subject and divert the attention off her and her illness. Mic held up a white bag. "Guess what," she grinned. "I stopped by Sally Belle's and picked us up a late lunch. Are you hungry because I'm starving?"

Peggy rolled her brown eyes and said, "Michaela McPherson, you know I'm hungry. I'm always hungry."

Mic laughed and hugged her old friend. "Shall we eat in the kitchen?"

"Yep, that's where I'm set up. I got the autopsy reports and the lab work you sent over. I think I might know what killed your friend, Camilla, and the woman at the bar. I suspect it's also what's going on with the children now."

Michaela gave Peggy an approving look and said, "You're the best, you're absolutely the best at what you do. I'm sure you know that," she said, her eyebrows raised. She detected a faint blush creeping up Peggy's face.

Peggy shrugged her shoulders and said, "Sometimes we just get lucky and this was one of those times." She moved over and sat down at her table as Mic made them each a glass of iced tea. The chicken salad biscuits and potato salad from Sally Bell's bakery smelled divine. "This is such a treat. I love Sally Bell's food. They've been around Richmond probably for over 100 years. I can remember when they were down on West Grace Street near VCU. My mother and I used to walk over from our house in the fan district."

"Wow, I don't remember that at all. That was way before my time," Mic said as she handed Peggy her plate. "I bought an extra pound of chicken salad and potato salad for you to eat later," she added with a smile.

"Oh, great! Thanks so much. Before we get started on the case, how's Biddy's doing?"

Mic's green eyes sparked, "Great. We've gotten a couple of great restaurant reviews, and we're a hot spot downtown for happy hour. Of course," she admitted, "I'm a little worried about security down there, if the perp knows it's where the police go to drink."

Peggy nodded, "Yeah, you should be worried. This perp is obviously a sicko – he murders old ladies, young women, and little children." She gave Mic another look, "And, I'm sure he knows all of the watering holes for the RPD officers."

Mic nodded and bit into her biscuit. "No question. I have increased security down there. The attack on the kids is particularly bad."

Peggy shook her head. "The death toll is three kids now and another of them is critical. I talked with one of my friends in the pediatric ICU at MCV and she said it was touch and go for another five or six. She's sure the death toll will increase in the next several days."

Mic shook her head, a sick feeling in the pit of her stomach. "What do you think? Any preliminary ideas?"

Peggy nodded and put down her chicken salad biscuit. "Whoever's doing this has a background in chemistry because they know exactly how to titrate the dosage. They know how much poison to mix and exactly what damage it'll do." Peggy eyes returned to her plate and added, "Honestly, the whole thing makes me sick. It's been a long time since we've had a string of crimes like this."

Michaela sat silently and she thought about Camilla's death and the deaths of the woman and children. It was odd to kill people of all ages. Some perps killed men, others women, but this guy was killing everyone. "Peggy, what do you think the purpose, the motive is?"

Peggy shook her head. "I don't think there is a specific motive other than to kill and to kill efficiently. Honestly, Mic, I think this perp or perps are just getting started. I think he's testing the water and seeing exactly what damage he can do – or they can do." She paused a moment for a sip of tea and added, "And, make no mistake, he's watching the law enforcement response… watching it closely."

"Scary isn't it. You think there's more than one perp?" Michaela murmured as she moved her potato salad around on the plate. "Do you think they're working up to a bigger crowd?"

"Oh yeah, most definitely. I think you have a mastermind guy and a muscle guy. The attack at Busy Burger essentially said, 'watch me, I can be anywhere' so I'm sure he or they have something big in mind. Most likely this weekend or early next week." Peggy predicted as she stopped and took another bite of her biscuit and said, "My guess is they'll do something this weekend since the rate of the crimes has escalated."

Mic's mind shot ahead. *What was happening this weekend in Richmond where a serial poisoner could kill large numbers of people?* "Oh no, Peggy. There're bunches of stuff happening this weekend. At least three or four outdoor festivals. There'll be thousands of people outside."

Peggy nodded, "I'm betting one of those is the next target."

Mic shook her head in dismay, "I'm meeting with the federal group that specializes in serial poisonings in about," she checked her watch, "an hour. Tell me what you think based on information I sent you earlier."

Peggy grinned. "I'll be at the same meeting. They called me a couple of hours ago," she said. "I consult with the federal forensics team on all types of poisons and gases."

Mic smiled, "Cool. They're lucky to have you. Need a ride? I've got my SUV."

"Sure, yeah, that'd be great," Peggy smiled. "Saves me a cab." Then she took a deep breath and asked, "Can you tell me one more time what your friends said about Camilla Rothrock just before she became ill."

Michaela searched her memory. "Pretty much they said she was fine and then she stopped talking. Her eyes got big and she could not respond to them. Then she fell forward on the table. That's pretty much it."

Peggy nodded. "Yeah. I thought so. More than likely it's some kind of plant poison that has chemicals that affect the parasympathetic nervous system. You know, the nervous system that slows down body responses. These chemicals can cause dilated pupils and blurred vision, an increased heart rate, balance issues, and confusion among other things."

Mic was thoughtful. "That sounds like what happened to Camilla. I do think Dottie said Camilla was reaching for her water or her cup before she passed out." She paused and said, "Could the same poison have affected the waitress at the Hotel Madison to the point where she fell down?"

Peggy pulled out a bound medical record. "It can. I've looked at the waitress's medical records and she has a seizure disorder that can be triggered by the poison. She's had several seizures since she's been in the hospital. The good news is she's still alive and breathing on her own. I think it's very possible she'll recover."

Mic considered this for a moment and asked, "Do you think it's possible the waitress somehow received a lesser dose of the poison and that's why she's doing better than Camilla?" She paused for a second and continued, "You know one of the ladies from the lunch group is apparently doing pretty well too. I wonder why some people die and others just become very ill?"

Peggy shuffled her papers around and studied some lab reports. "Medications are made from potentially poisonous substances," she stopped and smiled at Mic and continued, "The poison is titrated according to weight and height. This report says the waitress takes Dilantin so she most likely has a seizure disorder. I don't have the medical histories for the other three women, but my guess is the poison hit the waitress where she was already vulnerable. I'll need to ask for the medical histories of the women in the bar," she added.

Michaela was confused for a moment and then studied the documents and said, "So it looks like the poison attacks any body system that's already weakened. Is that right?"

Peggy nodded. "That's the gist of it. Camilla was tall, thin and much older so it's more likely that she'd be affected by smaller doses meaning she could have ingested less poison and had greater symptoms. Plus, Camilla had what we call a 'pre-existing condition' a cardiac condition so the heart effects from the poison most likely predisposed her to heart attack."

Mic was definitely out of her league in this conversation. "I see, so the fact the waitress had a neurological condition, a seizure disorder, predisposed her to balance issues and maybe that's why she fell down?"

Peggy raised her eyebrows and nodded. "Yeah, possibly, but we can't say for sure. Generally, people react to medicines at the cellular level so if there's already damage, say like Camilla's heart disease, the poison seems to zero in there first to incapacitate them or cause them more serious issues."

Mic nodded. "I think I see."

Peggy pushed several more papers towards Mic. "Anyway, there are tons of poisons that this could be. I think I have a pretty good idea what this poison is."

Michaela's phone alarm sounded. "We've got to get going, Peggy. We need to be in town in about fifteen minutes. Let me clean up the dishes, you get your stuff together and we'll take my car," Mic directed as she rinsed dishes and put them in the dishwasher.

"Thanks, Michaela. It'll be interesting to see if the federal poison team has come to the same conclusion as I have," she said as she grabbed her crutches and moved slowly out of the kitchen into the hall to gather her things.

Mic watched Peggy slowly navigate the long hallway towards her office and the front door with Angel by her side. She didn't know which one of them she loved or respected more. Peggy or Angel. She decided it was a tie as she placed the last dish in the dishwasher and pushed the start button.

Chapter 31

Snake was drinking in his favorite bar. He signaled the waitress, a bleached, buxom blonde with ginormous boobs, for his fifth shot of whiskey. He'd been drinking solidly for over an hour as he watched the news soundbites from the poisonings at Busy Burger. His tattooed hand squeezed his whiskey glass and the tattooed reptile eyes gazed at him angrily. In a fit of rage, Snake threw the glass on the floor and it shattered into a million pieces. In less than sixty seconds, a muscled bouncer with upper arms as big as tree trunks stood over him.

The bouncer grabbed Snake by the neck of his shirt. "What's the problem here, man? Do I need to cut you off?" The bouncer's eyes were close together and half closed. He was stoned and Snake thought he was juiced on something else as well. He decided not to tangle with the big guy who was high as a kite. Too unpredictable.

Snake looked up at him and smiled, "Nah, just havin' a problem with my girlfriend. Just a little fit of temper on my part. Sorry, man," he apologized. "Promise I'll keep it down," he said and signaled for another whiskey.

The bouncer looked around and pointed at a stripper gyrating on a pole. "Forget the girlfriend, man. That's what you need," he said with a wide, leering smile. "I can fix you up a lot cheaper than you think."

Snake shook his head. "Nah, thanks. I'm just gonna have one more drink and be on my way." He nodded at the broken glass. "Sorry about that," he wisecracked with a brief smile.

The bouncer didn't smile. "Okay, my man. I don't care how many drinks you have, just behave yourself. I don't want to have to hurt you cuz I gotta good buzz goin' and I don't wanna ruin it," he said as he headed to the back door of the bar for another toke.

Snake stared after him and accepted the drink from the blond waitress. The woman smiled at him, her porcelain teeth gleaming in the low light and her breasts practically smothering him. He looked up at her and said, "Thanks."

The waitress batted her eyes at him and asked, "Anything special I can do for you today?" her meaning clear as she stared at Snake's crotch.

Snake shook his head and focused on his drink. He looked up when a shaft of sunlight blinded him. The bar door opened and Boris's tall, skinny frame filled the doorway. He spied Snake in his booth and moved towards his table.

Snake stared at him through half-closed eyes and said, "You've been pretty busy, haven't you?"

Boris gave him a half smile and signaled for the waitress who ran over, her boobs jumping out of her halter top.

The blonde smiled at Boris and asked, "What can I getcha?"

Boris winked at her and pointed to Snake's glass. "The same," he said as he gestured rudely under the table and grinned at Snake who looked the other way.

"I've come to take you back into the fold, ole boy and cut you in on my new grand plan," Boris said as he looked hungrily at the waitress. "This job will make us famous forever," he assured Snake as he accepted his shot glass from the waitress who beamed down at him.

Snake pointed at his glass, looked up at Blondie and said, "One more."

Chapter 32

Dottie pulled off the road and entered Madame Toulescent's address into her GPS. She hated the robot lady that gave the instructions on her GPS but didn't want to get lost in Amelia County. The country roads looked the same to her. She mulled over Camilla's death as she tried to remember every single detail. If she got to Madame's home early, she decided to jot them all down on her calendar. She didn't want to miss anything important. She jumped as her cell phone rang. It was Michaela.

"Hello, Michaela. Is this going to be long? If it is, I'm gonna have to pull off the road. I'm in my car driving in the country south of Richmond."

"What are you going over there for? I thought you never crossed the river. You know what they say about old Richmond crossing the James, don't you."

Dorothy shook her head. *Honestly, Mic never gets it.* "Really, Michaela," she said in an exasperated voice, "I'm not old Richmond. Never will be. At best, I'm old Rome. I wasn't born and bred in Richmond. I was born and bred in a villa in Italy. Can you get that through your thick skull?" she asked crossly as she pulled over into an abandoned gas station.

"Whoops, who messed with your Cheerios this morning? You're grumpy," Mic observed. "I have Dr. Peggy Grey with me and we're heading downtown to meet with the federal poison people to identify the poison that's been used in these murders."

Dottie's mood brightened and she said, "Hello, Peggy. I know Michaela appreciates your help and so do I. This has just been awful. I feel so sorry for Camilla's family and everyone else, including myself," she added. "I am going to miss my friend dreadfully." Dorothy's hand left the steering wheel to wipe a tear from her eye. Camilla had been her dear friend.

Peggy sighed deeply. "I'm so sorry about all of this, Dottie. I think I've isolated the poison that's being used. I want to see if the federal authorities agree with me. If so, it'll help us prevent other killings," Peggy said. "We can at least avenge Camilla's death and the other women and children who've died.

"That's great," Dottie said. "Then Mic and I just have to find the killer or killers. Right, Michaela?"

Mic rolled her eyes smiled over at Peggy. "Yep, that's right, Dottie. Now, where are you headed over in Southside?"

Dottie was quiet for a moment and didn't reply. "To see a friend. I'm working on this case too, as we speak."

Realization dawned as Mic figured out where Dottie was headed. It would be the only reason Dorothy Borghase would ever cross the James River. "Oh no," she wailed,

"You're not going to go see that psychic person?" *But of course she is.*

Anger flared through Dottie's body. *Why couldn't Mic admit that Madame Toulescent had helped them in the past? Why was she so obstinate?* "What's that, Michaela? I can't hear you, you're breaking up on me," Dottie said as she clicked off her Bluetooth and smiled to herself. Michaela just wouldn't admit it, but Dottie knew that Madame Toulescent could help them. She certainly had in the past, but Michaela just called it coincidence. She looked both ways and pulled carefully on to the road.

Chapter 33

Traffic was light and Michaela and Peggy arrived at FBI headquarters faster than they'd expected. Mic pulled her SUV into the loading zone and helped Peggy out of the vehicle. "Wait for me in the reception area and we'll take the elevator up."

"Okay, sounds good to me," Peggy agreed as she adjusted her crutches and grabbed her briefcase. "I'll see you in a couple of minutes."

Mic nodded as she scanned the parking area, "Yeah, I'm gonna park right over there in the guest area." She glanced in her rear view mirror and saw Slade McKane park his police cruiser. "Hey, Peggy, there's Slade. Just wait a moment and walk in with him." Mic waved Slade over to her SUV. Angel's tail wagged happily in the backseat as Slade came to Michaela's window.

"Slade, you know Peggy Grey. She's a consultant on the poison case. We're all going to the same meeting," Mic winked at him.

Slade looked over at Peggy and said, "Of course I know the famous Dr. Grey. I'd be delighted to escort you into the building, Peggy," Slade said in his Southern manner. He looked back at Mic and said, "We'll catch you inside." Slade heard Angel whimper and looked at him in the backseat. "Mic, lower your back window so I can pat Angel. He looks like he's in need of some attention."

Mic rolled her eyes and lowered the window and Slade roughed up the fur on Angel's neck. "You ready, Dr. Grey? Let's go," he said as he took her briefcase. They walked up the handicapped ramp into the building, stopped at the counter, signed in and got temporary badges.

Peggy smiled at Slade as she took a seat on the bench while they waited for Michaela. "It's good to see you, Slade. I heard you'd accepted a promotion over in major crimes. Are you missing vice at all?" she asked with a grin.

Slade laughed and said, "Nope, not a bit. This is a nice change for me, at least right now. But I gotta tell you these poison murders are bad, real bad. Killing those kids is a whole new low for crime in Richmond."

Peggy nodded her deeply set eyes serious. "You've got that, Slade. These are some bad guys who've cooked up this poison that's easy to mix in food and beverages – or to stick most anywhere." She turned her head as the electric door opened and said, "Oh, here comes Michaela. That was quick. So we can head for the elevators."

Slade nodded and grinned. Peggy couldn't help but notice how ruggedly handsome he was with his dark Irish looks. "Knowing Mic, she's parked illegally. Want to make a bet with me?"

Peggy shook her head and smiled. "Nope, I'd lose," she said with a laugh. "You forget that I know Michaela as well as you do," she reminded him. "Punch the button will you, Slade? It'll get here just about the time Mic does."

Mic jumped in the elevator just in time and they were greeted on the third floor by an agent who ushered them into a conference room. Mic looked around and noticed members of the FBI and local law enforcement gathered around a polished walnut table. After introductions, the chairman of the committee, an official in the American Association of Poison Control Centers, Dr. Duncan, spent time and reviewed the confirmed poison cases. "Let me dispel one myth right up front – there are no untraceable poisons. It may take time, but with the sophisticated equipment we currently have, we'll be able to identify the poison, most likely soon."

Slade asked, "Have you been able to rule out the common poisonous agents?"

Dr. Duncan nodded his head slightly and said, "Yes, Detective McKane. We have eliminated narcotics, amphetamines, barbiturates and sedatives since they are a part of every drug screen. These poisons are easily found on a routine toxicology analysis. It's harder to identify other poisons and plant toxins. These poisons require the medical examiner to have a suspicion that a particular toxin is involved. These tests are often expensive. In this case we have five confirmed deaths so we will go to any expense to identify the poison."

"So, do you know what it is? We need to know what the poison is," Richmond Police Chief Herndon said impatiently. Mic noted the lines around Herndon's eyes. She knew he was under tremendous stress.

Dr. Duncan hesitated and said, "We believe it's a plant alkaloid, or plant poison. I don't think we're prepared to narrow it down at this point."

"A plant poison? What does that mean?" the chief asked. Mic could hear irritation in his voice.

"It means the poison came from a plant. There are hundreds of plant poisons out there. Many grow in our backyards," Dr. Grey responded. "I know you're anxious, Chief Herndon, but I assure you we will get to the bottom of this, but we need a little time."

"I'm not sure we're prepared to narrow the poison yet." He turned to Peggy Grey and asked, "Do you have a guess, Dr. Grey. You're as experienced as anyone with plant poisons."

Peggy looked around the table and said, "Yes, I think I know what our killer is using. I think he's killing people with atropa belladonna."

"Belladonna, is that something that grows in our backyard?" asked Michaela, a quizzical look on her face. "I didn't know that."

Peggy nodded. "Yes, Ms. McPherson. It does. Atropa belladonna is one of the most toxic plants found in the world and it grows in our own backyards. All parts of the plant contain tropane alkaloids and can be lethal. The berries pose the greatest danger to children because they have a sweet taste and easily mistaken for blueberries. The consumption of two to five berries by a human adult is often lethal."

"Do the berries taste good?" asked a FBI agent working the case.

"Yes, they're sweet. And they're lethal, as I said. Children are lured to belladonna plants because of the berries and they'll pick and eat one or two berries and die. They're delicious and they make excellent sweet tea. In the 1800s, belladonna tea was a lethal murder weapon."

"Really?" Slade asked. "I think I may have heard of that."

"Yes," Detective McKane. "You probably have," Dr. Duncan said. "belladonna is popular or I should say was a popular poison in the Middle Ages. It was a weapon of war. Many warriors perished from arrows soaked in belladonna. History tells us that King Macbeth of Scotland infused belladonna in tea to kill an entire army of Danes." He paused for a moment and looked around the room. He had everyone's attention. "These are just a few stories of how this innocent, very beautiful but equally lethal plant has been used as in instrument of murder."

The room was quiet as the law enforcement officials considered the enormity of the poison and the crimes.

Peggy studied the group around the table and added, "There's no better way we know of to poison someone either quickly or slowly and make them suffer at every step along the way," she added.

“Wow," said Michaela. "Isn't this the same poisonous berry that will dilate your pupils? Because Mrs. Rothrock’s friends say her eyes were big and she was thirsty before her death."

Dr. Grey nodded and said, "It surely is. Atropa belladonna has been used cosmetically by women for centuries. In fact, the name “belladonna” means “beautiful lady,” in Italian. The berry juice was used in Italy to enlarge the women’s pupils, giving them a striking, doe-eyed appearance. Of course, this wasn’t smart because the plant was poisonous. Nevertheless, the ladies were lovely as long as they lived,” he said with a smile.

“My mother always told me that beauty suffers pain,” a young female agent said cynically. “I had no idea what she meant.”

“I’d say that’s vanity to the extreme. I don’t think looking good is worth your life, or a slow, painful death,” a male FBI agent exclaimed.

“No argument from me,” Dr. Grey said. “However, we’ve used belladonna in medicine for years and it has many useful properties as an anesthetic and sedative. Currently it’s regarded as unsafe. But we still use it infrequently in medicine. Right, Dr. Duncan?”

“Yes,” Dr. Duncan said. “As Dr. Grey mentioned, belladonna is used as a sedative, or as an anti-spasmodic to stop bronchial spasms in respiratory disease. Sometimes it is used in ointments prescribed for joint pain or leg pain caused by back injury. But, it is used with caution. Other medications have been developed that are much safer.” He looked at Peggy for affirmation.

Peggy nodded and continued, "Dr. Duncan is correct. Also, belladonna has anticholinergic properties and can cause interruptions in thinking, memory, and learning. It can also cause seizures which can be life threatening. As we said, the consumption of just a few berries by a human adult can be lethal."

"That's not much," Michaela noted.

Peggy shook her head. "You're right. It's not much at all, but the roots are the most toxic part of the plant."

"So, the roots are the most poisonous part? What do people do, boil them and make another potion?" an agent questioned.

"The creativity of the criminal mind never ceases to amaze us," Dr. Duncan added. "Serial poisoners are creative. What's important to remember is that belladonna is a weapon of stealth and can be used by just about anyone. In the 1800s, a nurse was convicted of the murder of seven patients using belladonna as her weapon. Also, a doctor murdered his wife with morphine and put atropine, a belladonna derivative, in her eyes to overcome the pinpoint pupils often seen with morphine use." Dr. Duncan noticed the looks of surprise on people's faces and added, "Amazing how cunning some killers are, isn't it?"

"No kidding," Slade said sarcastically. "And devious. Anything else we need to know about this killer plant?"

"It can be found just about anywhere," Dr. Grey said. "It goes under the name of Nightshade and it's a popular garden plant. It can be found at many landscape dealerships and nurseries."

"That's just great," Slade said under his breath as Mic kicked him on his shin under the table. Peggy Grey smiled at him.

"I'm wondering," Michaela said out loud, "just how big is the problem of serial poisoners? Honestly, I've been chasing perps and murderers for years and have never had a poison case."

"That's a great question," Dr. Duncan responded. "They're actually more common than you would think. Experts believe the number of convicted poisoners is the tip of the iceberg and in actuality, the number is much higher, possibly thirty to forty percent higher."

"Is there a profile of this poisoner or poisoners?" Slade asked, as he looked at the special-agent-in-charge, a tall man by the name of Burnley who looked to be about fifty with gray hair. Burnley stood by the door.

Agent Burnley shook his head. "We don't have an 'official' profile. Contrary to popular belief, most convicted poisoners are men, almost always when the victim is a woman. If the victims are females, as they are so far in these cases, the poisoner is equally likely to be male or female. Perpetrators rarely cross racial lines when they decide to kill, meaning African Americans tend to be poisoned by other African Americans, Caucasians by other Caucasians and so on. We think on the average, a homicidal poisoner is five to ten years younger than his or her victim. However, this wouldn't apply here since this poisoner has killed an elder, a young adult, and children."

"Could I interrupt you for just a moment, Agent Burnley?" Peggy Grey asked.

"Of course, Dr. Grey," Agent Burnley said with a smile.

Peggy flashed him a smile, "As Agent Burnley suggested, our poisoner appears to be rogue. He's killing everyone he can and has no particular agenda except to kill. Killing with poison requires careful planning and specific knowledge of the poison. There's no surprise that poisoners tend to be cunning, sneaky and creative. Poisoners avoid physical confrontation and rely on verbal and emotional manipulation to get what they want from others. Some folks describe poisoning as a 'chicken' crime."

Mic interrupted. "But, it seems to me that this poisoner is acting like a terrorist. These are not crimes of jealously, passion, revenge, or even specific hate crimes. This poisoner is killing, just to kill," Michaela observed. "Or at least, it seems that way to me."

Peggy nodded her head. "That's true, Michaela. Sometimes poisoners are caregivers of the person they're trying to poison. Consider the loving husband who is poisoning his wife or mother over time or the doting mother who is slowly poisoning her children, most likely for her own self-gain."

"Like in Munchausen's syndrome?" asked a FBI agent.

Dr. Grey nodded, "Yes, Munchausen's by Proxy. Poisoners may act the role of tender, loving caregiver to the person they're slowly killing with poison. In this case, as Ms. McPherson suggested, we're not seeing the most common motives of poisoners – which is significant from a profiling aspect."

"Oh, this is serious and has huge implications," Slade observed.

Peggy nodded. "Our poisoner or poisoners may have a political or mass-assassination motive. There's no revenge, no love triangle, no insurance money, no gainful reason we've been able to ascertain other than just the need and/or the desire to kill." Dr. Grey watched the faces of the law enforcement officials as they digested her words. Their faces reflected anger and disgust.

"While we don't have a profile in these cases, we're working on one," Agent Burnley reported. "We profile based on what we know, in general, and from information obtained from research on convicted poisoners. So, we can only talk about the personalities of poisoners *who get caught*. We can make *some* hypotheses about the personalities of poisoners by studying the nature of the crime, in this case multiple crimes."

"So what do you think?" Mic asked, leaning in toward Burnley.

As Agent Burnley continued to speak, Mic pegged him as a psychologist, probably part of the famous, elite FBI profiling team. "Convicted poisoners have a sense of inadequacy and they compensate through a high disregard for authority and a strong need for control. Most research suggests incarcerated, convicted poisoners report wish-fulfillment fantasies, and exhibit a self-centered, exploitive interpersonal style." Burnley looked around the room and added, "Based on experience, we think these criminals will be about the same."

"So, they all came from broken homes, were poor, did badly in school, have juvie records and the like?" Slade asked. "What's new?"

"Yeah," Burnley said and gave Slade a half-smile. "Pretty much, Detective. Some psychologists compare the poisoner's personality to an amoral, incorrigible child who always wants his own way. This personality trait leads him or her to try to control and manipulate the world."

Slade rolled his eyes and Michaela whispered to him to behave.

Burnley looked around the table and noted rapt interest in the group. He continued, "Serial poisoners have been described as developmentally stunted and without empathy, concern or consideration for others. The poisoner's internal compass is guided instead by greed or lust rather than morals, hence the revenge poisoner or the one who murders for money. In fact, they get joy and pleasure out of watching their victims suffer," he added.

"Don't a lot of poisoners get by with their crimes for a long time?" Mic asked.

Burnley nodded. "Yeah, they do. Most likely because poison is often not detected initially at death. The poisoner continues to escalate his or her murders. The power and control poisoners experience with successful kills tends to increase their confidence in committing future murders."

"So, they're sociopaths, right? Just like any other repeat offender… murderers, rapists and the like?" Slade said.

Burnley cracked a smile. "Pretty much. In some ways, they share some of the same traits of a sociopathic personality," Burnley agreed.

Chief Herndon had been listening intently to the conversation. "So, Agent Burnley, how old do you think these perps are?"

Agent Burnley shook his head. "Hard to say, Chief. As noted earlier, the poisoner is usually ten or so years older than the victim, but in this case, that doesn't apply because of the attack on the school children. So, basically, we have no idea. But, I do think these killers – and yes I think there's more than one – have some specialized knowledge of poison. And based on that assumption it leads me to wonder if either one or both of them are somehow connected to the medical profession or at least in the physical sciences."

Dr. Duncan raised his eyebrow and asked, "What makes you think this, Agent Burnley?"

"While my knowledge of atropa belladonna is limited, it would appear the killers titrated the dose quite effectively... enough to make two of the victims, the ladies at lunch, suffer immensely, while Mrs. Rothrock died fairly quickly. We know several school children have passed away from the poison and we've yet to know about the others."

Dr. Duncan nodded, "There's truth in what you say, but it could just be the pre-existing health states of the victims." He turned to Dr. Grey and asked, "Peggy, what do you think?"

Peggy thought for a moment before she responded. "I honestly don't know. I don't think we can say with any degree of certainty. Mrs. Rothrock's heart condition was pivotal in her demise and we know the waitress at the Hotel Madison had a seizure disorder. Quite possibly the belladonna affected her neurological status causing her to lose balance and fall." She paused for a moment and added,

"You know, there's so much we don't know, but I believe we can conclude that premorbid health status did contribute to or hasten debilitation and death."

"What about the kids? Were the ones that died sick?" Burnley asked.

Peggy shook her head. "Too early. We don't know yet about the school children who have died, but we'll keep you in the loop as we find out."

"But, do you think the perps are members of the medical community?" Michaela persisted.

Peggy pondered before she replied. "I don't know, but it's possible. History has proven that." She paused for a moment and added, "I do agree it's someone with a science background, though, possibly chemistry or biology."

"Can you tell us more about how the poison affects people?" Slade asked.

Peggy nodded, "Sure, Detective. It's difficult to quantify the dose because symptoms may be slow to appear. The poison is affected by the state of health and size of the victims." She saw confusion on several of the police officers' faces and said, "A tall, heavy individual will require more poison than a child."

"So, what are the symptoms we're looking for, then?" an agent asked.

Peggy smiled apologetically and said, "There's really no defined set of symptoms, wouldn't you agree, Dr. Duncan?"

Duncan nodded. "Yes. There are no symptoms defined by research, but there are a few we can look for. Symptoms are varied but may include dryness in the mouth, thirst, problems swallowing and speaking."

Peggy continued, "Other victims become drowsy, have slurred speech, hallucinations, confusion, disorientation, delirium, and agitation. Coma and convulsions often occur prior to death."

"Isn't some of this what happened to Mrs. Rothrock before her death?" Mic questioned.

Peggy nodded. "We know that Mrs. Rothrock had heart issues and was confused before she died. The same is true of the female victim at St. Mary's. She had the same confusion before her death. Another woman is currently ill and unresponsive."

"So, is there an actual fatal dose?" Chief Herndon asked. "I'm finding this a little confusing."

Peggy shook her head. "We don't know the fatal dose. It's variable." Peggy paused for a second and added, "As we've mentioned before." Peggy knew it was hard for lay people to understand medical diagnoses and effects. She'd figured that out years ago while a medical examiner in

Richmond. She smiled and spoke, "I know you guys like your cause of death all wrapped up nicely with a ballistics match, the smoking gun or a bloody knife." She shrugged her shoulders apologetically. "We just can't give you that in this case."

Dr. Duncan intervened and said, "Dr. Grey is correct. When you work with poison, it's all relative to health status, age, and weight of the victim and dose. Research describes a fatal dose for a child who ate a half a berry dying alongside a nine-year-old boy who ate between twenty and twenty-five berries and survived."

"So, basically, we just don't know," Peggy added.

"Does anyone have any further questions, or should we summarize?" Dr. Duncan asked.

There was silence and no questions so Dr. Duncan began to summarize. "Okay, so I'm going to summarize from my notes. Dr. Grey has a strong suspicion the poison is atropa belladonna and at this point, I tentatively agree. We'll confirm this through further testing using some colorimetrics and other advanced tests. Special-Agent-in-Charge Burnley believes there may be more than one serial poisoner. At this point, we can't identify the age of the poisoners because of the range in the ages of the victims. We've covered the general motives of serial poisoners along with a history of the use of belladonna as a poison. Have I missed anything?"

Dr. Grey nodded her head and said, "That's pretty much what I have as well. We'll continue to gather data from the dead and monitor the progress of the victims in the hospital." She turned to SAC Burnley and asked, "Will there be a profile soon?"

SAC Burnley nodded his head. "I hope so. But for now, unofficially, I say we look for several murderers. These guys, and I do believe our killers are male, are murdering people in bars and restaurants. Basically, they'll kill anywhere they can. There's a possibility they are medical professionals. Any questions?" he asked as he looked around the table.

He heard Slade whispering to Mic. "Do you have a question, McKane?"

Slade shook his head, "No. Just want to get them before they kill again."

Burnley nodded. "Yeah, we all do. Let's continue to work together, share information and catch these killers."

"Here, here," said an agent in the back of the room. "Let's go get them."

Slade looked into Mic's eyes and shook his head. His gut burned with rage. Both knew they were dealing with a couple of sickos. "Let's get outta here," he said to Mic and Peggy.

Chapter 34

Dottie turned off the main highway and headed south to Blackstone Virginia. Madame Toulescent lived just outside of Blackstone and that's where she conducted her psychic readings. She wished away the butterflies that cramped her stomach. She had a sense that what she was going to hear wasn't good. She wished she didn't believe in the value of psychics or the unknown, but she did, and that was that. She'd seen psychic readings and prophecies come true time after time during her life. Mic wasn't a believer at all but had grudgingly admitted psychics had helped them in a case about ten years ago.

The speedometer on her car registered over sixty miles an hour on a forty-five mile limit stretch of highway. *I'd better slow down. The last thing I need is a Virginia State Trooper on my tail.* She braked and her car skidded, but she handled it skillfully. The Cadillac was a big, monster car, but she really liked it. Since Dottie had lived in the US, she had always preferred German-made cars and previously owned multiple Mercedes Benz. Of course, when Count Borghase had been alive, they'd always driven Italian cars, mainly Ferraris. But now she was pretty much American and she loved her Caddy. There was something about the Cadillac that was so plush and so American that she bought a new one every couple of years.

She saw an old gray mule in the pasture out of the corner of her eye and saw the fence that was lying on the side. Dottie didn't know what she'd do if they ever repaired that fence. She'd been looking fo that fence on the ground for years and it was her landmark just before she turned onto Madame's private road. She knew her turn was just up ahead. She slowed for a farmer carrying a load of hay in an old truck. He was hogging the entire road. *Now where in the hell am I supposed to go?* She steered her big car to the side of the road as far as she could without falling into the ditch. She cursed and held her breath as the farmer passed her. She swore the farmer missed her by less than an inch. The old codger hadn't even looked her way. She shook her head and cursed again softly. She threw her white Caddy into first gear and roared out of the ditch spewing gravel, dirt, and mud all over the road. She saw three rabbits running for their life and hoped she hadn't interrupted their nest. Dottie drove a little further and made her left turn. She turned right on the first road and started the difficult trip along the horrible, rutted road to Madame Toulescent's tiny home. The road was almost a mile long. Dottie's tall, thin frame bounced all over her plush leather seat and her hair fell out of her neatly arranged bun. *I'm going to have to take a pain pill. All this jumping around is killing my hips.* Secretly Dottie knew she needed to have her hips replaced but there was no way she was willing to do that, at least not while she could walk. *I wouldn't be able to help Michaela. And then, what would she do?*

Madame Toulescent waved at Dottie from her front porch filled with flowers and beautiful hanging baskets of petunias and begonias. Her small white cottage was immaculate. Madame Toulescent watched her painstakingly steer her huge Cadillac down her battered road. Dottie brought the iron beast to a stop, looked in her rearview mirror and re-pinned a piece of white hair that had worked its way out of her perfect updo. Even though Madame lived in a house that was little better than a house trailer, Dottie had been trained from birth to always look perfect when visiting. This task had become monumental at age eighty-two. She reached for her purse and checked to make sure her Glock was nestled in its special pocket. She checked her lipstick in the mirror, pinched her lips together, cursed the fine lines around her mouth and got out of the car.

"Hello, Madame Toulescent. Thank you for seeing me today on short notice." Dorothy smiled her gracious smile at the psychic, showing her beautiful white veneers, once available for a large price from the famous, dentist-to-the-stars Dr. Michael Smirkowitz.

"You are so welcome, Countess Borghase." Madame Toulescent looked around the empty fields and through the trees and gestured with her arm. "As you can see, there is no waiting line. Please come in. I've made us some tea." She paused for a moment and said, "Watch the steps. They're in need of repair," she cautioned.

In need of repair, my butt, they need to be rebuilt! Dottie climbed the rickety steps dodging rusty nails and wood splinters. She grasped the loose railing and posts that held up the old front porch. The last thing she wanted to do was fall and break something. She followed Madame Toulescent into her small but neat and cozy home. There was a wonderful scent in the air and Dottie's mouth watered.

"Please have a seat in the easy chair," the Madame offered. "I'll bring us some tea and sweet bread."

Dottie nodded and smiled her thanks as she carefully studied Madame Toulescent. She wasn't sure of her nationality. She thought she was Eastern European, but she seemed very much like the French and her house had several amazing pieces of French country furniture. In years past she had asked Madame about her former life, but the psychic seemed unwilling to share her past. Her voice had a strange accent Dottie couldn't identify which frustrated her. Dottie had traveled the world and she knew the languages and dialects of most ethnic populations. But she couldn't figure out Madame Toulescent's origins. That puzzled her.

Madame handed Dottie a cup of herb tea. The aroma alerted her senses and she immediately felt more awake and inspired. The tea had given her energy and awareness. She took a sip. It was delicious.

Whatever is in this tea? I feel a million times better just from smelling it. You've got to tell me where you got it because I know Cookie would love it too," Dottie gushed as she sipped her tea.

Madame Toulescent smiled and said. "I made the tea. It's a blend of ginger, mint, lemon verbena and a few other things I grow in my herb garden. I'll send some home with you. It's sweetened with honey I collected from my bees yesterday." She smiled briefly, and her lips stretched over teeth that could benefit from a cosmetic dentist. "That's probably what you love so much."

Dottie nodded and studied the Madame. The years hadn't treated her so well. Dottie didn't know her age, but her face was a mass of wrinkles that blended one into the other. Dottie guessed each wrinkle had its own story. Her skin appeared soft but deeply creased. Her jet black hair was streaked with gray and hung freely past her shoulders. She wore a simple blue shift with a silver belt and wore tennis shoes and socks. She smelled of lemon and freesia.

Dottie, as usual, smelled of Chanel No. 5. "It's so lovely out here, Madame. Do you ever come to town?"

Madame Toulescent shook her head. "Very rarely. My neighbor collects my groceries for me when I need them and as you know, I have a huge vegetable garden and I can and freeze most everything I need. I like it here and I like to stay with my animals — my dogs, cats, cow, mules and horses. It's quiet here and my love is nature."

Dottie nodded. She couldn't imagine staying in these four walls every single day. She supposed she didn't have the patience and gentleness of spirit that Madame had. But that was okay. Dottie was very happy in her own way.

The two women shared a comfortable silence and continued to sip their tea until Madame asked, "How can I help you today, Countess?" She smiled at her and said, "I can tell you have some significant things on your mind and that you are troubled."

Dottie put her teacup down and said, "Yes, I do. Have you been watching the news?" Dottie saw the woman pale under her sun-darkened skin.

Madame Toulescent nodded. "You're here about the poisonings, aren't you?"

Dottie held Madame's dark eyes with her own and said, "Yes, I am. Camilla Rothrock was one of my dearest friends and I need to know who poisoned her."

Madame shifted her gaze to the floor and said, "Countess Borghase, this is a very bad business that is happening. I've had some visions and they are upsetting. It reminds me of the evil work of Hitler in Germany."

This time it was Dottie who paled, her heart beating so hard she could hardly breathe. "Oh my God, Madame. We both remember his devastation in Europe and the millions of people he murdered."

Madame Toulescent rubbed her hands together, her face grim. "Indeed we do. A sad and sorry time. Let's move into the back where I work and see what we can see."

Dottie stood and followed Madame to the room in the far back of her modest home. It was a glass room with beautiful views into the forest. She left her teacup on the coffee table. Her heart thumped dangerously in her chest and she was short of breath. She was so terrified she almost lost her balance. She gripped her purse and cell phone in her hand. She was scared and just the idea of having the Glock made her feel safer. Could the evil be so strong it permeated her soul?

"Countess, why are you so upset? What can I do to help you?" Madame Toulescent looked at Dottie with concern.

Dottie stared at her, but her eyes said it all.

"Let me get you something to calm you down so we can have a good reading. Please stay in the chair and I'll be right back," Madame Toulescent said as she left Dottie and walked to her kitchen.

Chapter 35

Dottie sat quietly in a large wing-backed chair in the calm serenity of Madame Toulescent's solarium. The herbs Madame Toulescent had given her had done the trick. She could feel herself calming down. She could hear the rushing of the James River in the distance and she was mesmerized by the cattle grazing in the field in the distance. Perhaps all was right with the world. She supposed she'd know soon enough.

Madame motioned her to a simple wooden table on the side of the room. Dottie arose from her chair and took the seat facing the psychic. Madame Toulescent's eyes glazed as she looked through the glass window out into the fields. Dottie wondered what she was seeing but sat quietly and watched.

"Countess Borghase, you know I'm a psychic. Generally, when we meet, I do psychic readings. But, I also function as a spiritual medium. Would you like for me to see if I could talk with your friend, Camilla?"

Dottie's stomach knotted up and she felt nauseous. She stared at Madame Toulescent and said, her voice hesitant, "I... I don't know. I've never done that before. Will it help?"

Madame Toulescent could sense her hesitation. "You seem frightened to talk with your friend or at least have your friend communicate with us. Let's see what else we can do."

"I didn't know you talked with spirits," Dottie said. "Can you tell me how that works?"

"Well, there are quite a few things I can do," Madame Toulescent said gently. She could see Dottie was upset about channeling Camilla. "We've mostly done psychic readings when you've visited. The psychic readings are about getting advice, guidance or direction around things that are happening in your life. There've been a couple of times when you've been here in crises and you wanted some help or direction. It is my belief that a reading is getting confirmation on what our own intuition is already telling us. Most of the time, I've simply confirmed what your intuition had already suggested. I've validated what you already knew. Often as a psychic, I only teach and help people confirm their own wisdom."

Dottie nodded, "Yes, I agree with that. Most of the time you've validated what I've thought and believed and have helped me decide what to do next."

Madame nodded. "Yes, this is true."

"But, Countess," she said taking Dottie's cold hand into her warm one, "I also work as a medium and I can contact your friend Camilla and we can learn about the last few moments of her life."

Dottie's eyes filled with tears, "But I don't know if I want to know about Camilla's last few minutes. She looked so horrible and I think she was scared and in pain," she ended with a choked sob.

Madame Toulescent nodded. "I understand what you are saying. I just want to tell you that it's possible we can learn from Camilla. Perhaps she can help us solve the poisonings."

Dottie was silent for a moment as she considered the possibilities. Certainly, she could be uncomfortable and upset for a few moments, particularly if she could help Michaela and the police solve these horrible murders. Besides, that would prove to Mic that she wasn't old and helpless... although she really didn't think Michaela thought that. That was her insecurity popping up. "Um, okay. I'll do it. But first, could we just look at the murders in general. Could you tell me what you see and perhaps give me some direction that I can share with the authorities?"

"Of course I can, Countess. In no way do I want to upset you or frighten you, but I'm sure your friend wants to send us a message. I can feel her trying to get though," Madame Toulescent said. "In the meantime, let me focus on the poisonings. Give me a few moments to think and commune."

It was a lovely day. The birds were singing, the cattle were grazing contently in the field. Dottie smiled and focused on a mother deer and her fawn that grazed in the grass about twenty yards from the back window. They were beautiful. The fawn was young and still had its spots. She watched as the mother nudged her and encouraged her to eat the grass, but the fawn just wanted to play. She smiled as she saw them frolic in the sunshine.

She heard a low moan come from deep in Madame's throat. The sound sent shivers up Dottie's back. She wondered what Madame Toulescent saw in her vision. The moaning became worse and Dottie could hardly sit still. Her eyes returned to the view outside. The mother and fawn were staring into the window. The birds were no longer chirping. *I think they know something is about to happen here.*

Madame Toulescent was in a trance and her body swayed from left to right as she moaned and said "no" over and over. She had a conversation with someone, smiled gently and said, "Yes, yes. I will."

Dottie's eyes returned to the bucolic scene in front of her. Everything was okay now. The mother deer and her baby were gone, and she could see several cardinals feasting on the seed in the birdfeeder. She could hear other birds chirping in the distance. The cows chewed their cud contentedly in the fields and the sun was bright on the early spring wild flowers. Something must be right with the world, she thought. *Yes, all is right with the world, at least for a moment.*

It seemed forever before Madame Toulescent rose from her trance. She looked at Dottie and asked, "Are you okay?"

Dottie shrugged her shoulders and said, "Yes, yes, I'm fine. Can you tell me what you saw?"

A dark shadow flashed across Madame's face and she said, "I saw a lot. I felt the fear of Camilla and the three young women at the bar. I could feel the pain the women endured as the poison struck their internal organs."

Dottie nodded and waited for more.

"Regrettably, I heard the screams and felt the fear of the school children. I talked with the children that had died and wiped their tears."

Madame Toulescent paused for a moment to rest. Dottie watched as her shoulders relaxed and her breathing returned to normal. She went into the living room and returned with the teapot. She refilled their cups and said, "There are two men who are killing these people. One man has an agenda to kill, but the other man kills for sport. They are evil and will stop at nothing to reach their goal." Madame Toulescent was silent for a moment and sipped her tea.

Dottie waited patiently which was one of the most difficult tasks ever for her. She was simply not patient and wanted what she wanted the second she wanted to have it. As she waited for Madam to continue, she found herself replacing the bobby pins in her hair and picking at her nails. She crossed and uncrossed her legs several times until Madame Toulescent reached under the table and put her hand on Dottie's knee to quiet her.

"Please stop that, Countess. I can't focus. I'm trying to remember things. We'll talk in a moment."

Dottie felt like a child in kindergarten. She hung her head in shame because she had interrupted Madame. A couple of minutes later, Madame said, "The two men will continue to kill as they have for a few more days. Then they plan to poison a large number of people, possibly thousands at a major event. I don't know where, but it is coming soon."

Dottie's heart jumped into her throat. She was so frightened she could hardly speak and beside herself with anxiety and fear. She stared at Madame Toulescent until she found her voice.

"But wait… when and where will they attack?"

Madame Toulescent repeated, "I do not know when the attack will be. Perhaps the men have not planned a date and they do not know."

Dottie could feel fear and anxiety creep up her spine and she asked, her voice quavering, "What else, what else is there that you won't tell me?"

Madame Toulescent stared into Dottie's ice blue eyes and said, "Camilla said to tell you the poison was in the tea. She said when she drank the tea she began to feel sick and then she couldn't talk or see anymore. She also said to tell you that she is okay now. She wants you to tell the general she's fine and not to worry."

Dottie nodded slowly and said, "I guess that's good, if you have to be dead, right?"

Madame Toulescent nodded as she watched Dottie pull herself together and gather her purse. She stood up and offered the Madam her hand. "Thank you. Thank you for seeing me on such short notice. I truly appreciate it."

Madame Toulescent nodded and said softly," There's one more thing, Countess. Do you want to hear it?"

Dottie nodded and said, "I suppose so."

"Michaela is in grave danger. You must watch out for her carefully."

Dottie's spine stiffened and she stood even straighter as she looked down at the psychic, "Danger how? What kind of danger?" Dottie's heart fluttered in her chest and she held on to the back of the chair for support. She couldn't let anything happen to Michaela.

Madame shook her head. "I don't know. I could not see her danger, but I can feel it and it's real. Please watch out for her. These men are cruel and evil. They will stop at nothing."

Dottie said simply, "I will. I always do."

"And, Dottie," Madame Toulescent added, "I believe you are in danger as well. So I urge you to take no chances and to stay safe."

Dottie grinned and flashed Madame Toulescent her favorite aristocratic smile. "I'll be fine, Madame. I'm always in danger. After all, I'm eighty-two years old."

Madame smiled, "I am serious, Dottie, please watch yourself and stay safe."

"I will, I promise, thank you." Dottie's voice sounded a lot stronger than she felt as she left Madame's modest home and walked the short distance to her car. She opened her door and sat down, grateful for the softness of the plush, soft leather cushions. She closed her eyes and a million rays of light invaded her head. She was stressed, deeply scared and worried. These were different feelings for Dottie who usually only feared forgetting something or losing her memory. *I've got to take care of Michaela.*

Madame Toulescent watched Dottie back up her big car and continue down the deeply rutted road. She felt intense fear for the Countess, but she feared mostly for Michaela McPherson. These were evil men.

Chapter 36

Michaela and Angel stood on Dottie's circular front porch and waited for someone to answer the door. Mic looked down at Angel and said, "Hey, buddy, I know you're tired and I know you want to go home, but I just gotta see what Dottie is up to. You know how she is," she said as she looked into the dog's eyes and scratched his ears.

Angel looked up at Michaela and smiled. He loved to come to Dottie's house because that meant he'd get great treats. Angel loved Cookie, Dottie's housekeeper, who always managed to find him a meaty bone or two while he was there.

"Michaela, Angel, what a wonderful, unexpected surprise. I'm delighted to see you both," Cookie said happily, a wide smile on her face. "Can you stay for dinner? We're cooking a lovely London broil on the grill, or at least Henry is," she said. "As you know, I don't cook on the grill."

The thought of London broil made Mic's stomach growl. She hadn't eaten since the chicken salad biscuits she had shared with Peggy Grey seven hours earlier. Plus, she hadn't taken anything out of the freezer or planned anything for her own dinner. "I'd love to stay, Cookie, if it's not too much trouble. I love London broil on the grill and I love every single thing you cook. I wish I'd known and bought something to share."

"No, not a problem. We have everything and it'll be wonderful to have you. The countess will be pleased." A scowl crossed Cookie's face. "She's in one of her 'moods' so maybe you can cheer her up."

Mic rolled her eyes and smiled. "I'll do my best, but you never know with Dottie. Where is she?"

Cookie gestured with her head. "She's back in the library having her before dinner sherry. Feel free to go back. Can I offer you a glass of white wine? We've some excellent sauvignon blanc that I just opened for myself."

Mic smiled and said, "That'd be great. I'd love some. It's been a long day."

Cookie leaned down and ruffled Angel's ears and said, "Come on, you old mongrel. I have just what you need in the kitchen. Thank goodness I kept one here just in case." She looked back at Michaela and said, "Henry dropped two bones off at your house today and put them in the freezer."

"Thanks, Cookie, and Angel thanks you too," she said as she looked down at her dog. Angel looked up and gave both Cookie and Michaela adoring looks and then dutifully followed Cookie to the kitchen his tail moving non-stop. He held his head and his tail high and had a spring in his step. He knew good stuff was in store for him. Mic glanced after him. She loved it when he looked so happy.

She watched the two walk down the hall and then covered the short distance to Dottie's enormously grand library where the countess sat in her recliner sipping her sherry and watching the seven o'clock news. She looked up and gave Mic a tight smile. "Michaela, I didn't know you were coming by this evening," she said as she gazed at her friend with hooded eyes.

Mic placed her hand on her hip and glared at her. "Now, Dottie. Do you honestly think I don't know that you hung up on me this afternoon?"

Dottie smiled at her and said, "I told you, and I'm gonna tell you again. I lost reception. I was out in the country and there wasn't a cell tower around."

Michaela shook her head. "I'll never believe that. You blew me off and we both know it."

Dottie did nothing but continued to sip her sherry. *Damn, she knows me like a book.*

Mic sat opposite Dottie and asked, "Where were you this afternoon, Dorothy? Where were you in your ginormous Cadillac where there were no cell towers?" Mic glared at her.

Dottie said nothing and continued to stare at the evening news. Mic reached for the remote and clicked off the TV.

Dottie glared at her and said, "That's my damned remote and it's my TV. Give it back. Give it back right now," she demanded.

Michaela held up the remote and taunted her with it. "I'll give it back as soon as you tell me where you were. I know you were south of the river because you told me that much."

Dottie continued to glare at her and said with defiance in her voice, "I went to visit Madame Toulescent. So there. Period. Now you know." She gave Mic her frostiest aristocratic stare. "I dare you to say anything."

Mic shook her head. "Honestly. Why do you run to the psychic every time there's something you can't figure out? You have to use your head and wits. But you, every time you have a question, you drive halfway to hell to try to find the answer from some sort of psychic medium or whatever she is."

Dottie was pissed. She stood up, knocking her sherry glass off the table. "You know Madame Toulescent has helped us before. She has an impeccable reputation and has helped us in the past. She narrowed the location before we apprehended that killer a couple of years ago and she helped us find the pervert that kidnapped that eleven-year-old boy."

Michaela was silent as she thought back to those cases. It was true they'd taken leads from psychics, particularly Madame Toulescent, and had hit pay dirt several times. But Mic was a believer in evidence, clues and science. Not seers or psychics. But she was also smart enough to know she wasn't going to win this argument with Dottie.

Dottie continued to stare at her as she eased back down in her chair.

"Okay, okay," she said wearily. "I give up. What did Madame Toulescent say?"

"It wasn't good," Dottie admitted. "Let me tell you," she said quietly as a knock sounded on the door and Cookie entered with Michaela's glass of wine on a silver tray.

Chapter 37

Boris held the beaker up to the light and inspected it. The liquid was crystal clear. He smiled and turned to Snake, "I think I've done it. I think this is it," a look of pride in his eyes.

Snake sat up quickly. He'd almost been asleep. They'd been in Boris's lab for hours. He looked around the room quickly and saw dozens of dead mice, cats and a few groundhogs. Boris had been experimenting on any animal or creature he could catch with his hands without fear of reprisal. He stood up, walked over to his partner and glanced at the liquid. "It's about time. Damn, we've been here all day," he said as he looked around at Boris's makeshift lab that was in a nasty garage over off Porter Street in Richmond's Southside. It was a neighborhood where no one would ask questions because they didn't care.

Boris glared at Snake from across the room. "What the hell do you expect? I'm making poison enough to kill thousands of people. Of course it's going to take time." His eyes glittered with anger.

Snake was silent. He'd just have to suck it up. He was too close to D-Day to fight with Boris again. After all, they'd just had a knockdown drag-out yesterday. Besides, in his mind, the dude was crazy and he didn't trust him as far as he could throw him. "Yeah, yeah, yeah. I hear you. What is it they say? Practice makes perfect?"

"Something like that," Boris said as he surveyed his handiwork. All around him were pieces of paper with formulas, ratios and symbols Snake didn't understand. He was curious. "What are you, man? Some chemist or physicist or something? How'd you know how to make up big batches of poison? It ain't something they teach in school," he said snidely as he stared at the five-gallon bucket of poison.

Boris smiled smugly, mostly to himself as he admired his work. "It's just something I picked up along the way. Don't worry about it. When I do something I do it right."

Snake stretched his limbs and walked idly around the garage scoping out the equipment. He had everything you could imagine. Microscopes, Bunsen burners, beakers, gradients, eye goggles, supplies, syringes, needles and pretty much everything else you'd expect to see in a lab. The place reminded him, sans air-conditioning and sanitation, of one of the big labs at MCV in Sanger Hall. Once again, he wondered who Boris worked for. The guy had never told him. *Who was the big boss in this deal?*

He decided to find out. "So, who are we working for this time, partner?" Snake asked hoping to learn where his paycheck would come from.

Boris continued to drop poison into small containers. "No need to know."

Anger shot through Snake. Of course, there was a need to know. He put his life out there every day for people and he had no idea who they were. "Ah, yeah… there's a need to know. I got my ass stuck out here every day so I think I got a right to know who's who." Snake paused for a moment and continued, "If I like them and do a better job, maybe I'll get a bonus," he joked.

Boris remained silent as he labeled his poison containers.

Snake moved closer to Boris and grabbed his shoulder, "Man, I'm talking to you. Pay attention. Who are we working for?"

Boris slowly turned his head until he was eye level with Snake. His eyes were cold and empty. They looked like the eyes of the dead man. "You ain't gonna know who you're working for. So shut up." He looked over at the beaker of poison and said, "If you ask me again, I'm going to shut you up," he threatened as he stared meaningfully at the poison.

Snake knew it was time to back down. He raised his hands up in surrender and said, "Okay, okay. I get it. I think I'm gonna leave for a while. Text me when you want to discuss our plans for the big one," he said with a big grin.

But Boris was once again focused on his test tubes. He didn't bother to respond, but Snake knew he was watching him out of the corner of his eye.

Snake moved across the room towards the door and said, "Later, man. Don't hurt yourself." He grinned and said, "I'd hate to see you die from your own poison." As he walked down Porter Street towards his car he wondered again who his employer was. He knew it was a terrorist group, but he didn't know if they were domestic or international. For some reason he thought they might be domestic. But he didn't know for sure. Maybe they were just trying to make the police look bad. He snorted and laughed. *That was easy enough to do.*

Chapter 38

Michaela loved the way the cut glass wine goblet felt in her hands. Sharp, edgy and cool. She sat on the silk upholstered chair opposite Dottie and listened to her story. Mic looked calm on the outside but her insides were being eaten alive by dread and terror. *Where would these perps strike*? The possibilities terrified her. Richmond had gotten so big and every Saturday in May was full of special events. The possibilities were endless. She needed to talk with Slade and the FBI. She believed they would take a serious hit in just a matter of a few days. It was pretty coincidental that Madame Toulescent corroborated what the FBI suspected.

"Michaela, honestly, are you listening to me? Did you understand what I said?" Dottie asked in an irritable voice. Mic did not respond and Dottie spoke loudly and asked, "MIC, ARE YOU LISTENING TO ME?"

Michaela was startled and turned her attention back to Dottie. "Oh, Dottie. I'm sorry. My mind had wandered with the possibility of a large attack. So far, we've just been thinking about restaurants and fast food joints. It terrifies me they can hit most anywhere." A dark shadow passed over Mic's face and her green eyes clouded with fear.

"Yes, of course they can, you ninny," Dottie snapped. "But I'm worried about the direct threat to you. That's first and foremost on my mind."

Mic looked surprised. "Threat, what direct threat to me? What are you talking about, Dottie?"

Dottie sighed and rolled her eyes. "Have you been listening to me at all? Madame Toulescent said you're in grave danger. She said you had to be very careful."

Michaela smiled and said, "I'm not too worried about that, I'll be okay. I'm a lot more concerned about where these terrorists are going to poison hundreds and potentially thousands of people."

Dottie jumped out of her chair and said, "Dammit, Michaela! You may not be worried about you, but I am. Without you there is no us. Don't you get that?"

Mic looked up at Dottie. *She's right. How can I be so callous? I'd be worried to death about Dottie if the shoe were reversed. Not because of the Thelma and Louise fantasy, but because I love her and I don't want anything to happen to her.* "Dottie, I'm so sorry. You're right and I am concerned about what Madame Toulescent said."

Dottie continued to stand and glare at Mic. "I am concerned for your safety, Michaela. I think we should hire some RPD guys to hang around your house. Maybe have one travel with you."

Mic held her flaming Irish temper and counted to ten. "Sit down, Dottie. First of all, I don't like to be talked down to and secondly, I don't want you to get dizzy from standing there gawking at me."

Dottie gave her another dirty look, walked over to the bar and refilled her sherry glass. She needed alcohol. It'd been a bad day. She was so angry with Michaela for being careless with her life that her hands were shaking. "I will be there in a second. I need a refill." She turned around and asked, "By the way, how is your white wine and do you need some more?"

Mic drank deeply and said. "Yeah, I'd like another glass. This is a sauvignon blanc. It's fruity and yet it's dry. It's good, crisp, and refreshing."

Dottie nodded. "Good, I'll ring for Cookie to bring in some more. I'm glad you like the wine. Henry purchased about six cases this afternoon to serve with lunch tomorrow afternoon after Camilla's funeral. Cookie went with him and taste-tested it and she liked it." Dottie sat down in her chair and reached her little silver bell to summon Cookie.

Michaela shook her head. "Don't ring that thing. I'll go into the kitchen and get it. It's not a big deal for me."

Dottie sighed deeply. "Okay, if you want to, but get back in here because we have stuff to talk about. The main thing being your safety."

Mic had almost gotten to the door of the library when she bumped into Cookie and Angel. Cookie had the bottle of wine cooling in a wine chiller. "I figured you'd be just about ready for another glass," she said beaming at Mic. "So I've brought the bottle. I've another one in the refrigerator. I also selected a cabernet to serve with the London broil."

Michaela bent over to pet Angel's neck as she accepted the wine. She smiled warmly at Cookie and said, "Honestly, Cookie, I need someone just like you in my life to keep me straight." She gave Dottie a sideways look and said, "I don't think the countess realizes what a gem you are."

"Yes, I do. I really do," Dottie snapped. "Cookie knows how much I need her. I tell her all the time don't I, Cookie?" Dottie said as she glared at her extraordinary housekeeper.

Cookie flashed Mic a look and said diplomatically, "I always like to hear it when you tell me that you need me. It means a lot," she finished with a smile.

Dottie nodded and said to Mic, "Get your wine and sit down. We've work to do."

Cookie gave Dottie a critical look and chided, "Really, Countess. You sound so bossy. Michaela is your guest. You need to show her a bit more respect."

Dottie was so mad her face turned beet red. "Thank you, Cookie. I know how to treat my guests," she said icily. She turned her attention back to Mic and said, her voice contrite, "Please, Michaela, let's take up where we left off."

Mic poured her wine and returned to her chair. She looked at Cookie, "Thanks for bringing the wine, Cookie. I can't wait until dinner. I know it's gonna be wonderful."

Cookie's face lit up in a smile. "It is. We're having fresh asparagus and new potatoes as well as strawberry shortcake for dessert." She looked at Dottie and said, "Henry just put the meat on the grill. Dinner will be served in about forty minutes."

Dottie offered Cookie a tight smile and said, "Thank you. We'll be ready." Dottie looked over at Michaela as Cookie left the room. She watched as Angel walked over, lay next to Mic's feet and said sarcastically, "It's a good thing that dog loves you because you make it damned hard for people to even like you!"

Angel lifted his head as he heard the word dog. He looked back and forth from Mic to Dottie as he tried to figure out what was going on. He gave each of the women a quizzical look, opened the library door with his nose and walked down the hall towards the kitchen.

Mic laughed and said, "Well, you gotta admit Angel's about as smart a dog as they come. He knew things were pretty tense here so he just decided to leave."

Dottie nodded but said nothing.

Mic laughed again, "That's pretty smart. No one wants to be around when we're in the middle of it."

Dottie sniffed and said, "If you ask me, he just wanted some more treats and he knows Cookie's a real pushover for great treats."

Mic laughed and sipped her wine. "Now that's the truth," she said with conviction. She looked across at Dottie and said, "I refuse to have police protection. I'm old enough to take care of myself. Besides, I've got Angel right beside me all the time and he's the best surveillance anybody could have."

Dottie nodded slowly and chose her words carefully. "I agree Angel is as good as it gets, but I know these creeps are intent on murdering people. I wouldn't put it past them to put some poison on a steak to kill or incapacitate him." She paused as she saw Mic's face pale with fear. It would kill Mic if something happened to Angel. The two of them were inseparable. Dottie hoped she was long gone before anything happened to the dog. She knew it would destroy Michaela and she wouldn't be able to stand that.

Mic remained quiet as she thought about the potential harm to her and Angel. At first, she'd only worried about someone sabotaging her, but now she worried about Angel too.

"What do you think, Michaela? Speak to me," Dorothy said quietly. "Honestly, I've already lost Camilla and I would just die if something happened to you or Angel. I'm scared about these people. They're evil and heinous."

Michaela nodded her head slowly. "Yeah, they are. It's not your rank-and-file murderer, mugger, or rapist. We understand those criminals. We know how they think." She remembered back to the meeting this afternoon. Even FBI SAC Burnley hadn't been able to profile the perps.

Mic looked at Dottie. "There was a meeting downtown at FBI headquarters. They had a FBI profiler named Burnley, a nice guy who seemed competent but could not profile the killers. We mostly talked about serial poisoners."

"A serial poisoner? I've never heard of such a thing," Dottie exploded. "I can only assume they're people who poison over and over again. Is it really that big of a crime? Do many people murder with poison?"

Michaela nodded her head and said, "Yep. Hard to say how many poison deaths there are yearly. Lots of poison crimes are undetected annually so it's hard to get a handle on how often murder by poison occurs. The FBI folks think we've only uncovered the tip of the iceberg as far as defining and recognizing serial poison as a murder instrument."

For once in her life, the Countess Dorothy Borghase was quiet and pensive as she considered the magnitude of the crime. Finally she said, "Well, isn't this the cat's meow. Never heard of it at all. Have you talked with Dr. Grey about this?"

Mic nodded. "Yeah. She was there today. She's consulting with the FBI and she's convinced she's identified the poison."

"Really, what does she think it is?

"She thinks its belladonna. It's a highly poisonous plant."

Dottie smiled broadly and said, "Yes, it certainly is. It's really toxic. I'm growing it in my back flower border. It's also called Nightshade and it's beautiful."

Mic's mouth fell open. "You're growing Nightshade in your backyard?" Her voice was incredulous.

Dottie nodded. "Yeah, I always have. What's the big deal? Hundreds of people, perhaps billions of people grow it. You can buy it in any plant catalog. I've grown it in the US for years and I grew it at our villa in Italy. The problem is that cows sometimes get in it and they die. You have to be sure you keep it away from livestock, house pets and children. I can remember a long time ago when two children ate belladonna berries in Germany and died."

Michaela shook her head but didn't say anything else. Sometimes she forgot Dottie had eighty years of wisdom and had seen a lot of stuff.

Dottie continued, "Years ago, the count got sick and they couldn't figure out what was wrong with him. So we took him to the Pope's Hospital, just outside Vatican City, in Rome, and they discovered he'd taken too much Donatal, a medicine they used to treat spasms in his stomach."

Mic arched her eyebrows. "So Count Borghase was poisoned by belladonna? Wow!"

Dottie nodded. "Yeah, I'd say he was poisoned by belladonna. He wasn't sick for very long - maybe a few days and then they let him come home and he was fine. But his symptoms were extreme weakness and he lost sensation in his lower legs. He couldn't walk. Of course, Borgy had a legal prescription ordered by a physician. He wasn't in some back alley with a bunch of perverts mixing up cauldrons of poison."

Mic shook her head, "Yeah, over the years it's had a ton of medical uses. I don't think they use it much anymore because it does have such dastardly effects." She paused for a second and reached for her cell phone. "It's Slade. He said he has some information for me. I need to see him," Mic said.

"Just invite him to dinner. We've got plenty. Ask him where he is and how soon he can get here." *Besides, I want to make sure he knows you're in danger. They can pooh pooh Madame Toulescent all they want, but I'm sure she's right.* Dottie shuddered as she remembered the psychic's distress at the visions she'd had.

"He's almost at my house so he should be here in ten minutes. I'll ask Cookie to set one more place."

"Sure. I'll be in there in a minute. I want to finish my sherry because I want a glass of cabernet sauvignon with dinner." Dottie gave her a malicious smile and waited for Mic to complain about her alcohol intake.

Michaela paused at the door and turned to face her much older friend. Dottie sat straight in her easy chair. She looked immaculate; every hair in place and her makeup was perfect. She looked as though she'd just stepped out of Vogue magazine. *You wouldn't know she'd had several glasses of sherry.* "All I can say to you, Dottie, is that I hope I can hold my booze like you can when I'm your age."

Dottie smiled at her sweetly and said, "You won't be able to, my dear. Because you haven't been conditioned to drink all your life and I have. The name of the game is everything in moderation built on tolerance over time."

Michaela rolled her eyes and shook her head as she walked down the hall to the kitchen to see Cookie.

Chapter 39

Boris and Snake left the lab and walked down Porter Street towards their vehicles. The early May sunshine was beautiful even in this dark, poor and dingy part of Richmond.

"Let's take a ride over to where our event is this weekend. It'll help us get a lay of the land," Boris suggested, a jovial smile on his face.

Snake stared at him. He'd never seen Boris smile about anything, much less look happy. At first, he was overtaken by a feeling of suspicion but then looked up and said, "Sure, man. Anything you want to do. My time is your time for the next few days.

They reached Boris's van and he said, "Hop in. We'll take my ride."

"Nah, I'll take my own car," Snake said. He never wanted to go anywhere without his own wheels. He never knew when he'd need to get the hell out of Dodge.

Boris shook his head. "No. Get in. I don't want our cars seen together so why take the chance?"

Snake gave him a taciturn look. "No. I don't leave my car, ever. I like my own wheels," he insisted, his voice louder.

"I said get in, now," Boris insisted, a look of impatience on his face.

Snake sneered at him. "I don't think that makes any difference, at least not in this gig. I'll meet you there."

Boris grabbed Snake's upper arm and held it in a vice-like grip. "Did you hear me, man? I said get in. Remember, I'm your boss."

Anger flashed through Snake as he grabbed Boris's hand and yanked it off his arm. "Okay, dude. But just this one time. I like having my own ride. Get it?" he added sarcastically.

Boris pointed to the passenger side of his vehicle and Snake walked around the van and hopped in. The vehicle was a filthy, nasty mess. It was full of fast food wrappers, old newspapers, drink cups, half-smoked cigarettes, dirt, mud and other things he couldn't identify. It also smelled like dead fish.

He shook his head and looked at Boris, "Phew, this van stinks like somebody's dead in it." As soon as he said it, he instinctively looked in the back of the van and saw a large tarp covering what suspiciously looked like a body. He shook his head and said, "Aw man, you gotta be kiddin' me. You don't have a stiff back there do you?"

Boris looked over his shoulder as if uncertain if he had a body in the back or not. He scratched his head and smiled. "It's no big deal. We'll drop 'em off on the way."

Snake swallowed hard to keep his lunch down. He didn't have an aversion to dead people, or to dead bodies in general. But he didn't want to ride around in a closed up van with one either. Besides, the car had been sitting in the sun all afternoon. "You know what, man, you're crazy. Nobody drives around in the middle of the day with a body in the back of their car." Snake reached for the door, but Boris grabbed his shoulder.

He stared at him and said, "If you don't settle down, you'll be the fresh body in the trunk. It's no big deal. I've done it before."

Snake shook his head and reached for his seatbelt to settle in for the ride. *How in the hell did I ever get hooked up with this whack job? This guy is totally nuts and I wouldn't put anything past him.* He wondered if his fat paycheck was worth the effort. Snake had worked with a lot of people in his day, but Boris was the most dangerous. The Russian was unbalanced and deranged. Snake had watched him inject the mice and cats in the lab with poison and watched them die horrible deaths. It was clear he loved killing. And, the way he'd mutilated fish was insane.

Neither man spoke during the short drive to the pump station on the James River. Snake stayed in the car and watched as Boris dragged the body from the van and kicked it off the riverbank into the water. *I'm never getting mixed up with this freak again.*

Boris stood on the bank of the river, wiped his hands on his pants and watched until the body disappeared underwater. Snake hoped no one crossing the Boulevard Bridge saw the body sinking slowly into the water.

Boris returned to the car and smiled at Snake, showing his rotting teeth. "See, that wasn't so bad. Easy as pie," he said as he backed his vehicle out of the wooded area.

Snake held his tongue although there was lots he could've said. He wondered who the dead man was but figured it was better if he didn't know.

Boris read his mind and said, "That man wasn't nobody important. I gave him twenty-five dollars and tried out poisons on him until I got the dose right, well, almost right. I didn't think he was gonna die, but he did. At least he had a couple bottles of cheap whiskey before he croaked," he said with a chuckle.

Snake nodded but didn't say anything. A few minutes later, they pulled into the parking lot at Richmond's Carillon, an open air theatre on Byrd Park Lake. There was obviously a play that evening and people were dressed in costumes. The Carillon was home to many outdoor festivals where artists came from all over the United States to market their talents. Thousands of Richmonders turned out for the festivals to spend the day in the park drinking beer and wine and perusing one-of-a-kind art creations from all over the country.

"So, this is where we're gonna do it?" Snake asked as he looked around.

Boris nodded as a large smile spread over his skeletal face. "This is one place. We should be able to hit hundreds of people here, no question."

Snake looked around again and asked, "What are you gonna do? Hit the food trucks?"

Boris gave him an enterprising look and a sardonic smile. "Among other things. Come on, let's walk over and check out where the food and beer will be. That's part of our staging area."

Snake said nothing but followed him under a grove of trees. Nobody paid attention to them. For all anyone knew, they were a couple of artists, perhaps a potter and a sculptor checking out their art space.

Boris pointed to a huge area near the lake. "That's where the beer tent will be and the beer trucks will be parked around it. That's our main kill area. We'll go over to the largest breweries after dark and scope out their tanks or kegs.

"Their tanks?"

"Yeah. The stainless steel tanks that hold the beer. Then we'll go back tomorrow evening and 'fix' them."

"Huh, I don't follow." Snake had lost interest and bent down to scratch his ankle.

"Yeah, you know, fix them, doctor them up so the beer will be memorable." Boris said with an evil wink, a happy smile stretched across his thin face.

Snake shrugged his shoulders. "Whatever. Do we need to stay here any longer?   I swear somethin' is biting me."

Boris grinned again and said, "Nah, let's go." He turned around, took one last look at the beer area and smiled. "Yeah, I'm done. Let's get outta here."

Chapter 40

Slade McKane rapped the heavy brass knocker on Dottie's impressive front door. He stood under the portico outside her entrance and wondered how anyone could live in such opulence. He always felt small in Dottie's mammoth Monument Avenue home that took up almost an entire city block and was three stories tall. For the life of him, he couldn't understand why someone would want to live in a house that big. He compared it to his small childhood home on the Irish Bayou in New Orleans East where he'd been born. His childhood home had been about the size of Dottie's front porch.

Slade could hear the sound of the chimes echo through the great entrance foyer into the rooms beyond. He supposed this house was smaller than the Villa Borghase where she'd lived in the Italian countryside. He smiled to himself as he thought of Dottie. He had never met anyone quite like her and although she was over eighty years old, she didn't look or act that old… a fact that drove Michaela out of her mind. He thought of Dottie as an attractive lady in her fifties who exercised and stayed in shape. In fact, after three brandies, a bottle of wine, and before dinner cocktails, they'd had cigars on her terrace and he decided she was a pretty hot old broad. He smiled to himself as he remembered that night and the three-day hangover that followed. They bonded that night and were now friends for life. There was one thing for sure about Dorothy Borghase. She was smart, tough, and made of steel. He admired and respected the heck out of her.

“Detective McKane, how good to see you. The countess is pleased you’re joining us for dinner. It’s a pleasant surprise,” Cookie gushed as she opened the door and smiled broadly at Slade.

Slade rewarded Cookie with a big smile that flashed his perfect teeth and lit up his dark eyes. "Thank you, Cookie. I'm delighted to be here. Dinner at Dottie’s is one of the best parts of my life."

Cookie practically giggled. She was fond of the tall Cajun detective and knew he loved Michaela and consequently, the countess. "I gotta tell you, Slade, Henry is cooking on the grill tonight so it's not just my cooking."

"Well, that's good enough for me! I can honestly say I've never had a bad meal here at the Villa Borghase on Monument Avenue."

Cookie flashed him a final smile as they walked down the long hall toward the library where Michaela and Dottie were still having drinks. "Oh, look. They’ve gone outside to sit in the garden. It's such a beautiful evening," Cookie exclaimed.

Slade nodded. "Yes, it is. Why don't we join them?"

"Can I have Henry get you a drink? I think you have time for one before dinner."

"No, I'll pass. I'm sort of on the clock and there's information coming in left and right about these poisonings. But I will take a rain check and promise to have a drink or two or maybe three," he said with a wink, "the next time I come over."

Cookie nodded. "How about I bring you a glass of mineral water? Will that be okay?"

“That'll be great," Slade said as he walked out onto the flagstone terrace. “Thank you, Cookie."

He walked over to Dottie's chair and gave her a swift kiss on both cheeks. She looked up at him and smiled, "Glad you could come on such short notice.” She paused for a moment, stared at him and asked, “What new information do you have? Come on and spill the beans." She looked at him expectantly.

Slade shook his head and smiled at Dottie. She was incorrigible. "Great to see you too, Countess." Then he leaned down and planted a big kiss Michaela’s forehead.

Michaela smiled up at the handsome Irishman and said, "I'll supply the manners for this evening, Slade. We're glad to see you and happy you could join us for dinner," she said as she stared at Dottie out of the corner of her eye. "Have a seat. Now, let's get to the point. What new information do you have?"

Slade shook his head and grinned. "You ladies are unbelievable! Do you want to see me or are you just interested in my info?" He feigned a hurt look.

“Hmm,” Mic said with a flirtatious smile. “Maybe a little of both.”

Slade turned and met Cookie at the door with a glass of mineral water. He thanked her and returned to his chair.

“Well, what do you have, Slade?” Dottie snapped. “Times a’passing.”

Slade settled slowly into his chair and took a sip of his water. It was good, refreshing, especially with the lemon slice. He played with the stem of the glass and looked around at the manicured courtyard. The tulips and daffodils were in full bloom and a redbud tree was beyond beautiful. He didn’t answer, just to irritate Dottie. He loved to get her going. She was feisty and he liked that.

“Dammit, Slade. What’s new?” Dottie exploded. “Speak up. I have a few things to tell you, too.”

Slade looked at Dottie, “What do you have?”

“You first,” she goaded him. She hoped he and Michaela would become a “thing” as she called it. Of course, Dottie only hoped that if their relationship didn’t interfere with her relationship with Mic. But, she had to admit he was devastatingly handsome in the dark ways of the Irish and a good guy to boot. His New Orleans heritage gave him a tad of the mysterious and unknown.

"Okay, I'll tell you, but it's not that exciting. They definitely confirmed the poison in Camilla's death as atropa belladonna, but they think the poisoner altered the poison when he poisoned the three women," Slade said as he took a sip of water.

Michaela thought about this. "But why? Why would he alter the poison? The original formula did the job on Camilla. I don't get it," she said, her face puzzled and her green eyes confused. She paused a moment and said, "But I think it has overall significance to the case."

"I don't get it either. I guess that's a job for Dr. Duncan and his poison forensic team," he offered. "I think they're working on it as we speak."

Dottie remained silent until Mic asked her what she thought.

Dottie shook her head. "I think he's still experimenting with his proportions. He probably, or they probably, knew it wouldn't take as much to kill an old lady as it would some young woman. And then, I imagine he figured it'd take even less to kill a kid." She paused for a moment and added, "You know, he's a sick son of a bitch. No question, and very dangerous. That's what Madame Toulescent said and I agree with her."

Slade's interest perked up. "You went to see Madame today? What did she have to say?" He leaned in closer.

Dottie shot Mic a look of triumph at Slade's interest in her trip to the psychic. Mic rolled her eyes. "Yes, I did. And Madame Toulescent was glad I came. She said she'd had bad visions about these killers, and by the way, she said there was more than one poisoner."

Slade nodded. "That fits. What else?"

Dottie cleared her throat and continued. "She said the killers were planning more murders. She believes they're gonna attack somewhere where they can kill a large number of people and she thinks they'll do it soon."

Michaela saw Slade pale under his tan. "So, Slade. What do you think?" She looked at him expectantly.

Slade thought for a moment and said, "I agree with Madame Toulescent. I think these perps will plot until they get it right. And then I agree they'll attack in the area where there is a large number of people."

Mic's heart beat erratically. This was terrorism and terrorism scared her. "Any ideas on the timetable?" She asked in a low voice.

Slade stared into her eyes. "Soon. We think it'll be soon. The FBI and RPD concur, we think the death of Camilla and the others are, in many ways, the way the poisoners are getting national attention – the attention of law enforcement and the media. Of course, they've managed to do that, no question."

"That they have," Dottie barked. "The bastards," she hissed. She studied her sherry glass and asked, "Any idea where? Where they may attack?"

Slade shook his head. "No, but there's internet chatter that suggests a large area with lots of people, maybe a park or festival or something like that."

Michaela felt a huge knot form in the pit of her stomach. "So, who is it?"

Slade raised his eyebrows. "What do you mean?"

"Do they suspect domestic or international terrorists?" Mic asked him, a hint of fear in her eyes. She'd thought her question was perfectly clear.

Slade shrugged his shoulders. "No idea. We're working on it. We don't have a clue yet."

Mic nodded, stared at the flagstone patio and imagined how horrific a massive poisoning of the population would be.

"Dottie, did Madame Toulescent say anything else about the poisonings? Anything we could use?" Slade asked.

Dottie thought for a moment and said, "Not really. She mostly told me she could feel the fear and terror of the victims and the pain when the poison hit their bodies." Dottie was quiet for a moment.

"What else, Dottie? I know there's more. I can tell by the way you look," Slade prodded her.

"Well, she told me about her visions and what she'd heard and seen. Oh, there is one thing!" Dottie was so excited she could hardly speak.

Slade looked at her expectantly, "What, what else, Dottie? We have a couple of maniacs here so anything could be helpful."

Dottie flashed Mic a triumphant look and said, "To tell you the truth, Slade, for the first time Madame Toulescent put me in touch with a dead person, specifically Camilla. I didn't ask for that to occur, but the Madame said she could feel Camilla reaching out to me." Dottie could see the flush of anger on Mic's face as she turned to Slade and rolled her eyes.

Dottie gave Mic a harsh look. "Stop it, just stop it, Michaela. You weren't there and you don't know what happened. So stop sitting in judgment because you don't even know what message Camilla sent me," she said defiantly, her vivid blue eyes flashed in anger.

Mic shook her head and looked away. Slade touched her arm and asked Dottie, "What did Camilla tell you via Madame Toulescent?"

"She told me the poison was in her hot tea. And, she's right. She's the only one of us that had tea that day and several of us had the exact same meal." She turned to Mic and spat, "So there, Michaela. Does that make you more of a believer?"

Mic shook her head and said in a low voice, "No, not really. I'm not sure I believe in any of that stuff. I think that anything that happened in the past based on any psychic readings, visions, Tarot cards or whatever is just coincidence."

Dottie gave Mic the dirtiest look she could and turned to Slade. "There is one other thing, Slade. Madame Toulescent said that Michaela is in grave danger." She raised her perfectly shaped eyebrows to press her point. "Very serious danger and that we should watch her carefully." She felt Mic's eyes boring into her and gave her a defiant look.

Mic rolled her eyes again. "Me, why me? We've talked about this and there's no reason I should be in any more danger than anyone else."

Slade was thoughtful. "Humph. That's interesting. Did the Madame say why Michaela was in danger? Did she give a specific reason?"

Dottie shook her head. "No, she didn't and I didn't ask. By then I was so shook up from the reading that I just wanted to get in my car and go home. It was so strange, so unnerving. There was dead silence all around us – the birds stopped chirping and the deer and cows stopped grazing in the fields. I was cold, freezing actually." Dottie's voice shook a little as she retold her story and she wiped the chill bumps from her arms.

Michaela wondered how high Dottie's blood pressure was and reached for her pills that Dottie immediately snatched away. "Leave me alone, Mic. I'm fine. Stop treating me like an invalid. You know it pisses me off."

Mic nodded and looked at Slade who was deep in thought.

"If Madame Toulescent is correct, and honestly, Michaela, she's given us great tips in the past that have panned out," he said as he stared into Michaela's green eyes. "It could only mean that you know at least one of the perps." He paused for a moment and searched Mic's eyes. "Have you ever worked on a suspected poison crime before?"

Mic shook her head and said, "No, not that I know of. Honestly, most of the people who would like to hurt me either are dead or locked up somewhere. I have no idea who this could be," she said stubbornly. "I'm not sure it's even worth another thought."

Slade shook his head. "It's worth a lot of thought," he disagreed. "It's virtually the only clue we have about anything to do with the killers."

"But," Mic protested. "I don't ever remember working with anyone suspected of poisoning, or even anyone who has a science background, like the FBI suggested today."

"Well," Dottie said flatly. "It's the best clue we've got, Mic, so you're gonna have to remember back to all of those perverts you chased and sent to jail," she said. Dottie flashed her a victorious smile. Her trip to Madame Toulescent was going to pay off. She knew it in her blood.

"Dottie's right," Slade said. "After dinner we're going down to the station to go through your old files. There's gotta be a clue in there somewhere. In the meantime, I'm gonna contact the FBI and let them know what Madame Toulescent said. Can you call Dr. Grey and tell her about the tea? See if she thinks that was the poison vehicle?"

Michaela nodded as Cookie opened the terrace door and called them in to dinner.

Cookie and Michaela walked ahead and Dottie whispering to Slade said, "I got a new shipment of excellent Cuban cigars. Let's have one in the smoking room after dinner. It'll be good for us," she promised him.

Slade smiled, "I'm in, Dottie, but you're a bad influence on me," he said with a laugh. All in all, the Countess Dorothy Many-Middle-Names Borghase was an incredible woman, but then so was Michaela, he remembered as his heart thudded in his chest. The smell was tantalizing as he entered the massive dining room.

Chapter 41

There was a light, late spring rain the morning of Camilla's funeral. The smell of the earth was damp, moist and permeated the senses. Michaela stood with Beau Massie and Adam Patrick Lee behind a row of metal chairs where family and close friends were seated. It was a somber crowd. Mic strained her neck and looked around for Slade McKane or any other members of the RPD. There were several police vehicles within view. She and Slade had worked until the wee hours of the morning reviewing her old case files. Nothing had turned up to indicate she was in grave danger. It was customary for the police to attend the services of someone who'd died violently. Law enforcement always hoped the actual perpetrator or perpetrators would show up to admire their handiwork.

Hollywood Cemetery, Richmond's oldest and famous cemetery, was the graveyard home of Virginia bluebloods. It also was the burial place of notables such as Presidents John Tyler, Jefferson Davis, and James Madison and General J.E.B. Stuart. As the minister droned on and on about the virtues of a good woman, Mic wished she'd worn lower heels. She focused on the spring beauty around her and the lush green of spring. She jumped as she felt an arm circle her waist. It was Slade. She nestled back into the comfort of his body and lowered her umbrella. She whispered quietly, "I wish this minister would get the job done. He keeps going on and on and on."

Slade touched Mic on the shoulder and said, "Shhh... You need to mind your manners," he said reproachfully with a twinkle in his eye.

"Do you see anything or anyone suspicious?" Mic whispered. "I've been looking, but honestly, I haven't seen anything questionable so far," she reported.

"There are a lot of people here so it's hard to tell. Lieutenant Stoddard and another officer are on the other side checking people. Chief Herndon is here, not particularly on duty, but to pay his respects to General Rothrock."

Michaela nodded. "I hope we get a lead."

"Will you two hush up? You're disturbing the ceremony," Dottie said as she turned around in her seat. She glared at both of them. "Show a little respect, would you?" she hissed angrily.

Mic glared back at Dottie. She knew the reason Dottie was mad was because she wasn't in on the conversation. She leaned down and whispered into Dottie's ear, "I'll catch you up after the service."

Dottie nodded her head and didn't turn around again. Kathryn Lee gave Michaela a quick smile and reached for her husband's hand. She could tell the congressman was getting impatient, as his leg was moving constantly. Mic wished their granddaughter, Alex, was around to help her grandmother, but Alex had returned to New Orleans for a few months to help out at Crescent City Medical Center where she was legal counsel. Mic noticed Congressman Lee as he constantly shifted in the chair. She'd heard stories about him and his impatience for years. Kathryn nudged her husband. Mic knew Kathryn thought the funeral had gone on long enough. And, she was afraid her husband would explode.

Slade grinned at the congressman's impatience, nudged Michaela and smiled at her. Michaela turned to look at him and saw someone about hundred yards away behind a tree. "Slade, do you see the guy over there behind the big oak tree?" she whispered.

Slade peered through the crowd and searched the trees. Sure enough, there was a man in a blue shirt hidden behind the wide trunk of the tree. He nodded and whispered quietly, "Yeah, I do." He moved to the back of the crowd and started walking swiftly around the circle of mourners, talking softly into his headset.

Mic focused her attention on the tree where she'd seen the man. He was still there. She caught a glimpse of Lieutenant Stoddard walking the opposite way and she knew they planned to converge upon the man. Her heart beat wildly and she thought how great it would be to catch the killers before anyone else died.

Her attention returned to the funeral and she noticed everyone was praying. She hoped that meant the funeral ceremony was over and thankfully, it was. Dottie stood and gave General Rothrock a big hug and told him she'd see him in a few minutes. The funeral guests were going to Dottie's mansion on Monument for a light lunch. She hoped Slade and Stoddard would be able to report that they had captured at least one of the killers.

Chapter 42

Snake stood behind the large oak tree and watched the mourners at the graveside ceremony. He enjoyed the agony of the bereaved at cemeteries. Sometimes, just for the fun of it, he'd check the newspaper, visit funeral parlors and loiter outside - even when he hadn't known the deceased. He guessed he just liked watching people cry. He loved the pomp and circumstance, the flowers and the music, the soft, hushed voices. But, most of all he liked watching the tears of the women and the stoic grimaces of the men. He liked people jerked apart by agony, sadness and grief. It excited him.

Snake liked graveside burials too. Sometimes it was a bit risky showing up inside the church or funeral home or even outside the church of someone you'd offed a few days ago. But outdoor burials were great. Hollywood Cemetery offered him a million places to watch the shenanigans without being observed. There were tall headstones, winged angels, century old trees, bushes and even mausoleums he could hide behind. He'd picked this current large tree because of its low branches and wide trunk. He doubted anybody could see him there.

As he peered around the tree, he noticed a petite woman with dark hair that glistened even in the gray morning. He'd watched her walk from her car and her movements were familiar to him. His attention wandered to other mourners, but repeatedly he returned to the woman under the black umbrella. Where had he seen her? He knew her and the feelings he had weren't good. Could she be with the police? Could she be someone who'd arrested him in the past or interviewed him about his foot-long rap sheet? He couldn't remember. He'd be back at Hollywood Cemetery in a couple of days for the funeral of one of the kids who died. He brought his hands together in anticipation. The kid's funeral would be a great circus. Emotions would be high with everyone sobbing. Sometimes the family members even passed out from grief, fatigue or both. He didn't care he just like to watch.

Once again, his eyes focused on the petite woman. How did he know her? It was eating at him. He watched as she whispered to a tall man whom he was sure was a detective from the Richmond Police Department. He figured the woman was a cop when suddenly it dawned on him. He froze in anger. She was the bitch who'd attacked him at the hospital a few months ago… back when he'd been trying to clean up a leftover mess for the Russian Bratva. He cursed as he remembered how she'd thrown a bedpan on the floor and attacked him while he waited for his victim to die. Fortunately, he'd been able to get away, but anger burned through him like someone had thrown scorching hot water in his face. He'd follow her after the funeral. She was dead meat. He'd hoped to see her again for months.

He continued to enjoy the service. He was stunned when a large hand grabbed him, slammed him to the ground and hissed, "What the hell are you doing here? Are you trying to get us caught and killed?"

Snake lay on the ground unable speak. Boris had knocked the wind from him.

The Russian kicked him with this foot and Snake grimaced in pain. "I asked you what you're doin' here. Other than trying to get killed." Boris spat on the ground next to Snake's head.

"I was watching," Snake said as he rubbed his leg and looked up from the ground. “I like funerals. I always have," he confessed. "What do you care?"

Boris ignored him as he scanned the crowd. A small smile spread across his thin lips.

"Dammit, get your foot off my chest. I wanna get up," Snake growled. "I'm missing all the fun. I like to watch the people cry."

Boris ignored him and watched the funeral across the way.

"I'm gonna ask you one more time to let me up," Snake threatened. "Or, I'm gonna break your leg," he promised.

Boris gazed down at him and said, "Okay. I guess. By the way, the place is crawling with cops."

"No screaming shit," Snake snorted as he got to his feet and brushed the mud, dead leaves and twigs off his jeans.

He glowered at his partner. "Duh. Do you think I missed that?"

"Yeah, cuz you're an idiot," Boris said, as he stared into the crowd. "You know that tall, dark headed cop in the back row? I've seen him around and I think he prides himself on always gittin' his man," he said with a smug look. "But not this time," he smiled thinly at Snake. "I can guarantee you that we'll get him this time."

Snake peered through the trees and said, "I don't give a damn about the cop," he said quietly, "it's the short dark-haired woman I want."

Boris gave him a sideways look and studied the woman. "Well, um, let's go git her," he said, licking his lips. Michaela looked good to him too.

Boris saw two police officers heading towards them. "Move, move, we gotta git outta here. They see us," he said as he pushed Snake low to the ground. The two men ran and dodged bushes and headstones until they were far down the bank of the James River. The mourners gathered to celebrate the life of Camilla Rothrock never saw them.

Chapter 43

Dottie stood at the head of her dining room table and looked every bit the aristocrat she was. People milled around Dottie's banquet-sized dining room table and feasted on Virginia ham and chicken salad biscuits, potato salad from Sally Belle's bakery and a host of other goodies, pick-up foods, petit fours and cookies. A beautiful floral arrangement adorned the center of the table. People spoke in soft, hushed voices. In her heart of hearts, this made Dottie even sadder because she knew Camilla would have preferred music from the fifties and sixties, singing, dancing, and laughter at her wake. *Oh well, I'm gonna have to make sure that Michaela makes my funeral a happy occasion. And, I need to remind her that I want the words "but she had a good time" etched on my tombstone.*

Dottie heard someone call her name and searched the room to see who it was. Finally, her eyes rested on one of Camilla's old friends, someone she'd never liked much. Dottie smiled as the woman rushed over to her and gushed on and on about Camilla and all the good times the three of them had enjoyed. Dottie nodded her head patiently, touched the woman on the shoulder and decided she needed a break – mainly a quick trip to her smoking room. She needed a nicotine fix. She looked around and saw Michaela talking with the FBI profiler named Burnley and Chief Herndon of the Richmond police. It was a good time for her to slip away. Not even the death of her good friend would make it okay for her to smoke in Mic's eyes. *If she only knew…*

Dottie opened the walnut door of her smoking room and saw Congressman Lee and General Rothrock seated in two velvet Queen Anne chairs that flanked the fireplace. They were deep in conversation. She hesitated for a moment but then walked over and interrupted them.

"Stu, Adam, is this a matter of national security or do you mind if I join you? You know how hard it is for me to be nice for a long period of time. I'm in dreadful need of a cigar."

Adam Lee, always ready to fire up a good Cuban, stood graciously to acknowledge Dottie's presence. He smiled at the countess. They were great friends and had been for years. The two of them were a lot alike in many ways. Both stubborn and hardheaded, they loved their bourbon and smokes. "Countess, of course we're delighted to have you join us."

"We are indeed, Dottie and I have to tell you that this is the best hideout I've ever been in," Stuart Rothrock echoed, "and, it's the best stocked bar I've seen in ages."

Dottie gave the two men her best smile. "You gentlemen come and check out my humidor. I've got some new Cubans that will knock your socks off," she said, her blue eyes sparkling with delight. She loved the companionship of men. For a moment, a tear popped into her eyes. She missed Borgy so much. The count had been dead for more than thirty years and she still missed him every day.

"Now, where did you get...?" Adam began.

Dottie shook her head. "Not telling, Congressman. I've managed to get cigars ever since the US ended diplomatic relations with Cuba. Been gettin' them unlawfully for fifty years and I'm not telling now, particularly since it's almost legal."

Adam's eyes gleamed at Dottie's selection. "Damn, Countess. I'm gonna have me one of these," he said as he selected a sedately-wrapped Cuban cigar and picked up the silver cigar cutter.

Dottie and Stuart selected cigars as well. The two men returned to their chairs and Dottie seated herself on a brocade sofa. They smoked together in silence. As the smoke thickened, Dottie opened the French doors that led to the terrace where they could watch the crowd milling around without chance of the crowd seeing them.

"Countess, you and Stu let me know if you see Kathryn," Adam said as he craned his neck to see outside. "She'd skin me alive if she saw me with a cigar. You both know how she is," he said with a wink and a smile on his face.

General Rothrock laughed. "Adam, if it wasn't for Kathryn, you'd have been dead thirty years ago. You got more vices than Dottie and I put together and yet, you're still going strong."

"Yup, no question," Adam agreed amicably as he continued to smoke.

Dottie smiled and returned to the sofa. She turned to Stuart and asked, "General, have you drunk any of Adam's white lightnin' lately?"

Stuart smiled and shook his head.

Adam roared with laughter and said, "I don't suspect he has, Dottie. He's been missing some of the bigger parties at Wyndley Farm lately."

Stuart picked up his bourbon, "Adam's right. I've been on liver rest and I haven't had any Virginia white lightnin' for years. But, from what I can remember, the stuff sends you to outer space after a couple of drinks."

Adam nodded and his eyes twinkled "Yup, that's what them guys said that came to the farm from NASA. Said we could use it to launch rockets."

Stuart laughed loudly and Dottie nodded her head emphatically and said, "That it can, General. That it can."

Adam grinned at Stuart and said, "When you come out to the farm tomorrow for lunch, we'll sneak out to the pool house and have a taste. I'll give you a bottle to take back with you to Florida," he promised as he smiled fondly at Stuart Rothrock. General Rothrock was a patriot. Probably the best general the Army had ever had in recent years. And, from a national intelligence standpoint, Stuart had saved the administration's tail more than a couple of times, often at great personal loss. Adam knew dozens of America's enemies would love to destroy the American hero. He shook his head and hoped the Russians weren't behind Camilla's death. Adam Lee hated the Russians. He'd never trusted them, and would never put anything past them, especially revenge, and Stuart had messed with them enough for them to want him big time.

"Where're you hiding that stuff now, Adam? I heard Kathryn found your Lightin' stock and took care of it," Dottie asked with a wry smile.

Adam grinned and shook his head. Dottie noticed what a handsome man he was. Adam Patrick Lee was well into his late seventies and going strong. Dottie thought he was five or six years younger than she was.

He shook his head. "Nah, Kathryn may have *thought* she found it and I'm sure she did find some of it. But, truthfully, I got so many stock piles and hiding places, she'll never find all of it," he declared. "Thank goodness I got Digger hangin' around to help me 'member where I hid it," he laughed.

"How's Digger doin', Adam? I haven't seen him since we were looking for Saddam." Stuart inquired about Adam's close friend. Digger Stildove was a Native American neighbor of Adam's who was a cyber expert and master tracker who did special ops projects for Adam and the NSA under the radar.

"Digger's good. He's over in the Middle East searching for somebody now. Mary's back at the farm watching over Kathryn when I'm in Washington. Two finer people are nowhere to be found," Adam said as he picked up his whiskey glass. "They were so good to us after the attack at the farm. It was Mary who helped Kathryn find Alex and save her life."

"Yeah. All that was bad business, no question," General Rothrock said. "Still think it was those scum, your buddies at Al Qaeda?"

Adam nodded, "Yeah, but today I'm putting that out of my mind and enjoying a drink with my friends," Adam said as he raised his glass.

Dottie and Stuart laughed again and the three smoked in silence as they watched Camilla's friends eat, drink, and mingle on Dottie's immaculate terrace. The more alcohol the guests consumed, the louder the grieving became. Dottie watched as the catering staff opened four more bottles of white wine. She knew Camilla would approve of this luncheon even though no one was dancing yet.

She turned to Stuart. "I'm going to miss your mother." Her eyes filled with tears as she continued. "Camilla has been my gym buddy and running partner for forty years. She's the only one of my old lady friends that would go to the gym to work out with me," Dottie finished with a weak smile.

General Rothrock reached for her hand and squeezed it. "I know, Dottie. Y'all were the best of friends for years. I know you'll miss her. I know how much she loved you."

Dottie wiped her tears away and tried to assume her aristocratic appearance. She stood. "I'd best get back to my hostess duties. You men feel free to stay in here out of the crowd, and count your blessings you're not out there," she said with a smile.

Stuart rose to his feet. "No, no, I must get up and mingle as well. These folks are here to pay respects to my mother so I should be available. I appreciate you hosting this lunch for her, Countess," Stuart said as he reached out and enveloped Dottie in a hug.

"You're welcome," she said. "Promise me you won't be a stranger now, down in Florida. Promise you'll come up for Christmas or at least Thanksgiving – like you always do." Dottie said and turned to Adam. "Congressman, help yourself. I've got to go back to my duties before Cookie comes in here and jerks me out," Dottie said as she smiled down at Adam, a descendant of Robert E. Lee.

Adam shook his head. "Nah, I gotta get up. Kathryn will come sniffing for me in a minute and there'll be all hell to pay for smoking this cigar. I'd best go find her first," he said gruffly, a twinkle in his eye as he thought of his beloved wife, his bride of fifty years. He knew he'd been missing long enough and she'd soon scout him out. At an event like this, thirty minutes was his maximum free time.

Dottie walked towards the door and wondered about General Rothrock's wife. She'd thought it strange she hadn't attended the funeral, but then, Camilla had said a year or so ago they weren't together.

A moment later, Michaela walked into the smoking room. She wrinkled her nose in distaste at the smell of smoke and said, "Henry noticed a man watching the house when he took some of the trash out. One of the caterers saw a dark-haired man out by the back garden wall. Guy had on a blue shirt. You see him before?" she questioned Dottie. "Could he work for someone in the neighborhood?"

Dottie shook her head, opened a drawer in a bookcase, picked up her Glock and walked towards the back of her home, her gun hidden in her pocket. Mic followed her and said, "Slade and a couple of others are already looking for him. Why don't you come back in and hang with the guests? We don't want them getting suspicious now, do we?" she asked in a smooth voice.

Dottie gave Mic a dirty look and returned to her dining room. *What the hell was going on*? She thought there was a lot more than met the eye with these murders. Why were they snooping around her house? This wasn't good at all.

The Case of the Dead Dowager

Chapter 44

It was after 5:00 when Dottie bid the last guest goodbye. She was exhausted. She passed by the kitchen where the caterers were packing up dishes under Cookie's watchful eye.

"Is Henry okay?" Dottie asked. She knew Henry had been upset by the trespasser loitering outside by the trashcans. Henry was a great guy and the couple had been loyal for many years. They were, in fact, along with Michaela, Dottie's "adopted" family. Of course, she had a few long-lost relatives in Italy and one great niece who couldn't wait for her to die so she would inherit her title. Dottie gritted her teeth when she thought about her. Dottie loved Cookie and Henry and knew she couldn't make it without the two of them.

"I think he's okay," Cookie said as she spooned potato salad in a plastic container. "I just went up and checked on him. He's fine. He took one nitroglycerin but honestly, I don't think he needed it. I made him take it," she said sheepishly.

"Oh, I didn't know he had chest pain," Dottie said, her eyebrows arched in concern.

"He didn't. I just thought he might. He wants to come down and help clean up, but I told him to rest," she said not looking Dottie in the eyes. She was more upset than she wanted the countess to realize.

"I'm sure the caterers can finish up here. Why not go up and stay with him," Dottie said in an unusual display of concern.

Cookie turned her back so Dottie wouldn't see the tears pop in her eyes and said, "I'll go up shortly, Countess. Would you like me to have the caterers bring some sandwiches and salads into the library? General Rothrock, Michaela, and Dr. Grey are in there now talking."

Dottie nodded. "Please, they're all probably hungry. I doubt any of them ate anything," Dottie said as she walked behind the enormous bar in the kitchen and put her arm around Cookie's shoulders. She whispered, "Promise me you'll go up and tend to Henry. You know I can't do without either of you," she admitted softly.

Cookie was surprised but nodded and said, "I will, Countess. You best go and visit with your guests. There's probably a lot of important stuff being said."

Dottie nodded at the caterers and left the kitchen. She wondered what was wrong with her. She'd teared up twice in the smoking room and gotten teary-eyed with Cookie. Was she losing it? Was something going to happen to her? Her feet were killing her. She'd worn high heels all day. She stopped at the butler's pantry and pulled out a pair of her bedroom shoes she stored there. No one would care. After all, she was among friends feeling humble and sad. Not feelings she often experienced, much less admitted to.

She mused over these feelings as she opened the door to the library. Michaela, General Rothrock, and Dr. Peggy Grey sat at the game table. Slade had returned to work.

"Countess, I don't know how to thank you for hosting the luncheon this afternoon. It was most kind of you and I know my mother would have loved it and had a great time," Stuart said as he stood when she entered the room.

Dottie smiled and flashed him a smile. "Stuart, your mother would have been the life of the party. By the way, I have it on good authority that she's doing fine and loving it up there," Dottie said as her eyes looked up. "But I'm pretty sure she's a big part of the dancing and partying in Heaven," Dottie said as she glanced at Michaela out of the corner of her eye. She saw Mic roll her eyes. Dottie stared at her but remained quiet.

Stuart pulled a chair up to the table and Dottie sat down. Peggy Grey touched her hand and said softly, "I'm so sorry, Countess Borghase. I know you'll miss her deeply." Dottie nodded and Peggy continued, "I was just giving General Rothrock the final information on his mother's death."

Dorothy raised her eyebrows. "Are there any surprises?"

Peggy shook her head. "No, not really. But there are a few things we've picked up from other laboratory reports we've analyzed."

Mic smiled to herself. She knew Peggy Grey so well. She didn't want to use the word "autopsy" or "victim" around survivors. She already missed Slade who'd left with Stoddard to work on the case. They hoped to locate the lab the perps were using and search hospital orders for large amounts of chemicals and pharmaceuticals.

“Dr. Grey, is there anything new on the other poison cases,” General Rothrock asked, “that may be related to my mother's case?”

Peggy put on her reading glasses and looked through a few papers. "Yes, sir. We picked up a few things. The poisoners are altering the poison each time they strike."

"What exactly do you mean?" Michaela asked. "I don't follow."

"What I'm trying to say is the killers are changing the strength and toxicity of the poison each time they strike. In other words, they're altering the poison each time – sort of like experimenting."

Rothrock was quiet for a moment as he digested the information. "Is the poison the same? Is it always the belladonna?"

Peggy nodded and said, "Yeah, so far it is, but what concerns us about these small chemical changes is there's a good chance they're still experimenting."

Rothrock's eyes met Mic's and the two of them stared at each other. “So, they're creating the perfect weapon?”

Peggy nodded. "Yeah, the perfect weapon… the poison compound that will kill the largest number of people the fastest, most efficient way."

Mic swallowed hard. This was bad, just as she'd feared it would be.

"What evidence do you have to validate this?" Rothrock asked as he looked at her.

"We've got a body. A John Doe. A floater we fished out of the James this morning. Looks like he was a live pin cushion for belladonna research."

Mic was quiet and could feel her heart begin to pound. Her body was cold all over.

Rothrock had heard about the floater earlier and he weighed the repercussion as Michaela felt the knot tighten in her stomach. Peggy Grey was never wrong. The killers were searching for the perfect potion and the perfect venue. It would be the perfect storm. And it was coming to Richmond.

Peggy interrupted her thoughts as she looked at the general and said, "These perps have gotta have a lab. They are using some sophisticated equipment to titrate these poisons. We've got to find it. RPD is looking for it as we speak."

Mic's cell vibrated and she reached in her pocket and pulled out her phone. She had a text. It was from Sean, her bar manager. Her heart raced in her chest as she read it.

She was dizzy and her shaking hands dropped the phone. "We've been hit, I've got people down. Three are dead. Down at Biddy's. I've gotta go."

Dottie glanced down at Angel who growled. He stood beside Michaela. His ears were back and his teeth bared. The hair stood up on his shoulders. He was on full alert. Dottie rubbed chill bumps from her arms. She'd forgotten how ferocious and terrifying Angel could become in an instant.

Peggy touched Mic's arm, "I don't know what you're saying. What's happened at Biddy's?"

Michaela was pale as a ghost. "They've hit Biddy's. The poisoners. There are already three people down." She stared calmly at Dottie. "Call 911. Keep Angel for me. I don't want him around any poison." She reached down to reassure her dog who remained on alert. "And call and tell Slade."

Rothrock grabbed her arm. "I'll go with you, Mic. I'll drive. I'll get my car," he said as Mic ordered Angel to stand down.

Mic nodded and said, "Will you stay with him, Dottie? He'll be okay after we leave. Maybe Cookie could give him a bone to entertain him. If you have to, give him a sedative. You have some right?

Dottie nodded. She was on the phone with Richmond 911. "Yeah, yeah. I have all of Angel's medicines here. Just in case, let's go ahead and give it to him."

Mic bent down, talked softly to Angel and then led him into the kitchen. He stood obediently next to Cookie but looked longingly at Mic. He wanted to go with her. He knew she was in danger. Mic leaned down, kissed him on the head and told him to stay with Dottie. She went into the kitchen and reached for his sedative. She wrapped it in a pill pocket. Mic gave Angel the pill and she and the general left quickly. Angel watched her sadly from the sidelights that flanked the front door.

Chapter 45

Snake stopped by his place and put his Suburban in his garage. He entered his house, sat at the kitchen table and took a couple of deep breaths. That had been close, as close as he'd ever been to getting caught. He looked up at the dirty, smudged fingerprints that stained the white cabinets yellowed with age. He couldn't wait until this gig was over and he could escape to the Caribbean. He was gonna retire. No question. He'd had enough close calls lately and his luck was running out.

He needed a drink and got up, pulled out a bottle of cheap whiskey and poured a tumbler full of the brown liquid in a short, greasy glass. He sat for a few minutes and then moved into the living room and flipped on the TV to the seven o'clock news. The banner across the bottom of the TV set said, "RICHMOND'S BELLADONNA BOYS STRIKE AGAIN. He listened as the reporter talked about breaking news at a Shockoe Slip restaurant. *Damned Boris. He was just a one-man show.* He tossed down his whiskey, jumped in his ride and headed towards Boris's lab. He was pissed. The SOB had struck without him… again.

He spotted the Russian's car outside, hollered his name and waited for Boris to open the door.

Boris gave him a broad smirk, "Did ya hear the news?"

Snake nodded and said, "What the hell? I didn't know you were going to hit any other places until the big one. You should've told me. We're partners," he said stubbornly as he glared at Boris's deformed head.

Boris shrugged his shoulders and said, "I was bored this afternoon. I drove downtown about three o'clock, picked a restaurant that had a few cars in the lot and spiced up their food."

Snake shook his head and said, "Dude, you're taking too many chances. The last thing we need is to get caught. You should've waited for me."

Boris jumped up from his bench and said, "Shut up. What do I need you for? You've no idea what I'm doing or what kind of poison I use."

Snake fought to keep his temper. "Man, use your head. I'm your backup, your muscle and your lookout. This is the second time in two days you've killed without me being around. What's up with that?" Snake stared at him defiantly.

Boris remained silent and transferred some fluid with an eyedropper.

Snake continued, "Whoever hired you is gonna kill us if you mess this up. The bosses are gonna get us. Whoever they are, man. Use your damn brain."

Boris shrugged his shoulders. "I told you. I was bored. I mixed up another batch of the good stuff and I wanted to try it out before tomorrow and I just happened to pass by this restaurant and decided to test it."

Snake shook his head. "You ain't listening, man. You're going rogue on me and you're gonna get both of us killed. I'm pissed about that. I like living."

Boris glared at him but remained silent. He shifted his body position on his lab bench and Snake watched him carefully. Boris was tall and his arms and legs were long. He could grab Snake and put him in a chokehold in a couple of seconds.

Snake sat backwards in an old wooden chair and stared at the scarred wooden desk. He ran his fingers over the deep scratches and indentations in the wood. He counted to ten to hold his temper. He had to give it to Boris. The guy was a genius at poison and concocting death. He was also good at taking care of himself. Not what you'd expect from a guy who had a background in science. He took a deep breath and said, "Man, you've been so lucky. Suppose something bad had come down. Then where'd we be?"

Boris gave him a sly smile and said, "Well, it didn't. Everything went fine. I just want you to shut up so I can see how many people I killed," he whined as he gestured at the TV and turned the volume up.

Snake shook his head and looked at the TV screen. Again, the local news anchor interrupted with breaking news. He reported three people confirmed dead at Biddy McPherson's pub located on Shockoe Slip. The news anchor identified one victim was a Richmond police officer.

Snake jumped up and said, "Dude, you done kilt yourself a cop. How'd you manage that?" Snake's heart raced with excitement as he high-fived his tall Russian partner.

Boris smiled broadly, his sunken, bald head shiny under the fluorescent light. He looked at Snake, a wicked gleam in his eye and said, "Partner you ain't heard the best part."

Snake smiled happily and said, "What I heard so far is pretty damned good! What's the rest?"

Boris let out a cackle. "What you don't know is that we're gonna bag ourselves another copper tonight but that ain't even the best part."

Snake felt like a kid on Christmas morning, especially after those sons of bitches had chased him all over Richmond just a few hours ago. "What can be better than killing a bunch of cops?"

Boris smiled and taunted him with the information. He wanted to watch Snake squirm a little bit.

But Snake wasn't buying and he asked Boris quietly, "So, what could be better than killing cops?"

Boris's face was a caricature of evil. His smile was hideous and he was practically salivating, "The owner of the bar. She's the dark-haired broad you were gawking at this morning at the funeral. She owns the bar and it's the booze hole for the Richmond Police Department. She's a former cop, and," Boris glanced at his watch, "I bet she's gettin' down there right about now," he said with another cruel smile.

Snake gave him a deadpan look, a clap on the back and said, "Let's go, partner. Let's go watch the action and then we'll get her. We'll have some fun. Yeah! We're gonna have a good night." He was so excited, that he could hardly walk.

Chapter 46

Slade stared across his desk at Steve Stoddard and said, "Lieutenant, what's going on? I thought this body was pumped full of belladonna. Now the ME's office is telling us they think there is another poison on board," he said as he slammed the lab reports on his metal desk.

Stoddard nodded his head as he stared out of the window. The late afternoon was dwindling away. He wearily reached for his coffee cup. It'd been a hell of a day. First the funeral of Camilla Rothrock, and then the chase of a potential perp at Hollywood Cemetery followed by another sighting, possibly the same guy, at the home of Countess Dorothy Borghase. No one was apprehended.

"Yeah, this case just gets more and more crazy," he agreed. "When did the medical examiner's office say that they'd finish analyzing the floater's body fluids?"

Slade shook his head. "They didn't. The Feds were all over the place and checkin' out body fluids with their own set of analytics. That guy, Dr. Duncan, the Fed that runs the poison forensics team, just sort of came in and took over."

Stoddard shook his head. "I bet everyone down there is having a fit. Ain't nothing that screws up any office, not to mention the office of the medical examiner, like a horde of Feds swarming in like crows, takin' over, second guessin' you and searching for your mistakes."

Slade laughed. "Do you ever give the Feds credit for doing anything right? There's been a time or two where they've actually helped us."

Stoddard's head bobbed up and down. "Maybe. Most of the time when they swarm in, they screw stuff up and you and I both know it. Why should this be any different?" he asked defensively as he tapped his pencil rapidly against his desk.

Slade stood up and walked across the room. He had to get out of there and do something. He felt useless. "I think they were going to call Dr. Peggy Grey and try to get her down there to identify, or at least confirm, several additional poisons they pulled from the corpse."

Stoddard's eyes brightened. "Well, that's a good idea. Grey is as good as it gets. She'll be able to figure it out."

"Yeah. I think she's still over at Countess Borghase's house. I heard they were sending a unit to take her down to the state crime lab." He paused for a moment and continued, "If I know Peggy, she'll have an answer for us in about twenty minutes, almost as soon as she gets her hands on the samples."

"Agreed. I guess we'll just have to wait," the lieutenant said. "We got anything else on possible locations for the big hit?"

Slade paced around his office. Stoddard could see the anxiety in his steps. "There's a million things going on in

Richmond this weekend and every weekend the rest of the month. SAC Burnley thought the attack might be at the ballpark since the team plays this weekend. Of course, there's always Beaux Arts over near the Carillon and Byrd Park."

Stoddard ran his fingers through his salt-and-pepper hair. He was anxious too, and scared. He'd never come across anything like these poisonings. He preferred murderers, muggers, rapists, burglars, and all kinds of petty criminals. But he was clearly out of his league with this poison stuff. Although he'd never admit it, he was glad to have Burnley and the Feds on board. He preferred criminals that used guns, left fingerprints and blood splatter – not psychopaths that stuck half-dead people with poison to see how long they'd live. He shuddered inwardly.

"Stoddard, why do you think these guys picked Richmond? What did this city do to deserve this kind of crime?" Slade asked. "I just don't get it. Could it be some retaliation against us?"

Stoddard shook his head slowly. "I don't know. But, funny you say that because I've wondered the same. It makes no sense. We're used to normal violent crime and white collar stuff like running cigarettes, counterfeit clothing and other scams and the routine policing stuff."

Slade smiled. "By 'routine' do you mean murder, drugs, and gang violence?"

Stoddard smiled and his face lit up. "Yeah, not to mention always being on the alert for terrorism. I understand that kind of crime. This poisoning stuff is scary." He shook his head.

Slade nodded. "This is terrorism. We've got local citizens and emergency responders and police scared to go out and eat or grab a beer or a drink," he muttered, anger in his voice.

"Yeah. I just wonder where it's coming from," Lieutenant Stoddard sighed. "We're gettin' nowhere." His cell beeped and he stopped to read a text message. "Oh, the FBI wants to meet with us soon about planning security for the ball field and the art show."

Slade nodded. "Guess they've determined those are the most vulnerable targets, right?"

Stoddard nodded. "So far as I know, but there could be dozens more," he said as impatience flashed across his face. "What is the media calling these guys? Isn't it something like the 'Poison Pair' or 'Poison Boys' or something like that?"

"It's the Poison Boys and the Belladonna Boys. The media's flashing the composite sketch the kid from Busy Burger provided all over the networks, the one of the tall, bald dude with the dented head. We gotta get a break sooner or later," Slade mused as he tried to relax. "I got a team out looking for the lab they're working out of and we're tracking down large orders of chemicals that may play a part in this."

Stoddard nodded and reared back in his chair as he shook his head. "I don't know about this one, Slade. I got some bad vibes. A bad feelin'. These perps have targeted the RPD and the city, and I don't know why. I guess there's still speculation about General Rothrock being targeted?" he questioned.

Slade was about to reply when his smart phone vibrated. It was a text. A sliver of fear ran through him as he read it. "They've hit again. It's Mic's bar. They got three, maybe four dead down at Biddy McPherson's." Slade could feel terror envelop him.

Stoddard slapped him on the back and said, "Dammit. Let's go." He paused for a minute and said, "This is personal now, this is where we drink."

Chapter 47

Mic's heart leapt into her throat when she reached her restaurant and bar in Shockoe bottom. She reached out to pat Angel, to comfort him, and remembered he wasn't there. "This looks bad, General," she said to Rothrock. Fear clutched her heart at the sight.

Rothrock nodded and said, "Yeah, it does. Let's stay calm," he advised as he looked at her.

There were eight police cars surrounding Biddy's pub and rescue vehicles were everywhere. She saw the ambulance transport from the Virginia morgue.

Mic identified herself and the general to the police and rushed through the police barricade. They entered through the kitchen door, and found the kitchen staff frightened and intimidated. She went over, hugged her executive and sous chefs and assured them they weren't responsible. She was speaking with her chefs when a team arrived from the federal forensic poison team who began to order her staff around. This just added more anxiety and chaos to the scene. Mic felt anger overtaking her fear as she searched for the head of the poison team. It was a heavyset man dressed in blue. She identified herself as the owner of the restaurant and introduced General Rothrock.

"Is there a way my restaurant staff can assist you to keep things calm?" Mic asked her voice tight and her green eyes furious.

The man gazed at her over his spectacles as though she were an alien. Never had a restaurant patron or owner interrupted a safety inspection. After all, there were already three dead people.

"No," he said crossly. "Now get out of my way," he said as he pushed her aside. "This is a crime scene."

General Rothrock took a step forward to intervene when Mic tried again. "Sir, my staff is traumatized. We're as upset about this as you are. Let us help you in an orderly inspection and sample collection so you don't miss anything at all that could possibly help us catch these murderers."

The man nodded as he saw Dr. Duncan, head of the fed poison team, headed his way, a look of anger on his face. He said, "Okay, lead the way," as he watched Dr. Duncan and General Rothrock shake hands.

Michaela motioned for her executive chef to come over and direct the man as he and his staff began collecting and labeling samples of all the foods in the kitchen, refrigerators and the walk-in freezer. When she was positive things were under control, she left the kitchen and entered the main dining room. She saw her waitstaff in one corner of the room while a few restaurant patrons were in another. Sean, her restaurant manager, was behind the bar with a uniformed RPD officer.

There were two shrouded bodies on the floor. Mic felt her stomach lurch and she swallowed and held on to a table for support.

Sean raised his hand in greeting. Michaela walked quickly to the bar and sat on a stool across from him. Sean started to apologize, but she waved her hand to silence him.

"Sean, just tell me what happened. What exactly did you see?" She smiled at him calmly, hoping to decrease his stress.

He shook his head, his faced etched with fear and concern. "It was after three. The bar was almost empty. I was in your office working when Ginger, our new hostess, came running in and told me to go see the women over at that table," he said pointing to the table near the bodies. “She said they were complaining of being sick and short of breath. I called 911, but by the time I got into the dining room, one woman had already fallen on the floor. Ginger said she’d stood up so she could breathe. The other lady told me she couldn't walk and then fell to the floor too. I told her that 911 was on the way. I got on the floor and held her head so she could breathe a little easier,” he said as he stopped to take a breath.

Michaela watched the muscles twitch in Sean's face. He was so upset. She saw tears swim in his eyes so she walked behind the bar, put her arm around him and said, "Sean, it's not your fault. There's nothing you could’ve done. Both women were poisoned and you had no way of knowing that."

He shook his head, his lip trembled. "They were so young. Probably just out of college." He stared at the floor and regained his composure and continued, "They were regulars and came in almost every Friday afternoon. I think they teach school over on Church Hill." He thought for a moment and said, "Yeah, they do. One of them teaches art and the other one teaches social studies." He looked over at the table where Mic's waitress sat and said, "I think Melinda knows both of them. I think they were in grad school together at VCU. She can probably tell you more about them."

Michaela asked the uniformed police officer if she and Sean could go into her office where they could talk quietly. She thought she recognized the young police officer but wasn't sure. As the years passed, she knew fewer and fewer young uniforms. But he knew her, "Sure thing, Ms. McPherson. By the way, I just heard on my scanner that Detective McKane and Lieutenant Stoddard are en route. They should be here momentarily."

Mic nodded and smiled at him. Michaela, Rothrock, and Sean went into her office and closed the door halfway. Mic watched as a forensic team took a million pictures of the bodies. Both young women were casually dressed. A fire burned in her belly and she was having a hard time keeping it together. *What monster was vile enough to murder elderly ladies, women, school children and now two young woman celebrating the end of their work week*? She shook her head and tried to swallow away the lump in her throat.

"What did they drink, Sean? Do you think the guy, or guys, got access to the keg room or the bar?" General Rothrock asked.

Sean shook his head vehemently. "No, sir, hell no," he said firmly. "We have a guard between the dining room and the keg room and I was behind the bar. We've been watching the keg area from the bar. We had a few people in for lunch and these ladies," he said as he gestured towards the bodies, "came in." He paused moment and said, "They weren't even drinking. One had iced tea and the other one had water with lemon." He stopped for a moment and a small moan escaped his mouth.

Mic looked at him, alarm on her face. "What, what did you remember, Sean? Is it important?"

General Rothrock asked again, "What is it, Sean? It's important so take your time and remember."

Sean's eyes locked on Mic. "The blonde. The woman with blond hair, the art teacher, told me she was expecting her first baby, she'd just found out yesterday, so she didn't have her normal Irish Red, her favorite brew. They were sharing Welch Rarebit."

Mic looked down at her desk and touched her stomach as if she was trying to push the pain away. She studied her fingernails as horror and disgust spread through her body. The young woman was pregnant. *How much worse could this get*? She looked at Sean and the general, "So the poison had to be in the Welsh Rarebit? Anything else?"

At that moment, Slade entered Mic's office and gave her a big hug. She could feel her body tremble against his as he whispered in her ear. "We're gonna get these guys, Mic. I promise you," he said huskily. "Just keep it together for a little while longer." He gave General Rothrock a tight smile.

Mic nodded and said with a shaky voice, "Sean thinks the poison is in the Welch Rarebit. Both woman were eating the rarebit and drinking different beverages."

Slade stared at Sean. "You sure, man?"

Sean nodded. "Positive. That's all they had."

Slade placed his hand on Sean's shoulder. "Good work, Sean. That helps a lot."

"Yes it does, son," General Rothrock agreed.

A confused look crossed Sean's face. "But, but, that means the guy got into the kitchen to poison the food. What about the police guard outside the kitchen in the alley? The off duty cop we hired? Where is he?"

Slade nodded and said, "We found Officer Smith behind the dumpster. He's dead. Looks like he was poisoned too. Of course, I'm guessing. I can tell you for sure he's not shot."

General Rothrock cursed under his breath.

Mic could hardly think. Her body felt as though it was in one big knot and she felt horror spreading over her. She covered her face with her hand. Even though the policeman was working overtime for her, she felt responsible.

Richmond had already lost several officers earlier in the year. She looked up at Slade with a tear-stained face. "I need a minute to pull myself together. I'll be out soon," she said.

Slade rubbed her back, "Okay, I'm gonna talk to the forensic people and the poison team in the kitchen. It might save them some time if I tell them about the rarebit."

Mic nodded as she took a deep breath.

Chapter 48

Boris and Snake crouched behind a concrete fountain near a brick wall. They were several blocks from Biddy's pub and watched the police activity with increasing glee. Police bubble lights bounced off the building and the air was tense with excitement. The red lights of rescue vehicles along with searchlights lit up the night. They high-fived one another each time a body was removed from the restaurant. They'd seen three stretchers.

"Looks like you only got three people this time. How come?" Snake asked. "You on a life-saving kick or somethin'?" he asked with a wide smile.

Boris didn't like Snake criticizing his work. A shot of anger consumed him. He continued to watch the police, local officials, and emergency personnel mill around the bar parking lot and talk. "What are those guys standin' around talkin' about? They took the last body out forty-five minutes ago," he whined. "There ain't no more to do over there. I don't believe it."

Snake shrugged his shoulders. "I don't know. Who cares? They're wasting taxpayers' money. Why didn't you kill more people with the new poison? You got a lot of it."

Boris jumped into Snake's face and hissed at him through gritted teeth. He pinned the shorter man against the brick wall with his body. His breath was foul and Snake figured the halitosis would kill him before Boris's gun. "There weren't that many people in the bar, dumbass. I was just hanging out. I was bored. I only decided to kill people a couple of seconds before I did it."

Boris continued to pin Snake to the wall and stare at him.

Snake put his hand on Boris's arm and said, "Take it easy man. I don't give a damn who or how many you kill. I'm going to get paid whether we kill five people or five thousand." He stared into Boris's lifeless eyes and added, "Now, move the hell out of my way!"

Boris didn't budge and continued to press him against the brick building, his long fingers digging into Snake's shoulders. "You gonna stop complaining about me?" he asked as he stepped closer. For half a second he considered snapping both of Snake's clavicles with his fingers but decided against it because he needed him for the weekend.

Snake nodded his head. "Yeah, man. No more complaints. Is that your phone I hear ringing?" He nodded towards Boris's shirt pocket.

Boris yanked the phone from his pocket and barked into it in Russian. Snake could hear the conversation on both ends. He wished he could understand Russian. He only knew a few words but picked up that Boris was angry. Boris slammed his cell phone onto the ground, breaking the case and the screen.

It was then they saw the dog. A huge German Shepherd the size of a small pony had come up behind them and stared at them. The dog's eyes were red and they followed the men as they spoke to one another.

Boris loosened his grip and backed a short away distance from Snake. The dog guarded each man and growled deeply, showing sharp teeth each time either of them tried to move. The fur bristled on the animal's back. The dog had pinned them in place.

Snake cursed the dog and hollered for him to go way. The dog remained still and looked back and forth from one man to the other daring them to make a move. The louder Snake cursed, the deeper the dog growled. His ears were up and his teeth bared. He was a frightening sight.

Boris lunged at the dog and tried to scare him away, but the dog didn't move. He kicked at the dog's chest and the dog jumped on him and knocked him to the street. The dog placed a massive paw on Boris's chest as if defying him to move. The dog's jaws were several inches from Boris's carotid arteries.

Snake could see the pulse beat rapidly in Boris's neck, as he stood paralyzed in place by the wall.

Boris reached for the vial of poison in his jeans pocket and planned how to throw the vial into the dog's mouth.

Snake watched the dog guard Boris with a gruesome fascination. Boris couldn't move. Boris slowly moved his hand in his pocket. The dog saw it as well. As soon as Boris's hand disappeared, the dog opened his jaws and bit down on the Russian's hand.

Boris howled in pain as the dog jumped off his body and walked across the street. He stared at the two men and watched their movements closely.

"What the hell!" Snake muttered, "Was that some sort of devil dog? Did you see those red eyes? I've never seen anything like that!" He paused for a minute as he watched the dog from across the street. A chill ran up his spine. There was something weird, metaphysical about the canine. He stared at them as though he could read their thoughts. Snake shook off his fear and looked down at Boris who remained on the ground.

"That damned dog bit me," Boris whined. He held up his hand and sure enough, the dog's canine teeth had caught his hand. Blood oozed from two puncture wounds, one near his knuckle and the other on his wrist. The hand was swelling quickly as blood dripped from the wounds.

Snake took a couple of steps closer and inspected the bite. "Dude, that looks bad. But truth is, that dog could have killed you with one bite to the neck. We'd better go and get that looked at," he said, as blood steadily dripped from Boris's hand. "Puncture wounds can be bad."

Boris shook his head. "Nah, it'll be okay. I've got stuff back at the lab that I can treat it with as well as bandages," he said as he wiped the blood on his jeans. "I just hope the damned bastard had his shots. I'd hate to die from rabies."

Snake smiled to himself. Wouldn't it be ironic if Boris died from rabies poisoning? Poetic even. He wondered how many dogs Boris had killed experimenting with poison.

"Let's get the hell out of here," Boris said, "I want to get this hand fixed. If you want to stay here, gawk at the police idiots and look for that woman you want so bad, do it. I'll meet you back at the lab."

Snake smiled broadly, looked over Boris's shoulder and said, "I don't have to wait. There she is right there," he said as he pointed and watched Michaela step out of the front door of the bar. She walked towards her SUV that the Richmond police had picked up for her. "I'm going to follow her home so I know where she lives. I'll pay her a visit tonight, you know, and surprise her," he said with a chuckle as he made lewd gestures with his hands.

Boris ignored him, his face gray with pain. He mumbled, "I'll see you later," as he hobbled off, his wounded hand sheltered in his pocket.

The dog continued to watch them from a distance. His eyes followed their every movement.

Chapter 49

Dottie sat alone in her library and reminisced the day. For some reason she felt sad and morose and she wasn't sure why. She knew she was grieving the death of Camilla so perhaps that was it. Maybe since the burial and luncheon were over, she was lost and let down. She reached for her house phone and dialed Michaela's cell. She had seen on the news where the death toll at Biddy's pub was three people, two young women and a police officer. She shook her head and cursed as a tear rolled down her face. She looked up as someone softly knocked on the library door.

"Come in, Cookie. I'm sure it's you," Dottie said, her voice more chipper than she felt.

"How are you, Countess?" Cookie asked as she inspected her employer from head to toe.

Dottie smiled and said, "Pretty good. How's Henry doing up there?" she asked as she pointed towards the ceiling. Dottie noticed the lines of fatigue on Cookie's face and said, "Come over here and have a seat, keep me company for a few minutes and tell me how you're doing."

Cookie moved across the room and sat on the sofa opposite Dottie's Queen Anne recliner. She put her feet up on a brocade hassock. "Doing okay. Just a little tired. It's getting late," she noted as she checked her watch.

Dottie's eyes looked out of the French door and said, "Yes, it is. It's pitch black outside." She checked the clock on the mantle. "It's a little after nine. I must've fallen asleep for an hour or so," she said as she yawned.

"Have you heard from Michaela? Do you know how things are down at the bar?"

Dottie shook her head and said, "I just called her, but she didn't pick up. It looks like there were three people killed," she said as a shadow passed over her face.

"Yeah, I saw that. The local news said it looks like a different kind of poison. Did you see anything about that?"

Dottie's eyes widened and she repeated, "A different type of poison? No, I missed that. What's different about it?"

Cookie shook her head and said, "I don't think they know. The local news said it looks different than the poison from the other restaurants. It kills very, very quickly. These women died within a few minutes."

Dottie's ice blue eyes locked with Cookie's brown ones. *What could this mean? Does this mean the kill time is escalating? That people die much quicker? It must!* Isn't that what we'd expected? Slade said this afternoon the FBI thought the first set of killings were "practice" killings and testing the poison in preparation for the big one.

Cookie shivered and rubbed chill bumps from her arms. "That's terrifying," she said slowly. "I hope nothing much is happening this weekend." She paused for a moment and said, "But, I know there's Beaux Arts and other things going on all over town. Is VCU graduating this weekend?"

Dottie paled at the thought of a mass poison attack at VCU's graduation. The hotels would be packed with parents and family of graduates. *Oh my God, I've gotta mention this to Mic and Slade.* She looked steadily at Cookie and said, "I don't know, but it's possible. They usually graduate early in May, but I'll have to check."

Cookie looked around the room and asked, "Where's Angel? He was in here with you, but I haven't seen him lately."

Dottie shook her head. "I'm not sure. As I said, I fell asleep. Maybe he's in the kitchen in his bed or outside. Doesn't he get his arthritis medicine in a little while?"

"Yes, he does. Let me check around for him. Lord have mercy, Michaela will kill us if anything happens to Angel," Cookie predicted.

"I'll get up and help you," Dottie offered. "Honestly, if I don't move every couple of hours I'm so stiff I can't move." She sighed deeply and said, "I'm gonna miss Camilla so much. She was my running partner. I've not been to the gym since she died and I'm really feeling it."

"I'll walk with you, Countess. I can't walk as fast, but I can walk and I need the exercise," Cookie offered.

Dottie nodded and smiled, "That's a great idea. It'll be good for both of us. Now let's go find Angel. You start. I want to try and call Michaela again."

"Okay, I'll look outside," Cookie offered, as she got up and went outside and searched for Angel on the terrace.

Dottie reached for her phone and dialed Michaela's cell but got her voicemail. She'd dialed Michaela's landline when Cookie reappeared in the doorway, a look of concern on her face.

Dottie hung up the phone. "What, what's wrong?"

"It's Angel. I can't find him anywhere!" she said, her eyes filled with fear as a sob escaped her throat. "What are we gonna do?"

"Oh my God," Dottie said as she rose from her chair. "Mic will kill us. He's got to be around here somewhere," she said with more reassurance than she felt. She pictured someone throwing Angel a poisoned steak. She returned to her chair. She knew whoever had stalked her house earlier today would most likely hurt Michaela's beloved dog. She lay against the velvet of her chair, closed her eyes and prayed.

Chapter 50

Slade sat back in his chair, his feet propped up on his desk, eyes closed and hands behind his head. He mentally processed the events of the day. First of all, they'd spotted several men at Camilla's funeral, but the chase had gone nowhere. Then, the RPD had fished a body out of the James, a man who had been repeatedly poisoned, a virtual experimental corpse. Then, at lunch, Henry had seen someone stalking or at least loitering behind Dottie's house. Police had chased the guy for over an hour but once again, he'd gotten away. *What the hell was going on?* He'd never known perps who wanted or needed a front row seat in all aspects of their crimes. It scared him. These were psychopaths. It was pretty obvious they didn't care much about their own lives but were simply killing for kicks. Slade continued to reflect on the day and became more concerned about the inevitability of what was going to happen next.

These guys were terrorists, they were going to launch a terror attack in Richmond and it was going to happen soon. But, when? Who did they work for? The Feds were right. They'd been saying the same thing for two days most likely based on intelligence they hadn't shared. He needed to ask Chief Herndon to have the governor activate the Virginia National Guard. He opened his eyes when his fax machine beeped. He walked over to the machine and pulled the paper out of the fax. It was the preliminary autopsy report on the floater. Before he could read the report, his cell phone rang and Peggy Grey's name flashed on his digital display. He grabbed the phone on the first ring.

"Dr. Grey. What have you got? I'm sure you're not calling to tell me how nice it was to see me at lunch today," he joked, a note of doubt in his voice.

Peggy smiled. She liked Slade McKane. Even though he was short tempered and had the personality of the black Irish, he was a damned good cop. "It was good to see you today as well, Detective McKane. As a matter of fact, it's always good to see you, but you're correct. I have some information to share with you," she said pleasantly, but Slade knew her voice was guarded.

"I'm sure it's not good, not if you have to call me at ten o'clock at night," Slade mused. "Spit it out."

Peggy sighed deeply and said, "It's not good. I just got off the phone with SAC Burnley and Dr. Duncan from the Fed's poison team." She paused and asked, "Did you get the fax I just sent you?"

Slade felt a knot form in his belly and said, "Yeah, just got it. It's in my hand as we speak."

"Well, it's the preliminary autopsy of the fluids from the floater they pulled out of the river today."

"Yeah, I figured that," Slade said as the knot in his belly intensified. He could feel the blood rushing through his heart and to his brain as his blood pressure skyrocketed. "Break it down for me, Peggy. How bad is it?"

Peggy was silent for a moment and said, "It's bad. It's pretty bad, Slade."

"Spit it out," he ordered. "Whatever it is, we gotta figure out how to deal with it."

"We've got several different poisons in the body of the floater," she said. "He was full of another lethal plant toxin. It's often referred to as heartbreak grass."

Slade's brain exploded. "Isn't that the stuff they used to assassinate that Russian exile – the guy that was going to testify against the Russians? The man who was killed in London last year?"

Peggy smiled to herself. *Slade was a good cop.* "Yeah. It's the same. Heartbreak grass leaves a chemical calling card in the stomach that we can identify easily now, particularly if we're looking for poison. Of course the floater was full of other types of poison as well... the belladonna that we identified in Camilla and the others. We think now that the murdered kids had heartbreak grass in them as well. We're gonna go back and check."

Slade was appalled that someone would use heartbreak grass on a bunch of school children. His heart raced with anger and he didn't reply. Peggy continued to speak as Slade got his anger under control.

"Heartbreak grass blocks the transmission of impulses where the muscles and nerves meet. It causes quick respiratory depression and death. Victims can die immediately depending on the dosage, or within an hour. They often complain of dizziness, nausea, and vomiting. They may say they can't walk or stand so they fall to the floor. Generalized instability of their feet is common. It's a very lethal poison," she ended in a soft voice.

Slade was working out the response in his mind. He hated to even suggest it because he was afraid it was correct. "Sounds like we may have a Russian terrorist here in Richmond."

"We can't rule that out," Peggy said, a note of resignation in her voice. "Heartbreak grass is a main assassination tool of the Russians and the Chinese. We know it's a weapon of the Russian Secret Service. We also know it's made or perhaps refined is a better word, in the poison labs of the Russian Secret Service, known to some as Kamera."

Slade gritted his teeth, every curse word he knew jumping through his mind. "Could this get any worse?" he asked, terror riveting his body as he ran his fingers through his dark curly hair. He quickly assessed the possibilities of a heartbreak grass terror attack in Richmond. It would be deadly.

"Well," Peggy said slowly, "It can always be worse, but this is bad, quite bad in fact. There's an early meeting down at FBI headquarters in the morning so you need to be there… unless they move it up to tonight," she added.

Slade's intestines went into spasm. He asked, "Anything else I need to know, Peggy?"

"Heartbreak grass, along with cyanide, is the main component in the 'suicide pills' you see in spy movies and in real life."

"That's great, that's just great," Slade muttered sarcastically. He paused for a second and asked, "What about the stuff used at Mic's restaurant? Is it the heartbreak grass or the belladonna?"

"Don't know. Probably a combination of a bunch of stuff. We haven't analyzed it yet. We've got to get them, Slade, we've just gotta get them," Peggy said quietly. "Or, it'll be the end of life as we know it in Richmond, Virginia."

"Yeah, I know," Slade said as he wiped sweat from his face with his handkerchief. He hadn't realized he was sweating so much.

Chapter 51

Michaela's heart was heavy as she backed her car out of her parking space on Shockoe Slip and drove home from Biddy's. She tried to focus on her driving, but it was an effort. Her thoughts kept returning to the events of the last three hours. *Three people dead in my bar*. Two young women, one of them pregnant, and a Richmond police officer killed outside. A tear slid down her cheek as she thought about the men that were on this killing spree. When would it stop? Would the police and FBI be able to stop it? Anger and fear traveled through her body like lightening and twisted in her gut.

She jumped when her car phone rang; she pushed the button on her steering wheel and answered. It was Slade.

"Hey, how are you doing?" Mic asked a note of forced cheerfulness in her voice.

"I'm okay. Just burning the midnight oil. Did you tie things up at Biddy's?" Slade asked, his voice low and serious.

"Yeah, yeah, I did," Mic said a little catch in her voice as she choked back a sob. "I think the forensic team got all the samples they needed, and eventually the morgue collected the bodies. I spent a bit of time trying to reassure my employees, but honestly, Slade, I think this is going to get much worse."

Slade listened and was quiet for a moment. He didn't respond or disagree with her.

"Slade, Slade, are you there?" Mic thought she had lost her connection.

"Yes, yeah, I'm here. I was just thinking," he said in a pensive voice.

"Thinking, thinking about what? Is there new evidence or news?" Mic asked, as her heart jumped in anticipation.

"No… Yes, there's news but none of is good."

Mic shuddered as a new wave of depression settled over her. She asked in a small voice, "What's new, Slade? What's come in?"

Slade sighed deeply. Mic could picture him staring out his window at the dark sky. "I just got off the phone with Peggy Grey. Obviously they analyzed the body fluids from the guy they pulled out of the James River today."

"The John Doe? Yeah, who is he? How does he fit into this?"

"Well," Slade said slowly, "We think he was a research project for the poison boys. As you know, Peggy had thought this earlier and now they've confirmed it." Slade paused for a moment and added, "They used this guy like a pin cushion to inject different poisons into - until he finally died."

"Yeah. That's more than sick," Mic said impatiently. She'd remembered this from earlier. "What else?"

"The murderers may have a new poison of choice. Unfortunately a poison that is more lethal," he said slowly.

"What?" Mic asked as she pulled her car off the side of the road. She didn't want to miss anything. "More toxic? It seems to me the belladonna did the job well," she said angrily, "based on what we've seen."

"You can say that again," Slade agreed. "Peggy said she thought they used this other poison, heartbreak grass, on some of the children at the Busy Burger the other day. She said depending on the dosage, people die almost immediately and that seemed to be the case with the kids. The floater was filled with heartbreak grass," Slade added.

Mic stared at her steering wheel as her brain raced. "I bet that's what they used tonight or, I guess I should say this afternoon. From what Sean told me, the two women said a few words and died almost immediately. They didn't last long at all," she said as sadness engulfed her as she remembered the two young women dead in her bar.

"Yeah, you're probably right. Peggy and I both think they used heartbreak grass at your place. Based on the preliminary reports that have come in it looks like the women who died at Biddy's were killed with a different poison. However, there's no medical evidence to support that yet, purely speculation at this point."

"What exactly is heartbreak grass? It rings a bell with me for some reason," Mic questioned as she searched her brain. "Have we come across it before?" she asked as she reached over to pat Angel who still wasn't in his seat. "Man, I'm crazy, I can hardly do without my dog. I've reached over two or three times to pat him and he's not there. I wonder if I should call Dottie and get him back for the night."

"That's up to you, but I bet Dottie's asleep. She looked tired this afternoon."

"True," Mic said. "I'll get him in the morning. Now, what about this new poison?"

"It's another plant toxin, it comes from Asia. I guess I should say grows wild in Asia. The Chinese and the Russians use it for assassinations, and it's a favorite kill drug of the Russians."

"Oh," Mic said as she remembered. "That's the stuff they think killed that guy in Europe last year, isn't it? And I think they had a couple of assassinations in China using heartbreak grass." As realization set in, Michaela's stomach turned from fire to ice.

"You're correct, Michaela. There's some thought here that they've laced it with cyanide. But... we don't know for sure yet. Still purely speculation," Slade added.

Mic's heart hammered in her chest, "Oh, no, do they think this is some sort of international terrorism plot, happening in Richmond?" Mic squeaked as fear overcame her.

Slade sighed deeply. "We can't rule that out. Where are you?"

"I pulled over in a gas station on the Boulevard. I didn't want to miss anything while you were talking," Michaela said. "I'm getting ready to pull out."

"Okay, stay safe. Have you talked to Dottie?"

"No, I can't say I have. She called me a couple of times on my cell, but I was so busy at the restaurant I didn't take the calls. I would like to pick up Angel, but I'm sure he's having a great time over there."

Slade laughed. "I bet you do miss him and I'm sure he misses you too, but life at Dottie's is pretty good - especially with Cookie around."

"I'll just have to miss him tonight," Mic decided. "I'll get him in the morning."

"I'm sure that's okay. Angel gets treated well at Dottie's house from everything I've seen. Will you be okay at home tonight? Do you want me to stop by?"

"Nah, I'm gonna hit the sack. I know you're as busy as you can possibly be. I need some sleep and time to think so maybe I can squeeze that in tonight," Mic said.

"Okay, Michaela. Be sure you put your alarm on."

"Well yeah, of course I will. I always do," she assured him.

"There is a meeting tomorrow at FBI headquarters about international terrorism and the new poisons. Do you want me to pick you up?"

"Sure, that's fine. I need to get to bed, it's already almost eleven o'clock. I need my beauty sleep," she joked.

Slade laughed. "You need the rest a lot more than you need the beauty sleep, Michaela. You got more beauty than you'll ever need, that I can assure you."

Mic felt a warm flush covering her body, "Wow, Slade, I gotta write this down. You're not one who's much on giving compliments," she teased. "The world isn't gonna end, is it?" she joked.

"No, I hope not," he guffawed. "But, we do have to get these guys. ASAP."

"Yeah, we do," Mic agreed as she pulled her SUV on to the road. She didn't notice the car ease in behind her as she continued to talk to Slade.

"Gotta go, Slade. I'm home," she said as she parked her car a couple of houses down the street. "Stay safe."

"You too, Michaela. See you at zero-crack-thirty in front of your house," Slade promised.

"Okay, good night."

Chapter 52

Dottie took the elevator up to her bedroom on the second floor of her home. She was worried about Angel who still hadn't returned. She'd convinced herself he'd found his way home in the fan district. She'd called Michaela a few times after the attack at Biddy's, but they hadn't spoken. Dottie knew Mic was overwhelmed with the murders at Biddy's. A thought flashed through her mind that Mic could have financial worries, but if she did, Dottie would take care of those right away.

She could hear her phone ringing, her landline, as soon as she walked out of the elevator. *It must be Michaela. She's probably going to want to come over and pick up Angel.* She rushed into her bedroom to pick up the phone, but when she got there, the phone was dead. She hit the redial button and a man said hello.

"Who is this?" Dottie asked an irritable, but strong voice.

"Dottie, it's Slade, did I wake you up?"

Dottie smiled as she recognized Slade's voice. "No, I was getting ready for bed. I just got off the elevator and that's why I couldn't pick up. What's up?"

"I saw you called me several hours ago and this is the first chance I've had to call you back. Are things okay?" Slade asked, never sure what to expect from the eighty-two-year-old countess who often intimidated the hell out of him.

"Oh, that's right. I did. I have a problem here, you see." she said, her voice nervous.

Slade heard the apprehension in Dottie's voice and asked, "What's up, Dottie? You sound upset. But I can assure you Michaela is okay. I just talked with her. She's at home."

Dottie was silent. She didn't say anything.

"Dottie, Dottie. Are you still there?"

"Yes, yeah, I'm here," Dottie croaked. "But Angel isn't. I can't find Angel."

Alarm bells sounded in Slade's head. "What do you mean, Dottie? You can't find Angel?"

"Precisely that," Dottie snapped. "I can't find the dog. I haven't been able to find the dog since seven o'clock this evening. He disappeared sometime after Michaela left to go down to Biddy's," she said. "He was having a fit to go with her and she wouldn't take him. She was afraid he'd get hurt, that someone would poison him. So, I agreed to keep him here, which, as you know, I have many times before."

"Yeah, I know that," Slade said quickly. "Did you look for him?"

"Of course I went and looked for him," she said, her voice peeved and angry. "You know how much I care about that dog and I know that he's the best thing in Michaela's life. She loves him and it will kill her if she learns he's missing!"

Slade took a deep breath and continued. He knew it would do no good to get Dottie angry or upset. "Okay," he said. "Let's start over and take it from the top. When did you notice Angel was gone?"

Dottie thought for a moment and said sharply, "As I said, about seven o'clock. Everyone had left and Cookie went up to check on Henry and I took a short nap in my chair. According to Cookie, Angel was outside on the terrace, sniffing and walking around when she came downstairs. Then he went to the back of the yard, near the alley where we saw the intruder today."

"Okay, so Angel was outside sniffing near the back gate, correct?"

Dottie sighed angrily, "Yes, yes, that's what I said." She hated it when people talked down to her, like she was some old lady moron. Her voice had an irritated edge to it. She was upset and couldn't understand why Slade was asking her the same thing over and over again.

"Then what happened?" Slade asked.

"I went outside and called him and he came into the library. Just before I fell asleep, Angel was laying by the door in the sunshine."

"Then what?" Slade asked.

"I fell asleep and a little while later Cookie came into the library and asked me if I'd seen him. I told her no. So we searched high and low for him and then got in the car to go out and look for him."

"Okay," Slade said slowly. "Where'd you go? Did you see him anywhere?"

"We drove down Monument Avenue, over to Michaela's house. I was hoping he'd be on the front porch, but he wasn't. Then we headed downtown. I thought I saw him, or at least a dog like him, on Main Street, but it was dark so I can't be sure. We pulled into a parking lot and I called his name, but the dog ran the other way."

"So, do you think it was Angel?"

Dottie paused and said, "I don't know. Both Cookie and I thought it was Angel, but Angel always comes when you call him. He's well trained... so I don't know," she demurred.

"Yeah. He usually obeys. But you know how attached he is to Michaela. It's possible he left to follow her. I'm sure he knows his way downtown to Biddy's," Slade said.

"Yeah. You know, we sedated him just before Mic left. He was anxious because I'm sure he read her body language. His ears were up and back, his fur was up, and honestly, I could see the whites of his eyes."

Slade knew that look. He'd seen it many times when the three of them were on patrol years ago. "He's ferocious when he has his hackles up. I'm not sure a pill would make a difference."

Dottie was quiet for a moment and said, "He calmed down after she left. And he did lie down for a few minutes. Just before I fell asleep," she said defensively.

Slade laughed and said, "Actually, Countess, I think Angel was waiting for *you* to go to sleep. I imagine as soon as he knew you were down for the count, he took off," Slade concluded.

"So, what do we do?" Dottie asked as she felt tears pop into her eyes. Mic would never forgive her if she'd lost her beloved dog. "Angel has saved all of our lives and I've got to find him," she lamented.

Slade cleared his throat. "We wait for him to come back. I think Angel has gone to look for Mic to make sure she's safe. I think he'll be back soon."

Dottie was silent.

"Just go to bed, Countess. Angel will be back before you know it," Slade chuckled. "He knows he has the Life of Riley and trust me, he's just out there looking for Michaela."

"Are you sure?" Dottie asked in a timid voice that was out of character for her.

"Positive. Good night, Dottie. Get some rest. It was a big day," Slade encouraged.

"Good night, Detective," Dottie said softly as she clicked off.

The Case of the Dead Dowager

Chapter 53

Snake had changed his mind about following Mic home and had tracked down her address instead. He'd broken into the house earlier and gone through every room. He knew the house like the back of his hand. He'd easily managed to get into the house by disarming the burglar alarm system with a simple flick of his wrist and a screwdriver. He'd covered every square inch of her home and planned his attack and escape. He'd even started running the water in the bathtub. He'd sat in her bathroom and watched it trickle in for over an hour, confident it wouldn't spill over and spoil his plan. Then he'd returned to Biddy's, watched her leave and followed her until she'd pulled into a gas station parking lot to talk on the phone.

He smiled to himself as he remembered how easy it'd been to disconnect the alarm system. There'd be no 911 call or emergency vehicles tonight for former homicide detective Michaela McPherson. It'd be way too late when the first responders showed up. He laughed out loud when he thought about the thousands of dollars homeowners spent on alarm systems. Burglar alarms were next to useless. All he'd had to do was a little bit of work with his wire cutter and screwdriver and he was in.

Snake got out of his car and stretched. It was close to eleven o'clock. *Where was she?* He wondered how Boris was coping with his dog bite. He punched his number into his cell.

"Hey, man, wuz up?" he asked when Boris answered on the third ring. "You sleepin'?" Snake noted the groggy sound of Boris's voice.

"Nah," Boris snapped. "My damned hand hurts like a bitch where that dog bit me. I took some pain medicine. I gotta get better so we can get the job done tomorrow." He paused for a moment, "Where'r you?"

"I'm over at the cop's house. Waiting for her to get home," he reported with a note of glee in his voice. "I'm planning a big night!" He knew Michaela would be along soon and he rubbed his groin in anticipation. It was going to be a long, satisfying night and he was more than ready.

Boris was in a foul mood and itching for a fight. "Did you get all the tanks and hoses taken care of at the Craft pub like we discussed?"

Snake sighed. "Yeah, man. I told you I'd get it done. I even went to RVA, the big brewery and got most of that stuff done. Piece of cake. Nobody was around and the place was deserted. We're all done except the shoutin'. Stuck the first dose of bad stuff in the tanks. It was a cinch," Snake assured him.

"It better be," Boris growled into the phone. "If something goes wrong, it's your ass, and I promise you, I'll cut it to pieces," he threatened.

Snake groaned inwardly. He was sick to death of Boris's threats and tirades. "Okay, man, I get it. Cut the crap," he said harshly.

"Don't stay up all night and be no good tomorrow. We got work to do and if you screw it up, you're dead," Boris spat. "I need you alert and rested."

"Take is easy, man. I'll be great tomorrow. Energized and ready," Snake promised in a low voice.

"You better be," Boris threatened. "If you're not, you can kiss your life goodbye," he snarled.

"Just take some more pain medicine and go to bed," Snake growled as he clicked off his cell. *Dumb Russian bastard. He won't be able to do anything without me.*

Snake jumped as his phone rang. It was Boris. "Yeah," he snarled into the receiver. "What do you want, asshole?"

"You'd better show up," Boris hissed and hung up.

Snake shook his head and cursed Boris. He fidgeted in his car and looked out the windows. He peered through his rear view mirror. *Where the hell is she? Where's the bitch? Could he have missed seeing her? Was she in her house by now? No way.* It was dark and quiet. Nothing to see. He stared at her home, angered by how nice it was. *How in the hell could a cop afford a house like this?* His anger burned as he remembered how she'd come after him in the hospital a few months ago and messed up the work he was doing for the Russian Bratva. His face flamed with anger as he remembered her kicking him in the balls and how he had to slide under the bed to get away from her. He couldn't wait to get his hands on her to pay her back. *Make her suffer, just as she'd made him.* The minutes ticked by and Snake slouched low in his vehicle.

He saw a set of headlights turn the corner. *Ah, there she was. The bitch was home... for the last time.* Snake rubbed his hands together in anticipation as he plotted and replotted his plans to enter the house. He decided to play with her for a little while, get her anxiety up, and maybe just terrorize her a bit. *Hmmm, maybe a little game of flashlight tag?* He loved to frighten people and Michaela McPherson was top on his list. He opened the door of his car, closed it softly and moved quietly and swiftly through the bushes down the narrow walkway next to her house. He missed the eyes that watched him carefully as he edged his way through the narrow space.

Chapter 54

Michaela's heart was heavy as she opened her car door in front of her home. Her home loomed dark and lonely. There were no lights and nothing welcoming about the tall stately home with the large evergreen tree in the front yard. She checked her watch. It was after eleven. She missed Angel. They always came home together and the pair had a bedtime ritual. She planned to pick him up first thing in the morning.

She trudged up the dark steps to her home missing the flashlight in her cell phone. She'd left her cell at Biddy's. Her only way to communicate was on the phone in her car. She usually had her porch light on, but she'd been gone since early morning. *Boy what a day this has been. I can't wait to get inside and get in bed.*

Mic struggled with the front door lock until she successfully maneuvered the key into the lock and opened the door. She quickly reached for the switch plate next to the door and flooded the entry with light. Next, she entered the five-digit code to her security system to prevent it from going off. She kicked off her high heels in the foyer and walked in stockinged feet to the kitchen where she reached into the cabinet and pulled out a bottle of Bushmill's Irish whiskey. She poured three fingers in a glass, added one ice cube and sat down at her large round oak table.

Mic looked around her kitchen as she felt the glass cool in her hand. She took a long drink of whiskey and grimaced as the cool fluid slid down her esophagus into her stomach and warmed her. She gazed sadly at Angel's empty food bowl and admitted to herself just how much she missed him. She looked around her kitchen and smiled. She'd designed the kitchen herself and loved it. Her kitchen had walnut base cabinets, a restaurant stainless steel cooking stove, stainless steel appliances and black granite counters. Mic had painted the ceramic tiles that adorned the back-splash behind her countertop. She picked up her glass of whiskey, walked to the back door and peered out. The night was dark and dense clouds filled the sky. She thought she saw the beam of a flashlight in the alley so she stood and watched a few moments more. There was a beam of light, but she figured it was her neighbor across the alley in his backyard with his flashlight emptying the trash. "The Old Geezer," as Mic and Dottie named him, was a strange man. He often walked at night with only his flashlight. Mic shook her head and made a mental note to talk to him again about safety. Her neighborhood was as safe as any inner-city neighborhood, but still, she wouldn't take walks alone at midnight. It just didn't make good sense. She almost jumped out of her skin when her house phone rang.

She walked to the wall phone near the kitchen cabinets and answered it. "Hey, Sean, what's up? Are you still at the bar?"

"Michaela, glad you got home. I'm sure you're tired," her restaurant manager said, a note of concern in his voice.

"Yeah, I'm blasted," she admitted. "The hit at the bar and all this death has wiped me out," she admitted in a quiet voice. "How are you, Sean? It was as hard on you as it was on me."

"I'm okay," the young man answered, but Mic could hear a note of fatigue in his voice. Sean was such a peaceful soul who lived to manage her restaurant and play Celtic music. She knew the poisonings had torn him to pieces.

"I'm okay, I'm okay," he said quickly, much too quickly for Michaela to believe him.

"Are you at home? How do you think the waitstaff is handling things?"

"Yeah, I got home a little bit ago and I think the staff is as good as they can be. I called because one of them told me she'd seen a couple of guys a block or so away from the restaurant standing around watching all the commotion... the police cars, the emergency vehicles and so on. She said they looked like they were laughing and having fun."

"Two men?" Mic's heartbeat accelerated. "Did she say what they looked like? Did she recognize them?"

Sean thought for a moment and said, "It was Melinda. She'd left the bar to go outside and smoke. She thought a smoke break might relax her."

"Okay, Sean. That's fine," Mic urged him along. "Did she say what the men looked like?"

Sean paused for a moment as he remembered his conversation with Melinda. "One was tall and had a bald head and she said the other guy was shorter with dark hair and a blue shirt."

Michaela's heart leaped. The description matched the perp at Busy Burger and man who was loitering near Dottie's house had on a blue shirt. She kept her voice steady as she responded to Sean, "That's good. Thanks for letting me know. Did she tell the police at the restaurant?"

"I don't think she did," Sean reported. "I asked her about that and she said as soon as she returned to Biddy's, her fear came back and she forgot. She just told me a little while ago. I thought you'd like to know."

"Yes, Sean. This is so important. That matches the description of the guy at Busy Burger, at least the tall, bald man. And, there was a guy in a blue shirt hanging around Dottie's house this afternoon the police chased, but never caught. I'm going to call Slade and tell him."

"Okay, Michaela, I'd appreciate that," Sean said. Mic detected a note of relief in his voice. He probably doesn't want to talk to the police anymore she decided. Who could blame him?

"Is there anything else?" Mic asked. "Anything at all, Sean? You never know what the police can discover with just a little info that seems trivial."

Sean reviewed his conversation with Melinda and said, "Yeah, but this may be nothing. Melinda said she saw a dog watching the two men. A dog that looked a lot like Angel. As a matter of fact, she thought it was Angel, but then she heard you tell someone that you left Angel somewhere."

Mic was stunned. She was quiet for a moment. "Angel? I don't think it was Angel. I left Angel at Dottie's house and as far as I know, he's still over there. Or, I hope he's over there," she repeated, a note of concern in her voice.

"I'm sure Angel is at Dottie's house," Sean reassured her. "After all, it was getting dark when Melinda saw these guys and Angel looks like a lot of German Shepherds so I'm sure everything is okay."

"I'm sure it is too," Mic agreed, her voice sounding normal although she was still apprehensive. "If you think of anything else, call me, no matter how trivial or unimportant it may seem," she repeated.

“Will do," Sean promised. "Get some sleep, now."

"You too," Mic encouraged. "Good night. See you tomorrow," she said as she clicked off the phone.

Mic picked up her drink and paced around her kitchen. She was overcome with apprehension. *Surely, Angel's at Dottie's house. Dottie would've called me if something was wrong. Maybe I should call Slade and tell him.* She walked over to the counter, poured herself one more finger of whiskey and added two more ice cubes. *I'm not going to call anybody. I'm overreacting and I need to finish my drink and go to bed, otherwise I'll never get through the next few days.*

Out of the corner of her eye, Mic saw a beam of light flash across her kitchen. She shook her head. *Damn that old geezer. I'm gonna have to talk to him.* She smiled to herself and walked down the hall. She checked to make sure her security system was activated and walked up the wide stairway towards her bedroom that faced the front of the house.

Chapter 55

Dottie tossed and turned in her four-poster bed on the second floor of her Monument Avenue mansion. She couldn't sleep. She was concerned about Angel. She and Cookie had taken a brief drive to search for the dog. *If that was Angel I saw down on Main Street, how come he didn't come when I called?* He was as well trained as any dog she'd ever seen. But of course, Slade said that if he was out looking for Mic, he may well have avoided her.

Dottie looked over at the alarm clock on her nightstand. It was after eleven and she knew she had to get some rest. She'd already taken her melatonin but sometimes that just didn't work. Damn these doctors! *While can't they just give me my Ambien. The Ambien always works and if I get addicted, who the hell cares? After all, I am eighty-two years old.*

Staring at the ceiling and counting sheep was getting old. Dottie reviewed the events of the day starting with Camilla's funeral. She turned over as tears oozed from her eyes. Camilla's death was a harbinger of things to come. She knew her time on earth was limited, but she stubbornly refused to spend it sitting in a convalescent home or being cared for in a nursing home. The thought of her age made her cringe and she became more determined to get to sleep. Finally, she fell into a restless slumber dreaming about a man in blue in her backyard.

A while later Dottie awoke to the sound of scratching on her door. She stayed in her bed and listened carefully. The scratching continued. There it was again. It was a persistent scratching sound. One thing Dottie hadn't lost was her hearing. She could hear a fly buzz a mile away. She got up slowly from her bed and felt around on her hardwood floor for her slippers. Best not fall and break a hip. She walked slowly over to her door and opened it. Angel sat outside in the hall. He looked up at Dottie with a frightened look in his eyes and whimpered.

"Angel, Angel, where've you been? I've been so worried about you. What's wrong?" she asked as she bent down and rubbed the thick fur on his neck. Angel stared at her again and gave a sharp bark, then turned around and headed toward the steps. *He wants me to follow him.* "Wait a minute, Angel. Let me put on some clothes. Then we can go down stairs." Angel looked back at Dottie and dutifully followed her back into her room where Dottie hastily put on a sweat suit, socks, and tennis shoes. She reached into her night table drawer and pulled out her Glock. She checked the chamber, picked up a clip of ammunition and stuck it into her sweat pants' pocket. *A girl never knows when she's going to need her gun.* Her eyes traveled over to her closet where she kept her shotgun. She smiled to herself when she remembered Michaela scolding her for carrying the shotgun the last time she'd gone out late at night and it had come in handy.

Angel looked up at her and moved his head repeatedly towards the stairway, gesturing for her to go. He was obviously anxious. Mic must be in danger Dottie admitted to herself. She considered calling Slade but decided against it. She reached down and patted Angel's head, "Come on, buddy, we're gonna sneak out of here, get the Caddy and go over to your house and check on Michaela.

Angel gave her his most tender look, licked her hand, and waited patiently by the elevator. Dottie and Angel rode the elevator to the first floor. Dottie grabbed the keys to her Cadillac and the two left quickly. Angel jumped into the passenger seat next to Dottie and waited patiently for her to raise the garage door and exit onto the street from her paved driveway.

Once Dottie turned onto Monument Avenue, she remembered she left her glasses at home. "Damn, you're going to have to help me see, Angel," she said softly as she scratched the German Shepherd's ear. He turned around and gave her a slight nod and a doggy smile as if to say, "No problem, Dottie. We're going to get this thing done."

Dottie stopped for a red light across the street from Michaela's fan district home. She inspected the house carefully, looking for signs of trouble. There were no lights on outside but there was a light on in the back of the house and several lights shone upstairs. A second later, Angel gave a ferocious growl as two shadowy figures passed in front of Michaela's front bedroom window.

Dottie saw the image and turned to ice. She looked over at Angel and said, "We’ve got company, Angel. Are you ready?" she asked as her heart jolted and an adrenalin rush gave her the energy of a woman much younger. Angel gave her a steady look and a slight nod.

"Let's go, buddy." She said as she texted Slade a message “911 Mic's house. NOW.”

Chapter 56

Mic stepped into her shower and cut on the hot water letting the steamy heat roll over her tired, aching bones. It had been a hell of a day. She stood in the shower for about ten minutes and for the first time, felt relaxed. She grabbed two large white bath towels and wrapped one around her head and the other around her body. *Thank God for Irish whiskey and hot water. I feel like a new person*. She toweled her hair dry and slipped on a pair of pajamas. She walked out of the bathroom, into her bedroom and over to the front windows. She reached to pull the draperies closed, but they were stuck. She looked down at the street below and noticed how dark and isolated it was. Her grandfather clock struck midnight and as she turned around to walk toward her bed a sound stopped her. Fear shot through her body. It was the sound of a man clearing his throat. Mic turned quickly and her eyes widened at the sight of a man staring at her from the foot of her bed. She looked into his eyes and was chilled by the reflected lust and cruelty. She saw the knife in his hand.

"Did you have a shower, Detective McPherson? Are you nice and clean now?" The man asked in a low, confident voice. "You smell good," he said, a lecherous look of his face. He lifted the knife, rubbed his finger against the sharp tip and said, "I've been waiting for you. I've waited for hours. What took you so long?" He laughed at her fear as he took a step forward decreasing the distance between them.

Mic was paralyzed with fright, felt her heart race and her blood heat the muscles of her body. Was that a tattoo on his hand? Somehow, he was familiar to her, but she couldn't think how. *Think, Mic, think. You've been in situations worse than this. Calm down and think. You can get out of this.*

The man took another step closer holding the shiny knife at his side. Michaela backed up until she was almost on top of her nightstand. She slid open the drawer and reached inside, her hand searching for her gun. She tried to shield her search with her body as her fingers covered every square inch of the drawer. Her fear increased when she realized the gun was gone.

"Oh, Detective, are you looking for this?" the man asked, a note of sarcasm in his voice as he reached in his jacket pocket and pulled out her Glock. Mic stared at him as terror spread throughout her body. He was a big, heavyset guy. He probably outweighed her by at least sixty pounds. She quickly realized her strength would be her agility and speed. She also remembered she had a second pistol tucked under her mattress.

She lifted her head and searched his eyes. "Who are you? Who the hell do you think you are coming into my house at midnight and sneaking up on me? What are you, crazy?" Mic's words were strong and forceful, but her fear was real as her heart slammed in her chest and her knees buckled with fear. She held his eyes with hers, unwavering.

The man smirked at her and said, "I've been here for hours. Before that I was down at your restaurant and bar watching them haul dead people out on stretchers." He smiled at her, an evil smirk on his face.

You're half of the poison boys or whatever they call you." She noticed his blue shirt. He was the guy at Dottie's house. "Who the hell are you?"

The man stared at her with lust as his eyes raked her body. He remained silent.

"Oh, so you were outside my friend's house today as well? You surely do get around," she taunted him. "Looks like we've pretty much spent our day together, only you were always looking in… and I was already in," she said sarcastically.

Snake smiled at her again, a slow sardonic smile.

"Didn't you 'drop in' at the luncheon after the funeral this afternoon?" Mic goaded him as she put her hands on her hips and spoke in a derogatory voice.

The man's eyes twitched and Michaela felt his gaze undressing her. She needed to get him to talk, to buy her some time until she could figure out a way to escape. She eyed the door but knew he'd shoot her before she could get there. Her mind searched all tactical means of escape. Maybe she'd play a few mind games with him. Anyone who went around poisoning kids had to be crazy.

She took a step closer to him and stared into his dark eyes. "You must be pretty tired. You had a busy day. First of all you showed up at my friend's funeral, my friend that you and your buddy poisoned where you were spotted and chased by the police. Then, you showed up at the luncheon over on Monument Avenue, where the police chased you again." She gave him a knowing look and said, "Oh my. I gotta give it to you. You've got some balls, but you must be a tired boy," she ended as she shook her head, a triumphant gleam in her eyes as she saw the pain flash over his face. Then she laughed, as loudly as she could. "You're always on the outside looking in, aren't you? What's the matter, asshole?" she taunted as she reverted to her Irish sing-song voice. "You havin' a hard time keepin' ahead of the police?"

Snake was pissed. He hated being made fun of and that's precisely what the bitch was doing... making fun and laughing at him. How dare she! His eyes glittered with anger as he picked up the knife and came towards her.

Mic saw his hesitation and continued, "Where's your tall, skinny friend? The one with half his head caved in? Is he comin' here to get you out of this mess?" She continued to bait him. "Or did he leave you on your own, to fight your own battles for a change?" she taunted as she shook her head and gave him a pitiful look.

Snake was white with fury and raised the knife. There was less than a foot between them and Mic, quick as a flash, pulled the lamp from her bedside table and slammed it into the side of his head. Snake staggered, his head poured blood, but he kept his balance and stayed upright. "You bitch," he hissed. "I was going to play with you for a while, but I think I'll just kill you," he said as he lunged towards her. Mic dodged the knife and rolled across her king-size bed, headed towards her bedroom door and hall. *If I can just get down the steps and get to a phone, I can call for help. I've got to get away from him. He's going to kill me.*

Michaela fled into the hall, and ran towards the wide stairway, but she wasn't fast enough. Within seconds, the man had overtaken her, and put her in a chokehold as he dragged her down the steps. Her body banged on every wooden step until they reached her entry foyer at the bottom. Snake pinned her to the floor, straddled her and looked down into her face. Mic turned her head away from his foul breath and evil eyes.

"You're not doing so well now are you?'" he sneered with a vicious grin. "It looks to me like you've run out of tricks... or at least police tricks," he added with a vicious grin. "But," he said as he inspected her, "I've got some other tricks in store for you," he threatened, his intent clear.

Mic looked into his face. “What do you want? Are you gonna rape me? Prove you're a man? Because you aren't! Real men don’t murder children and old ladies." she hissed.

Snake jabbed his knee between her legs causing a pain which Mic likened to riding a boy’s bike and slipping off onto the cross bar. Agony poured through her body, but she didn't let it show. She'd never let this bastard know he'd caused her any pain.

She looked up into his eyes. "What the hell is wrong with you that you run around poisoning old ladies and little kids? You're some kind of a lunatic, a sick son of a bitch," she spat as she challenged him with her eyes. "You can kill me if that's what you want to do, but that's all you can do to me. My mind is shut off from you and what you're trying to do," she assured him. She stiffened her body as she felt him pulling at her pajama bottoms.

"Shut up, shut up, bitch," Snake hissed as he fumbled with her nightclothes.

Mic turned her head and saw the brass umbrella stand next to the front door, but it was too far away. Then she saw her front door was cracked open. *But why. Then she realized he'd entered through her front door. What the hell had happened to her burglar alarm?* Then her eyes wandered and she noticed her high heel shoes, the stilettos she'd kicked off when she'd entered the house earlier. They were down by her feet. She strained her body and kicked one of the shoes up towards her hand. Almost. Her fingers were within a half an inch of the shoe. She had to get it. It was her only way out. She arched her body closer to Snake's and wiggled under him.

Snake looked down at her and smiled, a lewd and lascivious grin on his face and said, "You're loving this, bitch, aren't you? You broads are all alike. You fight, moan and groan, and then you can't do without it. You just gotta have it. I can see right now I'm not gonna be able to keep you off me." He gave her a vulgar grin.

Michaela gave him a satisfied smile, let him grind his body into hers for a few seconds and then reached for the pale blue shoe. She grabbed it tightly in both hands and arched her body as high as she could. She reached over Snake's head and ground the sharp end of the stiletto heel into the bottom of his head, into his hindbrain. She could feel the crunch of bone and tendon as the heel penetrated the skin and pierced his brain.

Snake howled in pain and surprise as he rolled off her as his hand grabbed the back of his neck. Michaela quickly sprung away from him and stood, running towards the kitchen, but Snake caught her foot with his free hand and pulled her down. She pulled away and seconds later, they were circling each other around the dining room table. Snake had the knife in his hand, and he waved it in the air. "I'm gonna cut you into little pieces, you bitch, you just wait. You're gonna know what pain feels like," Snake promised in a hoarse voice, almost a whisper. He held one hand behind his head in an effort to stop the bleeding and pain.

Mic was silent as she studied Snake. She could hear blood droplets splatter on the marble floor from the wound in the back of his neck. Snake grasped the table for support and weaved back and forth, as he looked at her. Michaela's heart leapt with hope. *He must be getting dizzy… he's lost a lot of blood. Maybe I can wait him out and he'll pass out…* Mic prayed to herself. She continued to watch him as a shadow in the front yard caught her attention. Did she hear something? She turned her head, looked out the front window and thought she saw a dog. Was it Angel? She heard Snake mutter something and looked back at him.

"What's out there, bitch? Do you see something?" he roared as he jumped across the table at her. Mic dodged him and quickly circled around the table, but her bare feet slipped on something slimy. Her feet slid from under her and she fell. She could see blood. She'd slipped in the blood from Snake's head wound. *Damn.*

"I'm coming to get you. You won't get away from me again," Snake promised as she scrambled to get off the floor. He grabbed her body and pulled her out of the dining room back into the center hall of the house, striking her head on the doorframe. Michaela was dizzied by the blow but struggled to stay conscious. But she wasn't sure she could.

Chapter 57

Dottie, her Glock at her side, crossed the street and climbed the steps up into Michaela's front yard with Angel at her side. The huge evergreen tree in the front yard kept them safe from prying eyes as they surveyed the house in the cloak of darkness. The front porch lights were out, but the front door was slightly ajar. Dottie reached down for Angel's collar and he looked up at her. He noticed the opened front door and growled softly. Dottie touched his collar and said, "We've got big trouble, buddy." Of course, Angel knew it. He was on full alert and ready to attack on command.

Dottie leaned down and whispered softly in his ear, "Let's go around back. I've got a back door key hidden under the first step. We'll go in that way," Dottie pointed as they walked through the front yard around the corner to the narrow path between Mic's house and the house next door. They had only walked a few feet when Angel stopped to sniff something. Dottie could tell it was a large, bulky shape but couldn't identify it from a distance. The smell of damp earth permeated her senses and again she wished she had her glasses. As she got closer, she saw it was a body. She looked down on the man and recognized him as Mic's neighbor from across the alley. "It's old Mr. Geezer, Angel. He must've known something was up and come to help." Angel whimpered quietly as the two continued down the path to the backyard. Dottie walked softly onto the first back porch step and fished out her key. "Let's go in, Angel," she ordered as she quietly opened the back door that led into Michaela's kitchen.

The smell of coffee lingered in the air and assaulted her senses as she entered the kitchen. The smell was familiar, safe and so typical of Mic that Dottie paused and smiled. The kitchen was undisturbed, and everything seemed to be in place. Dottie motioned Angel forward into the back hall. It was then that they heard the short scream and the sounds of a scuffle. Angel growled again and bared his teeth.

Dottie flattened her body against the refrigerator and peered into the center hall. Mic was on the floor. She was still and appeared unconscious. A dark-headed man stood over her with a knife. Dottie watched mesmerized as the man lifted the knife to stab Mic.

"Attack," she screamed at the top of her lungs.

Angel leapt into the hall, jumped on the man's chest and knocked him to the floor. The man turned the knife on Angel and plunged it into the dog's hind leg, but Angel didn't let up. He stayed on the man's chest. Mic struggled to sit up as Dottie swiftly moved into the hall, her Glock in front of her. "Down, Angel," she ordered and when the dog desisted, she fired a slug into the man's shoulder. He struggled on the floor for a few seconds, pulled Mic's pistol from his back pocket and fired at Dottie who pivoted and quickly fell to the floor. Mic watched mesmerized as Angel moved quickly to break her fall. Dottie lay unconscious on top of Angel. Mic didn't know who was bleeding the most. Blood was everywhere. Her body hammered with pain. She felt defeated and useless as she saw the two people she loved most in the world on the floor dying. The man quickly got to his feet and ran towards the front door. He turned back to her and said, "I'm gonna get you, bitch. I'm gonna kill you. This isn't over." Mic's heart raced even harder in her chest as she saw the look of hate and malice in his eyes. She knew he'd be back. To kill her.

She got to her feet and frantically bent over Dottie and Angel. Angel seemed in better shape than Dottie who stared at Michaela with huge, dark blue eyes. "Hang in there, Dottie. Help is coming," she promised as she turned her on her side and examined her bullet wound. It was in her right lower back near her kidneys. Mic ran to the kitchen for towels to pack in Dottie's wound and wrap Angel's leg. She reached for the house phone, but it was silent. She frantically jammed the button, but the phone was dead. That damned bastard cut my phone line.

She ran back into the hall and asked Dottie for her cell. Dottie was weak and bleeding heavily, but she understood and pointed to her purse. She was trying to tell Mic something. Mic leaned in closer as Dottie gasped, "Slade on his way." Mic gave Dottie a hug and quipped, "I sure hope he's bringing a bus because both of you need one." Dottie gave her a half smile and offered up a scary sounding lung crackle. Mic was terrified by the sound, afraid her lung had collapsed, but she patted Dottie's shoulder. She rubbed

Angel's neck for a couple of seconds and released the makeshift tourniquet she'd placed on his leg to allow blood to permeate the tissues. Seconds later, Slade burst into her front door with two of Richmond's finest behind him. Mic's eyes filled with tears when she saw him. She pointed out the door and said, "That way!" and the uniformed police began a search for Snake. Ten minutes later Dottie was on her way to MCV and a police escort had gone to pick up Cookie to stay with Dottie. Slade and Michaela were on their way to the emergency police vet with Angel in the backseat of Mic's SUV, his head in Mic's lap. Tears of reality streamed down Michaela's face as she looked into Angel's face.

It has been a hell of a twenty-four hours.

Chapter 58

"Thank you so much for seeing us at this time of night, Dr. Vest," Michaela said with tears in her eyes as she watched the police vet carefully examine Angel's hind leg. She saw Angel wince as the veterinarian's practiced fingers got close to the stab wound. She reached for Slade's hand and squeezed it tightly.

"You're welcome, Michaela," Dr. Vest said as he looked over his bifocals at her, his kindly eyes noting her pain. "This is a bad wound and you've done a great job at giving Angel first aid." He turned his back to them and spoke to his vet assistant. He ordered a bunch of medicine and then glanced back at Angel who was watching him with a guarded expression.

Michaela was paralyzed with anxiety as she waited for Dr. Vest's diagnosis and treatment plan. He continued to push and prod around Angel's leg as Angel whimpered and Mic's heart twisted in pain. She rubbed his neck and ears to comfort him.

"Well, what do you think?" she finally asked, her heart beating at twice its normal beat. "Can you fix him?" she questioned, her voice strained and choked as she studied the vet's kind face.

Dr. Vest nodded and said, "Yeah, I think we can. But, as much as I hate to, I'm gonna have to put him under general anesthesia. I wanna make sure I'm able to stitch the wound correctly because it's deep and jagged." He peered again at Angel's leg and said, "Plus, I want to be certain there's no nerve damage, particularly since this is close to the place where he took the bullet." He paused and looked at Mic and Slade and added, "I need to be careful and avoid any scar tissue that might build up and get us in trouble later." He ruffled Angel's fur and asked, "Is that okay with you, old boy?"

Angel gave the vet a searching look and then looked at Michaela for assurance. She smiled and lowered her face to his eye level. "It'll be okay, Angel," she promised him. "You're going to have an operation and while that's happening, Slade and I are going down to MCV and check on Dottie. Is that okay with you?"

"Seems to be," Dr. Vest noted as Angel thumped his tail weakly against the examining table.

Slade asked, "Are you sure you have to give him an anesthetic. Angel seems pretty old to be put under."

Michaela poked him in the ribs and admonished, "Don't say that, Slade. Think about Dottie. She's going to have to have anesthesia too." She looked at him tearfully, "We can't think like that now," she added stubbornly.

Slade nodded and said, "Yeah, Mic, I hadn't thought of that."

Dr. Vest looked at the detective and said, "Slade, I think we'll be okay. Of course, there's more risk than there was a few years ago when we did surgery on his leg for the bullet, but honestly, I've got to see the extent of this wound and be sure I stitch it up properly so it heals. The last thing we need is Angel getting a wound infection."

Slade nodded slowly. "Yeah, okay, I guess."

Mic narrowed her eyes. "What's up, Slade? Do you have a bad feeling about this or what?" she asked, her emerald eyes stared into his.

Slade didn't respond and scratched Angel's ears.

Mic could feel anxiety shooting up her back and knew she had to stay calm for Angel. She looked away from Slade.

Dr. Vest intervened. "Both of you know that if anything happens to Angel, I'm gonna be run out of town by one hundred percent of Richmond's police force. This is," he said as he looked down at Angel, "the most famous, decorated, and celebrated dog in Richmond's long history of canine officers!"

Slade grinned, "Yup, ain't that the truth. I know he'll be fine, Dr. Vest. Right, Angel?" he said looking at the dog.

Angel thumped his tail again and Mic laughed. "Yeah, he's gonna be okay." She gave Dr. Vest a grateful look, "Thanks, Doctor."

Vest looked at Mic and Slade. "I actually think Angel will be better than the two of you," he quipped. "Now get out of here and let me get to work."

"Angel's a real trooper and he'll be fine," Slade agreed.

Michaela looked up at the vet with tearful eyes. "Thank you so much. How long do you think this'll take?"

Dr. Vest considered the question and said, "The surgery will probably take a couple of hours and then he'll be groggy for a couple more. I'm planning to keep him pretty sedated for the first twenty-four hours, but you are certainly welcome to come and visit him anytime you want."

"Well," Michaela smiled. "You know we'll do just that. When do you think I can take him home?"

Dr. Vest shrugged his shoulders and said, "Let's play it by ear, Michaela. I'm hopeful he can go home in a few days, but let's be careful. I want to make sure when I discharge him, he's as good as he was before he came in here."

"Okay, fair enough," Michaela said as tears streamed down her face. "We'll be back a little later to check on him right, Slade?"

"Absolutely, thank you, Doctor," Slade said as he shook the older man's hand.

Michaela looked into Angel's eyes and said, "Buddy, we'll be back in a little while. You'll be feeling better then, I promise," she said as she wiped the tears from her eyes with her fist.

Angel gave her a doubtful look and laid his chin on his paws. He really wasn't too sure about any of this, but he raised his head, licked Mic's nose and the tears from her cheek. He laid his head down again and closed his eyes, resigned to what was to come. Angel had dismissed them. It was time for them to leave.

"We'll be back when you wake up, Angel. I promise," she assured him as Angel feebly wagged his tail. She turned to Dr. Vest and asked, "Will you text me when he's out of surgery and I'll come back down here to see him?"

"Of course I will," he answered in his kindly voice as he waved them towards the door. "Now get out of here. Go catch some bad guys. I've got work to do." Slade opened the door for Michaela and they walked down the hall and out of the door in silence.

Slade steered Mic to her car and helped her in. He noticed the tears glistening on her face as she fastened her seatbelt he walked around to the other side of the car and got in.

"I really think he's going to be fine, Mic. We both know Dr. Vest is the best and knows what he's doing, right?"

Mic nodded her head and reached for her purse. She removed a new package of tissues and blew her nose. "Yeah, I know. He'll be okay, I'm sure of that. I'm just worried, that's all."

Slade nodded and backed the SUV out of the parking space. "I'm gonna have somebody else pick up my vehicle. Are you able to talk about what happened tonight? We haven't talked about that yet."

Mic was silent for a moment and said, "Yeah, I can. Basically, I came home, I went into the kitchen, poured myself a whiskey and sat at the table for a few minutes. Then I saw a light through my back door so I got up and figured out it was the old guy across the alley out in his backyard."

Slade nodded and said, "What happened next?"

Michaela shrugged her shoulders and said, "I went upstairs, took a shower, put on my pajamas and walked over to get into bed. I heard a noise and someone cleared their throat. It was him. I looked up and he was at the foot of my bed. He had a knife."

"Okay, then what happened?" Slade asked as he watched her carefully.

Mic's face was pale and glistened with sweat. Her voice was almost a whisper. "He came toward me and I backed away from him, toward the head of my bed. I tried to get my gun out of the bedside table, but he already had it. It was in his pocket." She paused for a moment. "Oh, I hit him in the side of the head with the lamp on my night table."

Slade nodded. "So he'd been up there a while, or at least cased the place. Particularly since he had your gun." Anger soared through Slade as he thought about a man in Mic's bedroom, especially a man with a knife. He fought for control and to stay objective.

"Oh, hell yeah," Mic said, "I'm sure he was in there the entire time I was in the shower," she said, as an involuntary shiver raced through her body. She saw the whites of Slade's knuckles as his hands clenched the steering wheel.

"Then he told me he'd been following me all day. I assumed he was one of the poisoners. I confronted him and he didn't deny it."

Slade watched the emotions flicker across Mic's face. Her vivid green eyes were dark with anger and fear as she told her story. Slade felt the anger rising and again wrestled for control. "Then what happened, Mic?" he asked in a soft voice.

She paused for a moment and said, "He looked like a whack job. I tried to psych him out and he lost it. I bolted for the door, but he caught me and dragged me down the steps. We struggled some more and I stabbed him in the back of his neck with my high heel." She paused for a moment and relived the scene in her mind.

Slade prodded her to continue. "Good for you," he said with a smile.

"Then I think he knocked me unconscious because when I came to, Angel was on his chest and Dottie had her gun aimed on him. The man fought Angel and stabbed him with his knife. Dottie saw, or I think she saw that Angel was injured and ordered him to desist. Then she shot the perp in the shoulder, but I think he shot her first." She paused and replayed the tapes in her mind. "This part's a little fuzzy. I need to think about it some more. I can put more of the pieces together in a little while."

Slade nodded and maneuvered the car skillfully onto the interstate headed for the Medical College of Virginia hospital. "Okay, but you're positive he's one of the poisoners?"

Michaela turned and stared at him. "Yeah. I'm absolutely positive he's one of them. There's no question in my mind."

Slade nodded, "Description?"

Mic closed her eyes to remember. "He was in his late thirties or early forties, still had on the same blue shirt, dark, kind of greasy hair and dark eyes. He's a big guy probably close to six feet and heavy... not fat, just big. I'm sure he outweighed me by sixty or seventy pounds. I imagine he's at least hundred ninety pounds or maybe bigger," she added as she thought about the huge man on top of her. She hadn't been able to use any of her defensive moves that had saved her so many times in the past. Her advantage over him had been speed and size, but she'd never had a chance. "He was a brute, just a brute," she finished.

Slade nodded. "That's the description that we had from someone who saw him running from your house. We've got an APB out on anyone who meets that description. I'm sure we'll get some hits. It's just a matter of time," he said confidently. "By the way, I am afraid the perp murdered your neighbor, the one you call the 'Old Geezer' who lives behind you."

Once again, tears popped into Mic's eyes as she looked at Slade and said in a choked voice. "Oh no, he was out walking last night. I saw him with his flashlight from my back door. You mean the guy killed him?" Mic stifled a sob and wiped her eyes with her hand.

Slade nodded. "Yeah, I'm afraid so. Looks like he stabbed the old guy. His body was found between your house and the house next door. We think he'd come over to investigate."

Mic shook her head as tears slid down her face.

"We'll get him, Mic. We'll get him, I promise," Slade said as he focused on driving.

Michaela looked at his calm face and said in a shaky voice, "Yeah, I know we'll get him. What I don't know is if we'll get him before he and his friend do something horrible with the poison and kill a thousand people."

Slade sighed heavily and nodded, his eyes on the road. There was little traffic on I-95 this time of the morning. "Are you feeling any better?" he asked as he reached over and placed his hand on her hand.

Mic shot him a quick smile. "Yeah. A little and you're right, we will, I know that look," she said. Suddenly, a huge realization raced through her head and she said, "Oh, Slade. I didn't tell you this. The guy has a snake tattoo on his hand."

"Yeah," Slade said softly. "A snake tattoo?" It sounded familiar to him.

Mic's eyes were wide with realization. "Slade, come on, don't you remember? The snake tattoo? It's the same tattoo the man had who tried to kill Danielle in the hospital a few months ago. Remember? The tattoo man. This has to be him. It's the same tattoo," she said excitedly. "I'd recognize it anywhere, anytime."

Slade stared at her out of the corner of his eye. He was excited. His heart rate picked up. "Of course! The tattoo man. He'd been the only loose end in their recent human trafficking case. RPD had killed most of the people, including a Bratva boss and other international criminals in a shoot-out at the port of Richmond. *What the hell is going on? Is this another international crime incident? Why was a human trafficker now poisoning people?* He picked up his phone, called SAC Burnley at the FBI and relayed Mic's information.

Mic looked over at him and said, "The plot thickens. But what's going on here, Slade? Do you have any ideas? Kidnapping, trafficking, poisoning? What's the tie-in?"

"My guess is international terrorism," Slade said as he pulled into the hospital emergency room entrance. He reached across her and opened the door. "Go on and get out," he instructed. "I'm gonna call the unit to pick me up. I need to get back to the station. I'll valet park the car. I need to get downtown and put all of this together."

Mic nodded. "Keep me posted. Wait, was that a text? Who is it?" she asked as she watched him grab his phone from the console.

"It's Cookie and she's waiting for you in the waiting area."

"Okay, thanks, Slade," Michaela said softly. She gave him a soft kiss on the cheek.

"You gonna be okay, babe?" he asked as he searched her eyes.

"Yeah, just worried about Angel and Dottie, that's all," she said.

"They're gonna be fine. Just hang tight and I'll see you soon," he promised.

Mic flashed him a strained smile as she reached the emergency room doors.

Chapter 59

Snake was exhausted by the time he got to Boris's lab. It had taken every ounce of energy he had to beat on the door. Finally, Boris opened the door and asked, "What the hell happened to you?" as he stared at Snake's beat up face, sagging shoulder and bleeding neck. "You got blood all over you!" Then he grinned and said, "Don't tell me the cop broad beat you up and shot you?"

Snake looked at him but said nothing as he staggered over to the faded, dirty couch. "Man, you got any whiskey. I'm about to pass out," he said in a weak voice.

Boris, his hand still painful from the dog bite, walked over to his lab cabinet and pulled out a bottle of cheap whiskey. He poured Snake a tumbler full and said, "Here, drink this, let me check your bullet wound."

"No, hell no, don't get near me," Snake roared with the last bit of strength he had. His eyes glittered dangerously and Boris could see he was half-crazed from pain and fatigue. "I can't be touched right this minute."

Boris sat in a chair across from Snake and said calmly, "Okay, man. Drink your whiskey. Then I gotta clean your wounds. We have a big day tomorrow and kickoff time is noon. I gotta have your hands doin' the work and they ain't gonna work like that," he said as he looked at the bloodied, swollen fingers on Snake's right hand. "If we don't perform, we don't get paid, and you know what that means."

Snake nodded and leaned his head against the back of the sofa. Boris sat across from him and saw that his shoulder was steadily pumping blood. His clothes were saturated. He asked calmly, "Can you use your arm, man?"

Snake's eyes flew open and he stared at Boris. "Hell, yeah, I can use my hand and my arm. It just hurts like a son of a bitch."

Boris nodded, "That's good. I was worried about nerve damage because you've got a lot of stuff to do tomorrow morning and you need dexterity. Do you remember any of that?"

"Yeah," Snake hissed. "What? You think I'm confused or somethin'? I know everything. Now just leave me alone and let me rest a minute. Then you can fix my shoulder. Okay?" Snake's eyes scanned the lab until they rested on the huge fish tank with the warm bluish-green water. The tank calmed him and he watched the fish swimming gracefully through the water dodging the brightly colored coral on the floor of the tank. *Humph. It looked like fewer fish and where was the small blue-colored octopus?* Snake continued to watch the fish as the whiskey numbed his brain and his shoulder. Then he noticed a bloody knife and the dead fish on the counter. "What the hell happened to all the fish?" he asked in a low voice.

"Nothing. Couple were sick. I cleaned out the tank," Boris muttered. "I'm gonna fix your shoulder now. Gotta stop the bleedin'. What the hell happened to your neck?"

"Bitch stabbed me with a high heeled shoe," he said tersely. "I'm gonna kill her. Just wait and see."

Boris laughed and got up and went over to the sink again. He removed a bag of IV fluids and a needle from a cabinet. He glanced at Snake whose eyes remained closed and said, "I'm gonna start an IV on you, give you some pain medicine and some sedation so I can get the bullet out. Then I'm gonna run some IV antibiotics so you don't get an infection. I need you as good as I can get you in just a few hours. Is that okay with you?" he asked as he peered at Snake's pale face. *Guy's in bad shape. Damn, I wish I had a few units of blood. May have to go steal some from the hospital.*

Sweat poured from Snake's face, "Yeah, are you a doctor now? Get that needle in me. I'm in some serious pain," he grimaced. "So much pain that I can't even think," he added. Snake reached for his whiskey with a trembling hand and wrapped his fingers around the glass. He took a deep drink and peered at Boris as he walked over towards him with the supplies he needed to start the IV.

Boris smiled his menacing look, his skeletal face puckered at an unusual angel. "Yeah, I'm a doctor and a lot of other things you don't know about," Boris said. "It's better you don't know, actually," he added with a grin.

"Yeah, so what the hell are you? You said you were a chemist and now you're a doctor?"

Boris shook his head and said, "Somethin' like that. Don't worry 'bout it. I'm gonna fix you up."

"Yeah, sure," Snake said as the needle pierced the flesh on his left hand. He felt the fluid entering his vein. For a moment he wondered if Boris was gonna kill him, not fix his shoulder.

"You're one sorry ass mess. I can't believe that stupid woman cop beat you up like this." *I should just pour some belladonna down his throat or inject some stuff in his IV. What an idiot he is. All for a woman*. Boris shook his head and hesitated for a moment before he plunged another needle into Snake's forearm. *It'd be so easy to kill him… maybe I can do without him.*

"You didn't put any poison in that, did you?" Snake asked softly.

Boris shook his head and said, "Nope, not yet."

"The cop didn't shoot me. It was the dog and the old lady," he slurred. "The same dog that got you."

It was then Boris saw the dog bites up and down Snake's opposite arm and leg. *Yeah, one pitiful, sorry bastard. I'll kill him tomorrow after it's all done.*

Chapter 60

Michaela's eyes searched the waiting area in MCV's trauma emergency department. She didn't see Cookie anywhere. The emergency department was buzzing with activity and there were people everywhere. Some were on stretchers, some in wheelchairs, a few were on their feet, but most were bedridden. Dozens of others, presumably family members, swarmed around the department. Paramedics pushed stretchers through the doors and a handful of Richmond's finest were on hand to take reports and keep order. An alarm sounded loudly and red lights flashed as a local rescue squad brought a red blanket through the side door. The patient was covered with blood. An obvious gunshot wound Michaela thought. She waited her turn in line to talk to the department clerk, lost in thought as she absently watched the controlled chaos around her.

"Yes, may I help you?" the middle-aged clerk finally asked as she studied Michaela above her half-glasses, her black hair gleaming in the florescent lights. The clerk's eyes traveled to Mic's fly-away hair and bloodstained pajamas as she silently assessed her. "Who are you looking for?" she asked slowly as her eyes darted to the left, making sure the security guard was at his station.

Michaela reached into her purse and pulled out her retired RPD shield. "Dorothy Borghase. She came in via rescue squad about an hour or so ago with a gunshot wound. She's quite elderly. Where is she?" Mic asked as she looked calmly at the woman.

The clerk searched her computer screen and said, "She's in the operating room. We sent her up to the OR. She'd lost a lot of blood from what I heard."

Mic's heart was racing. "Where's the OR? Where do I go?" she asked, as she attempted to keep hysteria out of her voice.

The clerk pointed towards the elevators and said, "Tenth floor. Stop at the glass window and they'll give you an update." She paused for a moment and added, "There's a nice waiting area up there and good snack machines. It's quiet. You'll have what you need," she assured her.

Michaela nodded and rushed to the elevators. She waited anxiously for the door to open and exited on the tenth floor. The clerk told her Dottie was still in surgery. The woman pointed her to the family waiting room and she headed over to see Cookie.

Cookie flashed her a smile and waved. She had a cup of coffee in her hand.

Mic sat beside Dottie's faithful housekeeper and gave her a big hug. She could feel Cookie's body shaking with sobs as she held her. "Oh, Mic. This is horrible," she wailed. "Dottie looked so bad when they took her back. She was confused and I don't think she knew who I was." Cookie's eyes again filled with tears.

Mic took Cookie's hand and said, "I think that's pretty normal. She'd lost a lot of blood and she is a little bit older than the rest of us, right?" she joked with a feeble smile.

Cookie returned her smile and said ruefully, "Well, she'd never admit that, but she *is* older than we are."

Mic swallowed the lump in her throat as she thought about her beloved, opinionated, crotchety but elegant older friend, "Well, Cookie. No one knows any more than you and I just how tough the old bird is. If anybody can pull through this, it's the Countess Dottie Many-Middle-Names Borghase, right?"

Cookie smiled broadly in agreement. "Absolutely. The doctor told me it was touch and go. He said she was having some heart problems so they were gonna proceed with the surgery with great caution." She paused again to reflect and added, "He said a few other things too, but honestly Michaela, I can't remember. I was pretty upset."

Michaela stroked Cookie's hand and studied her pale, tired face. Cookie wasn't a spring chicken either. She was probably in her mid to late sixties. Her face was etched with pain and grief. "You did the best you could, Cookie. All you could possibly do." Michaela reassured her and added, "You must believe that," she insisted.

Cookie shook her head and said, "No, no I didn't. I didn't do my best. I didn't hear her leave the house tonight. Possibly I could've stopped her."

Mic gave her a tight smile, shook head and said, "Cookie, you and I both know there was no way to stop Dottie, short of double blazing six shooters when she has her mind made up. She was coming to my house – do or die – with Angel. I suspect Angel sensed I was in trouble," she lamented as anxiety seared through her brain.

Cookie gave Mic a confused look and said, "Angel? Was Angel with Dottie at your house tonight? We couldn't find him earlier," she said as she thought back to the events of the previous evening.

Mic gave her a stunned look, her eyebrows arched with surprise. "What do you mean? Was Angel missing? Do you mean you couldn't find him?"

Cookie nodded impatiently. "Yes, yes, he was missing. We noticed he was gone around six o'clock or so. The Countess and I went searching for him in her car but… well, he was nowhere to be found. We figured he'd followed you down to Biddy's," she said as her voice trailed off. "We thought he'd gone home."

Michaela thought for a moment and said, "Well, they were together at my house tonight around midnight." She paused and added, "And once again, Dottie and Angel saved my life. I guess we'll find out more and put the pieces together when Dottie wakes up."

"We will for sure. Where's Angel? Is he at home?"

Mic shook her head and tears filled her eyes, "No, he's having surgery at the vet's. The perp stabbed him in the leg just before Dottie shot him," she said barely able to hold back the sobs that were straining her throat. "He's in pretty bad shape."

Cookie's eyes filled with tears too as she hugged Mic and said, "I'm so sorry, Mic. This has been a horrible few days, hasn't it?" she said as she wrung her hands together.

Michaela nodded her head and said, "Yeah, but better days are comin'. I'm sure Dottie and Angel will be just fine. Angel most likely saved Dottie's life. He jumped off the perp and broke her fall after she was shot. Otherwise, she'd probably have broken a bunch of bones. We just have to wait and pray."

Cookie rolled her eyes and said, "I've done plenty of that, don't you worry. Enough for both of us," she assured her. "How was Angel when you left? He is an amazing dog." She heard a phone alarm. "That's my phone. It's probably Henry. He about had a fit when I left a few hours ago."

"Yeah, I bet," Michaela said with a smile. "Can I use it when you're done to call Slade? I don't have mine with me. I need to check on Angel."

"Sure, no problem. Let me just reassure him we're okay," she said as she pressed the green button on her phone. After she spoke to Henry, she passed her cell to Mic. Cookie sat quietly and pretended to look at a magazine as she listened to Michaela as she talked softly to Slade. Finally she asked, "Who shot Dottie and stabbed Angel?"

Mic shrugged her shoulders and shook her head. "We don't know yet. The man was in my house when I got home last night from the restaurant. We struggled and somehow he knocked me out. When I came to Angel was on top of him and Dottie had her gun out." She paused for a few seconds as she relived the frightening story and continued, "The rest is history. That being said I'm positive the man at my house was one of the poisoners."

“But, why? Why do you think that? Did he say so, or did you see poison?”

Mic shook her head and said, “Nah, it’s just a feeling I have. You know how I get those, right?” she said with a grin.

Cookie nodded but remained silent as the two women sat together and waited for news of their friend. An hour later Michaela pushed herself out of her chair and started pacing around the waiting room. She went over to the clerk and asked, "Any news on the Countess Borghase? Is she still in surgery?"

The clerk yawned, picked up the phone and called the OR. She spoke briefly with someone, then hung the phone up and said, "They’re finishing up. The doctor will be out shortly to speak with you."

Mic nodded her thanks, checked her watch, returned to the waiting room and gave Cookie the news. "I'm going to listen to what the doctor says and then probably go check on Angel. He should be out from surgery pretty soon, too. But first, I want to take you home," Mic said, as she looked into Cookie's eyes.

Cookie shook her head vehemently. "You just go see Angel. Henry will pick me up in a little while. He's texted me about five times and I'm sure he hasn't slept at all."

Michaela smiled, "I'm sure he hasn't. Henry likes his girls to be at home. On time, every night," she joked. "And besides, he gets up at zero-crack-thirty, right?"

Cookie smiled and nodded. "That he does." She paused and added, "Look, this must be her doctor," she said softly as they watched a tall surgeon dressed in green scrubs walk towards them. He extended his hand and said, "I'm Dr. Borland. And you are Countess Borghase's friends?"

Mic and Cookie nodded. "How is she, Dr. Borland?" Mic asked, her heart beating wildly in her chest. She was so frantic she thought she would suffocate. She was surprised at how soft her voice was.

The surgeon smiled at the two women and said, "She's doing remarkably well. She tolerated the surgery well and we removed the bullet. We've given her several units of blood and she'll probably continue to receive blood the rest of the night. She was anemic to begin with, and she lost quite a bit of blood due to the bullet wound."

Cookie breathed a huge sigh of relief and said, "So, you think she'll be okay?"

Dr. Borland nodded and said, "I hope so, but she did have some cardiac issues prior to the surgery and she is up in intensive care, but all in all, in my judgment, I think she'll be fine."

Mic was so relieved she wanted to jump in the man's arms and kiss him, but she restrained herself. "Thank you so much, Doctor. Dottie's a tough old girl, but she surely had us worried."

The doctor nodded. "She's going to be in the ICU a while longer, for at least twenty-four to forty-eight hours and we'll take it from there. Any other questions?" he asked as he looked from one woman to the other.

Cookie shook her head and Mic asked, "When do you think we can see her?"

"Probably not until midmorning or just before lunch. She's pretty well out of it so I don't expect her to be alert for quite a few hours."

"Well," Michaela said as she smiled in relief, "You'd best tell the ICU nurses they've got a real tyrant on their hands. Dottie can be quite irritating when she doesn't feel well."

Cookie shook her head, flashed Mic a look and said, "Dr. Borland, Detective McPherson is being kind. The real truth is that Countess Dorothy Borghase can be quite uppity and difficult whether she's sick or well, and especially when she doesn't get her way." Cookie stopped for a breath and added, "So, it's best to tell your nurses to gird their loins."

Dr. Borland laughed and said, "So I've heard. I think she showed a few of the emergency room nurses a touch of that aristocratic behavior. But don't worry," he said with a smile, "they can handle just about anything in the emergency department and up here in ICU for that matter," he assured them. "I'll be in touch," he promised as his cell beeped and he headed for the door. He turned around and added, "I can't wait to meet her actually. I hear she's a former Olympic Gold Medal swimmer?"

Mic grinned and said, "Yep, she sure is and I'm positive she'd love to tell you about it when she wakes up."

"I'll look forward to that. She strikes me as a pretty impressive lady."

Cookie rolled her eyes and said, "Oh my, that she is. And, she'll tell you that as well!"

Dr. Borland smiled and waved from the door.

"Good night, Doctor," Mic said as Dr. Borland left the room.

Michaela hugged Cookie and said, "That's sounds really good. Don't you think?"

Cookie smiled broadly and said, "For sure, you go now and check on Angel. Tell him I have a big steak bone waiting for him when he gets home, will you?"

"I will indeed," Mic promised as she left the waiting room. She was happy about Dottie but had a nagging worry about Angel. *I've gotta get down there soon.* It had been over two hours since Angel went for surgery.

Chapter 61

Mic's gut told her something was wrong when she pulled her SUV into the vet's parking lot. Slade's police cruiser was parked next to Dr. Vest's car. *I wonder why he's here. He didn't call me on Dottie's phone.* She steadied her hands as fear tightened in her chest.

She walked into the vet's office and sat next to a lady who clutched a tissue in one hand. There was no one at the reception desk. *Where is Slade? Where is Dr. Vest? Where is anybody*? Mic wondered as hysteria paralyzed her body. Mic's anxiety increased as she watched the lady next to her. She could see her shoulders shaking and knew she was crying.

Michaela stood up, touched her shoulder and asked, "Is there something I can do for you? Is there someone I can call? I think there's a drink machine at the end of the hall," she offered.

The lady raised her head and Michaela saw her tear-streaked face. She shook her head and said, "No, thank you. It's my dog. I think I'm going to have to put him down. They're telling me there's nothing they can do for him and I'm trying to make the decision about whether to do it." The woman's face crumpled and she reached for tissues from the table. She looked away from Michaela and blew her nose. "I'm so sorry," she apologized.

Michaela shook her head and her eyes filled with tears, "There's no need to apologize. I feel the same way. I may be in the same situation. I'm sorry. I'm so, so sorry. I know you will make the right choice." Mic paused for a moment and added, "I think… I think you just have to follow your heart."

The lady looked at her and said, "You know, isn't it funny how some people don't understand that our pets are our family members? One of my friends told me today, 'He's just a dog, we can get you another one.'"

Michaela was speechless and just shook her head. She said without thinking, "I think I'd rethink that friendship."

The lady nodded as the vet tech came to the door and motioned for Mic to come in.

"Ms. McPherson, could you come back? Dr. Vest wants to see you." the young receptionist said. "Mr. McKane is already back there."

"Yes, of course," Mic said as a feeling of dread permeated her body. She felt paralyzed and unable to stand but was finally successful. She touched the woman's shoulder as she passed and whispered, "I'm rooting for you."

Mic opened the door to Dr. Vest's office. Dr. Vest and Slade were sitting at a table. Slade's face was drawn and tight. Mic's anxiety spiraled. "What's wrong, what's wrong with Angel?" Her green eyes filled with fear and unshed tears. "Tell me. Is he okay?" Mic was panicked and unable to think.

Dr. Vest rose and pulled a chair from under the table for Mic. "Sit down, Michaela. Angel came through the surgery well. The wound should heal without any complications that I can foresee."

Mic said, "And... what then?" She looked at Slade, "Why are you upset then, Slade? I can see it in your face," Mic demanded, her green eyes focused on him.

Slade held Mic's green eyes with his dark ones. "There's a complication. A potentially complex one."

"What? Tell me." Mic demanded as her fear rose even higher.

"Angel's in renal failure. His blood work came back and his kidney blood values are high. He also has pancreatitis. He's sick," Slade said as he squeezed Mic's hands in his.

Mic was frantic. "Renal failure? But how? He was stabbed in the leg? Not in the kidney? Why are his kidney's failing? What's gonna happen?" Her eyes darted between Slade and Dr. Vest as she searched for answers.

"I'm hoping he will recover," Dr. Vest said with a tight smile. "We're treating him with medicine and IVs. Hopefully, we can detoxify his kidneys and he'll get better. We'll know in a few days whether it's acute or chronic kidney failure."

"Chronic? How could it be chronic? His kidneys were okay six months ago when he had his yearly physical," Mic insisted, her voice rising to a level of hysteria.

"Yes, I know. That's good. I hope it is acute renal failure. That's a better prognosis. He'll be better in a few days, hopefully," Dr. Vest added calmly. "If not, we'll treat him for chronic kidney disease."

"Can I see him? Is he awake," Mic asked.

"Of course you can. He's been awake several times since his surgery. He's probably pretty groggy though, and he has a lot of pain medicine on board. We still plan to keep him doped up for a day or so."

"Okay, let's go then," Mic insisted as she stood.

Dr. Vest opened the door to the ICU area of the emergency vet clinic. There were four patients. Angel was on the floor in a huge kennel. He had an IV in his front paw with medicine running through it. His hind leg was bandaged. Mic ran over, sat on the floor and called his name.

Angel lifted his head slightly and looked at her. His tail started to move slowly and Mic knew he tried to smile.

"Can you open the kennel so I can pet him?" she asked in a tearful voice as hope rushed into her soul.

"Of course. Here you go," Dr. Vest said. "You can stay with him as long as you like."

Mic reached inside and talked softly to Angel, stroking the fur on his neck. Angel sighed deeply and watched her. He tried to lift his head, but Mic persuaded him to lie back down. She laid her head in the kennel next to him and said,

"We're gonna get through this, buddy, and I'm gonna take you home as soon as I can."

Angel licked her hand and Mic knew he'd smiled at her. She looked up at Slade and Dr. Vest and said, "I'm feeling good about this."

Dr. Vest nodded. "Good. That's great. You know him best. We're gonna get his blood again in a few hours and we can see if his kidney values have come down. If you're here, I'll tell you the results," he promised. "But for now, I've got to go, I have another patient."

Slade squatted down next to Mic and ruffled the fur on Angel's back and neck. "Hey, he looks pretty good, Mic," he said as he stroked her shoulder. "Not bad for a dog that was stabbed and had surgery a few hours ago," he added.

Mic nodded and continued to stroke Angel's back.

Slade scratched Angel's ears for a few more moments and said, "I've gotta go, Mic. I need to go home and take a shower so I can get downtown for the FBI meeting."

Mic nodded. "Okay, take notes for me. I'm gonna divide my time between here and Dottie. Is there anything new happenin'? Anything I need to catch up on?"

Slade nodded and said in a low voice, "Yeah, FBI intercepted some internet chatter. Looks like it's some sort of loosely organized terror group and they plan to hit us tomorrow... or today I guess it is now. We're sure the man who attacked you is in the middle of all of it."

"But who and why?" she asked as she watched Angel's chest rise up and down.

Slade shrugged his shoulders. "Who knows? FBI thinks it's a Russian group. We'll know soon enough." He leaned over and kissed her on the cheek. "They'll take good care of him here. I'd like you to go home and get some rest. I may need you later today."

She smiled and said, "Yeah, okay, I will. Stay safe."

"What about Dottie? How's she?"

"They said she did well. Not out of the woods, but she's doing pretty well. Just like Angel," she murmured.

"Let me tell you something, Michaela. The Countess has about forty-two lives. She'll be partying and hangin' out when you and I are six feet under," he said with a relieved smile.

Mic laughed, "Yep, she will be. No question."

Chapter 62

The Richmond skies dawned gray and dismal as a spring rain fell softly to the earth. Snake, dressed as a Richmond city maintenance worker, watched as workmen assembled the large tent almost directly in front of the Carillon monument. Pain hummed through his body. The tent would house ten Virginia breweries at the art festival. He looked across the street at the traffic on the Boulevard and saw two huge beer trucks, the size of tractor-trailers, waiting to turn into the Carillon to set up for the day. His heart thudded with anticipation. It always did on a mission day. He watched as the workmen attached sides on the beer tent and lowered them to keep out the rain. A breeze ruffled his hair and he looked up and saw six ceiling fans buzz to life. His cell phone vibrated in his pocket. He checked the digital display and noted it was Boris. He pushed the button, "Yeah. What?"

"What's going on over there? Is the tent up?" Boris barked impatiently. "Are the beer trucks there?" he growled in a low voice.

"Yeah." Snake sighed deeply and said, "Tent's almost up and trucks are arriving." He paused for a moment and added, "Man, you're gonna love this. This tent has ceiling fans. Six of them to be exact. All the better to blow stuff around."

Boris snickered. "All the better to cool you when you hit the ground," he joked viciously.

"Yeah. Guess so. Man, I got some terrible pain. You got any pills for me?" he asked in a flat voice as he rubbed his painful shoulder. His hand was swollen and his fingers would hardly move. The dog bites felt like needles sticking into his swollen flesh.

Boris's temper flared. "I got the pills, man. But first, we've got to make sure all the valves are working on the tanks and the hoses are injected. I need you fully alert so we don't miss anything. A lot of time has gone into this mission and I don't want any screw ups."

Snake's temper raged, but he kept his mouth shut. He didn't know how much longer he could stand the pain in his arm. "Okay, man," he said evenly. "They're directing the big trucks around the perimeter of the tent and the smaller breweries are going in the middle. I'm gonna do a sneak and peek up close and check the hoses on the tanks I worked on yesterday evening at the breweries. Make sure they're okay."

"You got the syringes with the stuff in them? I want you to inject them again, this time into the black hose that runs into the keg and the siphon hose that hooks into the tap. Like we did yesterday, but this time inject twice the amount in both hoses. Just think of it as insurance. Overkill, even. We want to keep the poison comin'," he said with an evil laugh.

Snake almost lost it. He was hot all over and his heart was pounding. "I gotta have the drugs, man. I can't hardly move my arm and hand. My arm is swollen from the shoulder down to the end of my fingers. If you want me to inject this siphon tubing, you gotta give me drugs NOW. It's hard to get that big gauge needle though any hose, much less the hard plastic siphon hose, especially when you can't move your dominant hand and fingers."

Boris could hardly contain his anger. "You do it or I'll kill you. Right here in front of everybody," he snarled as his head pounded with anxiety. He paused, but Snake remained silent.

"Answer me," Boris screamed into the phone.

Silence.

Boris could hear the younger man breathe heavily into the phone. He relented and said in a hushed voice. "Okay, meet me over by the restrooms. I'll give you a shot that'll work fast so you can use your hand and get the juice in the hoses."

"Okay, give me a minute to get there," Snake said, his voice low and strained. "Let's watch these guys set up the tanks. I may be able to get this big truck with ten kegs on it before I come," he said, a note of hope in his voice. "Nobody's guarding the truck. They're over there shootin' the crap with the boys from RVA's Finest Craft Brewery."

Boris smiled into the phone. "Excellent. If you get that one done, I'll give you more pain medicine. RVA's Finest Craft is our biggest brewery," he ended on a lighter note. "If we can hit the hoses on that one, we'll knock off a bunch of folks." Boris sounded excited and ended on a high note. Snake shook his head. He couldn't wait for this day to be done. After this, he was gettin' the hell out of the US for a while. Maybe go to the Caribbean for some sunshine, women and rum.

"Okay," Snake muttered as he walked painfully towards the huge beverage truck. He knew he'd need some pain medicine first. He'd never have the strength in his shoulder or fingers to push the big barrel of the syringe into the thick, plastic hose. He took a syringe of morphine from his pocket he'd stolen when Boris wasn't looking. It was a six cc dose. He injected it into his injured shoulder. Hopefully it would help him move his fingers. He leaned against the side of the beer wagon for a few minutes and felt the throbbing pain ease up. He flexed his fingers. There, he could move them better. He'd be able to push the plunger down into the hoses without difficulty. He smiled to himself and walked toward the hoses and moved around the chillers and kegs attached at the center of the truck. The hoses spiraled like spaghetti the full length of the truck.

"Man, what're you doing?" a sharp voice bit through the clouds and gloom. Snake jerked his head around and saw a man with long oily black hair dressed in a private security uniform. "Ain't nobody supposed to be back here behind the beer trucks. It's a secure area," he grunted as he glared at Snake, his eyes taking in Snake's disheveled appearance.

Snake swallowed deeply as anxiety fueled his body. He pointed to his RVA City Maintenance identification badge and said, "My boss sent me back here. Somebody reported they'd seen a copperhead earlier. Wanted to be sure I got all the weeds down," he explained. "I hurt my shoulder last night in a car wreck and am gonna go to the hospital after work," he said as he opened his jacket and showed the security guard his temporary cast. "I think it may be broken," he lamented. "It hurts like hell," he added with a lopsided smile.

The guard peered at him through suspicious eyes. "Yeah, may be broken. You ain't holding your shoulders level. Your right side's drooping," he said. "It looks kinda like my son's did when he broke his shoulder bone."

Snake nodded. "Yeah. Goin' to the hospital as soon as I get off," he repeated as he picked up his trash bag and weed eater and limped away from the truck.

The guard nodded and watched him weed whack for a couple of minutes and then wandered over to the other side of beer tent.

Snake breathed a sigh of relief and watched him disappear. As he waited, he checked out the RVA Brewery and the activity around the beer truck. RVA was Richmond's premier, signature craft brew beer house. Most of the beer consumed today would be tapped from that truck. He sauntered near the truck, picked up some trash on the ground and worked his way to the end of the RVA Beer vehicles. He pulled four sealed syringes from his garbage bag and quickly injected them into the first row of RVA Brewery keg hoses. He emptied four additional syringes into the second line of hoses. He heard a voice. *Is that man yelling at me?* Snake's heart stopped in his chest. He was gripped with fear but didn't hear anything else.

Several seconds later, he sauntered nonchalantly over to the trees and lit a cigarette. He inhaled the smoke and scanned the beer tent area. No one seemed interested in him. He finished his cigarette and waited for his heart to settle down. He reached inside his bag and felt around for the other three syringes. The RVA Finest Beer truck was the biggest beer wagon. It had multiple serving stations with five kegs at each station. That meant he'd have to poison the other side as well. That'd been the plan. He'd inject the hoses in a couple of minutes. He was already half done. He breathed a sigh of relief. A second later, his phone vibrated.

It was Boris. Snake was irritated. He'd like to kill the tall, bald SOB. He gritted his teeth and growled, "What now?" he hissed into the phone. "I'm trying to work, dammit."

"Where are you?" Boris asked in a cold voice. "I've been waiting for you over here."

Snake could see Boris in his mind's eye. An ugly skeleton of a man with a crushed skull – like something from a horror flick – looking down his nose at him through squinty little pig eyes. Anger engulfed him and he was incensed. "I'll be there when I get there," he retorted angrily. "Now, shut up. I'm getting stuff done," he said as he clicked the red button on his cell.

Boris cursed as the phone went dead. Anger pulsed through his body. He was as mad as he'd ever been. Snake was a dead man.

Snake finished his cigarette and moved inconspicuously to the other side of the tent. He turned his back and pulled two syringes from his bag, uncapped them and quickly plunged the poison into the hoses attached to the kegs on two smaller trucks that represented several of Richmond's craft-breweries. No one seemed to notice him. He stopped, suddenly fatigued. He was sweating profusely and dizzy. Once again, the pain in his shoulder made it impossible for him to use his fingers to work well enough to guide the syringe into the hose and press the plunger in the syringe. *I've gotta give myself more morphine.* He'd get more pain syringes from Boris in a few minutes. He could barely function. He snuck into the men's room, quickly pulled out a pair of gloves and injected himself once again with a full ten cc syringe of morphine. Then he sat on the toilet and lit a cigarette. As the drug spread through his body, he allowed himself to dream about his new life in the Caribbean, a life he intended to begin this afternoon after he got his dough and his shoulder fixed. He'd leave the US and move to the Caribbean. *Screw this kinda work. I've got enough money for the rest of my life.*

He left the bathroom and picked up grass and trash from around another beer truck from another small craft brewery. He shook his head. These damned craft-breweries were everywhere. He paused, looked around and quickly injected the ten cc's of lethal solution into each of the three hoses and siphons. Then he continued to make his way slowly down to the next truck with his trash bag and weed eater. He stood behind the second truck and searched the hoses with his eyes He glanced around as his eyes darted and searched for trouble. Then he headed towards the restrooms as his phone blew up his pocket. *That bastard better give me a bunch more morphine if he wants the rest of those damned hoses injected.*

His phone vibrated in his pocket. He reached for it but fumbled the phone in his hand. It fell into the grass.

"Where the hell are you?" Boris barked.

"Over on the left side of the tent. I'm almost done. Leave me alone," he said through gritted teeth as he fought to stay upright.

"Okay, keep me posted," Boris demanded. "I'm going to be over there in a few minutes. I'll switch the tanks on these small keg trucks we didn't get to yesterday. I have the canisters with the gas set out." Boris was quiet for a second and said, "That way, we'll kill more people. Then, I'm on my way back to you."

Snake grunted into the phone and walked painfully back into the beer tent. *Already the ground was damp and muddy. It would be a Woodstock in a couple of hours. But it will be a crime scene before then. No Woodstock today,* he thought as he grinned to himself.

Snake trudged over to the final beer trucks, the trucks awarded medals by beer officials. He walked around them to check the hoses he'd already injected. They looked fine, no leakage anywhere. The beer tanks were loaded and ready to go. The stainless steel shined, even in the low daylight. Snake checked around carefully to see if anyone had noticed him. No one had. The brewery employees were standing around talking, comparing brewery disasters, telling jokes and clapping each other on the back. He checked his watch. It was still early. He knew the poison would permeate the beer in plenty of time before the first beer was tapped. He turned on the first tank valve and heard the soft "whoosh" as the poison entered the liquid. Snake emerged from behind the first two stainless tanks and saw Boris as he unloaded a load of carbon dioxide containers that contained highly poisonous gas. Boris placed the stainless steel containers in groups of five about every ten to twelve feet in the massive circus-styled tent. Boris wore an identical RVA city maintenance uniform. Snake pointed to the door and left the tent.

Boris joined him outside in the drizzling rain and the two sat on a concrete wall smoking cigarettes. They looked like two ordinary maintenance workers. Boris looked at Snake's shoulder and grimaced. The thing had to hurt like hell. He needed surgery. "You get 'em turned on yet?"

Snake shook his head and cradled his painful arm against his chest. "Nah, not all. I got the first three. Didn't want anybody to notice me. I'll get the other three in a few minutes. How 'bout you?"

Boris nodded, took his hat off and mopped his forehead. He was sweating and it wasn't even hot yet. "I got one more side to do. I figure they'll hook those carbon dioxide containers up to the small kegs an hour or so before the alcohol permit starts, probably about eleven o'clock. That gives the gas plenty of time to circulate. The CO2 should saturate in the beer quickly based on my calculations."

Snake shook his head. "I hope your arithmetic is right because we've worked hard on this and if your poison concoction doesn't work, we're dead in the grass."

Boris leaned his head close to Snake's face. He smelled of smoke, dental decay and sweat. Snake turned his head in disgust as Boris said, "Don't worry. There's plenty of the potion in that CO2 and with the stuff you put in the hoses, they'll be dropping like flies in no time. I just hope the first few sips of beer is good for them cuz that's the last taste of anything they'll ever have," he said with a short laugh.

Snake looked into Boris's wild, crazed eyes, the eyes of a madman. For a moment he was unnerved and said, "You like doing this, don't cha, you crazy bastard? I never knew you loved killing so much until now."

Boris squinted at him as though he was stupid. "Hell yes. I want to kill as many of these people as I can. That's my job."

Snake shook his head. "But man, you're a doctor and a scientist. What the hell did these people ever do to you? These people we're gonna kill today."

Boris shot him a disgusted look and said, "Nothing. Nobody did nothing to me. I became a scientist and a doctor so I could learn from bodies, dead or alive. I've spent my life doing experiments that end life or save life."

Snake shot him a confused look. The pain in his shoulder was killing him. "Huh? What are you talkin' about?"

"I kill people who interfere in my way of life. My country's kind of life. The Americans interfere in everyone's way of life. They are so stupid they think all terrorists who attack them live in the Middle East and come from Afghanistan, Iraq or Syria, but they couldn't be more mistaken. It's my country who trains the insurgents, finances their missions, and makes sure the job is done."

Snake said nothing but stared at the ground. He noticed a small frog hopping in the grass and wondered if Boris's poison would kill animals too. He flashed back to the tank of half dead fish in the lab. *What was he doing with those fish*? There wasn't a decent, ethical bone in Snake's body and he had killed his share of people over the years. But it didn't excite him and he didn't look forward to it. It was just a job for him. It was what he did for a living. On the other hand,

Boris loved killing, relished it and looked forward to it. Snake didn't have a lot of love for humans. They'd hurt and disappointed him all his life. But he loved animals and creatures. He'd never hurt an animal, except that damned killer dog who'd bitten Boris and tried to kill him. *But damn, what's up with the fish? It looked like he had dissected them.*

Chapter 63

Mic turned her head back and forth and then buried it in the pillow as she tried to make the knocking sound go away. She tossed, turned and pulled the covers over her head as she tried to escape the noise. She was tired, weary and sore. Every bone, joint, tendon, and muscle in her body hurt. The knocking persisted and she flipped over onto her right side and pulled the king size pillow over her head to muffle the sound. *I wish those people would just go away. I'm so tired.* After a few minutes of sleep, a voice called out to her.

"Michaela, Michaela, I hate to bother you, but we need to talk. Can you hear me?"

Michaela thought she recognized the voice, but she wasn't sure.

“I have coffee,” the voice cajoled. "Please, Mic. I know you're tired, but we have decisions to make."

Mic opened one eye and looked up at Cookie. Then it all came back to her, everything that had happened since the day before - her attacker, Dottie and Angel. She sat straight up in the bed.

"Cookie, Cookie, what's going on? Is anything wrong?" she asked, her heart thudding deep within her chest, her voice a fearful croak.

Cookie shook her head and said, "No, I don't think so. The hospital called and they think Dottie might have pneumonia so they want us to come up there and see her."

"What? Pneumonia? How can she have pneumonia? She's been there less than sixteen hours," Michaela cried out in a frightened, uncertain voice.

Cookie nodded. "Yeah, I know. Pneumonia in anyone Dottie's age isn't good so I'm thinking we better eat quickly and get down to the hospital." Fear strangled Mic. She knew pneumonia in someone Dottie's age was often a kiss of death.

Michaela reached for her coffee and asked, "What else did they say?"

Cookie shook her head. "Nothing, really. Said she was doing pretty well from the surgery and that they got her up this morning on the side of her bed, much to Dottie's dismay."

"Oh, my," Mic said with a huge smile and a quick laugh. "I can only imagine how that went. I bet Dottie burned them a new one. I can't imagine getting her up on the side of the bed so soon after surgery," she mused. "Although, I think it's the movement that keeps them from getting sicker."

"That's exactly right. That's what they told me." Cookie smiled broadly and said, "And I heard the countess did give the nursing staff a piece of her mind, so we best get down there and run damage control."

Mic laughed. "Yeah, for sure. Because you and I both know how to take her but those nurses..." Mic shook her head. "They're liable to kill her, she'll make them so mad."

Mic and Dottie shared a quick laugh as they imagined how furious Countess Dorothy Borghase could make the ICU staff at one of the best hospitals in the country. "Tell you what," Cookie said. "Once you eat and grab a shower, I'll have Henry run us down there and we can check on her. I know she's getting a ton of IV antibiotics for her pneumonia."

Michaela nodded and asked eagerly. "Would you and Henry like to go see Angel after we see Dottie? We can stop by the vet's and see how he's doing."

"Absolutely. I would love to see Angel. I want to see how he is," Cookie said sadly, as tears sprang up in her eyes. "I hope you don't think I didn't take care of him, Mic, and that's why he got away," she said as her voice ended with a sob.

Mic reached out and put her arm around the distressed woman. "No, of course not. I know you, Henry, and Dottie love Angel. The real truth is that if Angel wants me he's going to come looking for me and there's nothing you or anyone else will be able to do." She paused and added, "I appreciate you and Dottie looking for him. He was smart enough to come back and get Dottie late last night to help him help me."

Cookie shook her head and said, "You know, that's amazing, right?"

"I absolutely do. Do get out of here, Cookie, so I can get dressed and we can leave," Mic teased and flashed her a smile.

"I'm gone, I promise. We'll be downstairs waiting for you in the foyer," she said as she closed the door to give Michaela privacy.

Chapter 64

Snake sat on the bench at a picnic table overlooking the lake at Byrd Park. The Carillon and the beer trucks were behind him. His work was done and it was all over but the shouting and payday. Boris had given him enough pain medicine to hold him until he could get medical care. He figured he'd go to the hospital later in the afternoon when he was long gone from Richmond. He watched the paddleboats on the lake and surveyed the enormous homes on the other side. He reflected on his life of crime, pain, and loneliness.

"Hello, mister." A small musical voice startled him. He jumped. "Did you hurt your arm? It looks like it might be bleeding," a child said as her brown eyes inspected the bandages on his right arm.

Snake looked down at the young child with short blond ringlets and serious brown eyes. He didn't think he'd spoken to a child before – at least not for thirty years. At first, he just stared at her unsure if she'd actually spoken to him.

The little girl walked a little closer and inspected his arm critically. She nodded her head and said, "Yeah. Just like I thought. It's still bleeding." She looked away from his arm up into his face and asked, "How'd you hurt it?"

"I… I got bitten by a dog, a big mean dog," Snake said as he pointed to his forearm. He looked at her carefully and said in a kind voice he hardly recognized, "You should always stay away from dogs you don't know, did you know that?"

The little girl nodded solemnly. "Yeah, I know." She looked at his arm again and said, "I think you need to go to the hospital. Especially if you did it yesterday and it's still bleeding. That's bad," she said as she pondered his injuries.

Snake cracked a smile. This was one smart little girl. He said, "You think I should? I'm going to go this afternoon when I get off work. As soon as my boss says I can go home, I'm gonna go see a doctor and get some stitches.

The little girl nodded and said, "My mama is an artist. My daddy's a doctor. My mama is over there," she said as she pointed towards the Carillon, "hanging up her big oil paintings. You want to come over and see them? They're beautiful," she offered. "Her name is Melodie and she paints all kinds of stuff, mostly big stuff with weird designs," the little girl announced.

Snake shook his head and said, "I'm sorry. I can't go. But, I'm sure they're very nice, just like you said. I'm on my lunch break and I have to get back to work cleaning up trash and sweeping the concrete."

The little girl looked disappointed.

"Tell you what though. I'll try to get over there before I get off work and say hi to you and your mother," he said. "Does that sound good to you?"

The little girl nodded, smiled and scampered off. Snake could see a tall dark-headed woman call and motion frantically to the child. *That's a stupid woman to let her child roam all over the park unsupervised.* No telling what could happen to her. *Or what will happen to her.* Snake felt a funny feeling come over him. Was he going soft? He'd never cared about anyone before, but this little girl had somehow touched him. He wondered if there was a way to save her. Or if she would die soon.

Snake continued to think about the little girl. He felt strange. He never spoke with children. He didn't like children and he didn't understand them. He shook his head and shivered slightly wondering if he was losing his mind. *Maybe it was all the drugs he'd taken.* He felt terrible all over. He wondered if he had a fever. Or even worse, if he could be getting lockjaw or rabies from that damned dog. He laid his head back against the bench and drifted off to sleep for a few seconds.

"Snake, get up. It's almost show time," a happy, excited Boris said to him. He sat down next to him on the bench, his smelly, skeletal body touching him. "We gotta move in five minutes. The beer tent opens at one and I don't want to miss anything." Snake could feel the excitement drifting off Boris and it disgusted him.

Snake ignored him as his thoughts returned to the innocent young child. He wondered how many kids would die today between the canisters of poison gas and the beer.

They wouldn't kill any kids with beer unless they drank from their parent's beer cups. His head raged with pain. He turned to Boris and asked, "Man, you got any Tylenol? I think I got a fever. I feel like hell. I can hardly move. My body hurts so much," he whined.

Boris picked up his backpack, reached inside and pulled out a bottle of acetaminophen. "Here, take it. After everything happens, you need to get to a doctor. You probably do have a fever. Those dog bites were bad," he said.

Snake swallowed four Tylenol and his thoughts returned to his conversation with the little girl. *What was wrong with him? Was he hallucinating? Maybe he was already dead.* He didn't know. But the conversation with the child was the brightest moment he could remember in his entire life. The only time his life had been totally shaped by innocence and honesty.

Boris stood and covered his face with the hood of his rain poncho. "Get up. I want to move over to that bench just outside the beer tent. I want a good view and the front row seat. I don't want to miss anything."

Snake stared at him with loathing. He shook his head and said, "You're a real sicko, you know that?"

Boris smiled happily. "I've been working towards this day for years. I've wanted to test this poison forever," he said with passion, his eyes bright.

Snake stared at Boris. He'd never seen him like this. Boris's eyes shone with happiness and his normally pale cheeks were flushed. He was ecstatic with glee. Snake recognized that killing people was more than a job for Boris. It was an experience he loved, cherished and enjoyed. Killing people wasn't just about survival or money, it was about science, research and experiments. It was twisted, but it was true.

Boris was impatient. "Get up, man. We gotta go," he urged him. "I want a front row seat to this show," he repeated happily. "I been in line with this ticket for my entire life," he gushed.

Snake shook his head. "Man, who are we working for? Who wants all these people killed? You can tell me. I deserve to know," Snake insisted.

Boris gave him a strange look and said, "You don't know?"

Snake shook his head. "No idea. Tell me."

"Me. It's me. I want them dead. What's wrong with you? I thought you'd figured that out by now," he snorted and laughed.

Snake was shocked. "You? But why? What did these people ever do to you?"

"It's personal. Now get up. I want a good seat," Boris ordered, an irrational, wild look on his face.

Snake shook his head and struggled to his feet, but his balance was off. He slipped in the wet grass. "You go ahead, Boris. Grab us the bench and I'll be there in a couple of minutes. As soon as I'm steady on my feet," Snake promised.

"Okay, no problem. I'll save you a seat," Boris said, his tall skinny body glowing, his bumpy head glistening with rain, excitement and passion. He looked like a crow in his dark rain poncho. Snake watched him grab a bag of popcorn from a vendor, walk nonchalantly over to a bench, and sit down to wait for the show. He looked back, gave Snake a final look and said, "It's not really me, Snake. Don't worry. You'll get paid."

What the hell is he talking about? The man is nuts. Nausea traveled up Snake's esophagus, but he swallowed it. He turned his face towards the drizzling rain. He looked over and saw the little girl helping her mother in her art booth. He wondered if they would survive. He wondered if he would survive. He wanted to live but most of all, he wanted his old self back. Snake wanted his cold, evil, uncaring, killer personality back in his body. He didn't like having feelings. They hurt. They were painful. He looked again at the little girl and she waved at him. He turned his head away and pretended he didn't see her.

Chapter 65

The Countess Dorothy Borghase looked dreadful. She looked like a little girl in her hospital bed. Michaela had never seen her look anything less than perfect, even when she'd had a serious case of the flu five years earlier. Dorothy's beautiful silver hair was a mass of tangles, her skin was dry and paper thin, and even her perfectly manicured fingernails had a bluish tint. Her hands and arms were covered with reddish-purple bruises from blood draws and IV injections. Michaela's heart cried for Dottie. She felt Cookie reach out for her hand and Mic clasped it warmly. They were both upset, but they could never let Dottie know that.

Dottie lay in her bed, attached to dozens of tubes and bottles and hoses and all kinds of stuff Michaela couldn't identify and couldn't explain. There were at least two IVs running and Dottie had an oxygen mask around her face. Mic's heart flip-flopped when she saw the ventilator next to Dottie's bed. *Oh my God. If they put her on this breathing machine, they'll never get her off.* Michaela moved to the other side of the bed, took Dottie's hand and squeezed it "Dottie, wake up. Cookie and I came all the way down here to see you."

Dottie's amazing, ice blue eyes fluttered open and she stared at Mic. For a second, Michaela thought she saw fear and confusion in Dottie's eyes and then, in an instant, the old sparkle returned. "Where in the hell have you been, Michaela? I've been here forever waiting for you and Cookie to show up."

Mic smiled from ear to ear and said, "You tough old goat. They told us you were pretty sick, but I'd never know it. You're as mean as ever." She turned to Cookie and said, "Cookie, look at this old broad. She's lying here doing nothing and you and I are practically running the world."

Cookie stood beside Michaela and took Dottie's other hand and said, "Oh, Countess. We've been so worried about you. They said you might have pneumonia." Dottie looked at her with her amazing eyes. They were unchanged by the years and still as blue as the sky. Dottie didn't miss a trick. She knew exactly what was going on.

Dottie smiled at Cookie and then started to cough. It sounded like a cough that wouldn't come all the way up. The alarm on her finger sounded and the digital display above her bed dropped from ninety-nine to eighty-four. Michaela guessed it was her pulse oximetry. A nurse came into the room and smiled, "Countess Borghase, how are you feeling? You've had a nice nap. And your fever is down. So," she said as she looked around at Mic and Cookie, "maybe your friends will like you well enough to take you home in a few days."

Dottie's eyes blazed with anger and she huffed, "A few days? Are you crazy? A few days my tail. I'm getting out of here just as soon as I can. You guys are a bunch of vampires! Look what you've done to me already," she said as she waved her bruised arms in the air.

The nurse smiled and patted Dottie on the shoulder.

Dottie continued, "You don't know how quickly my aristocratic arse can move do they, Cookie?"

Cookie smiled and remained quiet.

"You nurses don't know how to show me any respect," Dottie snapped. "You don't do anything I ask you to do," she said with a frown.

"Oh yes we do, Countess. I gave you ice cream three times this morning when you were not supposed to have it," the nurse said as she smiled down at her.

"Pssst. You call that mess ice cream?" Dottie asked. "It tastes like nothing. Absolutely nothing," she repeated.

The nurse laughed and said, "It's sugar-free ice cream. I told you that. It doesn't have sugar in it. We've got you on steroids and your blood sugar is high. You can't have any sugar or real ice cream for a while," she reminded Dottie.

"Sit me up," Dottie demanded. "I want to see my friends. They're both very busy ladies," she insisted.

Michaela shook her head and said, "Dottie, we can't stay. They told us we could only see you for five minutes. I promise we'll be back later this afternoon. We just want you to get better. Promise?"

Dottie stared up at the nurse with her ice blue eyes and arched eyebrows and said, "Put my bed up."

The nurse stared back at Dottie and asked with a smile, "Now, what's the magic word, Countess?"

"Please," Dottie hissed. "PLEASE put my damned bed up, NOW." Dottie's tantrum ended in a fit of coughing.

The nurse smiled at Cookie and Michaela and said, "You can stay for a few more minutes. She's riled up now and I actually think it's good for her. She's better. Her fever is down and her oxygen is holding steady at about ninety-five so all in all, that's pretty good."

Cookie smiled gratefully at the nurse and said, "Please don't mind her. She's a little arrogant from time to time, but she's truly a wonderful woman."

"No, she's not," Mic said and laughed. "She's not nice at all."

Dottie glared at both of them, her eyes reflected anger, but she remained silent so she wouldn't cough anymore.

"I got the Countess's number. As a matter of fact, all of us do up here. We heard about her from the nurses in the emergency department last night." She patted Dottie on the shoulder and said, "Now, Countess, I'm here with you until four o'clock this afternoon and then another nurse is coming in. After your friends leave, I want you to rest for a while and then I'll introduce you. Does that sound like a plan?" the nurse asked.

Dottie nodded and asked icily, "Do I have a choice?"

"Nope, you don't," the young nurse said, "but I'm giving you the next best nurse in the entire ICU because I kinda like you," she said. "Oh, by the way, I'm the best nurse, just so you know."

Dottie smiled briefly and warmth returned to her blue eyes, "I like you too, Shorty," she said. "You're not too bad. Now, get out of here so I can visit with my friends."

Shorty feigned a hurt look, laughed and said, "I've been called a lot worse. And by the way, Countess, you can thank your Olympic gold medal lungs and good clean living for saving your life. Most folks probably wouldn't have made it, but you're pretty tough," she said as she stared at the octogenarian, a look of admiration on her face.

Dottie smiled and said, "Yeah, and I'm a runner too," she said proudly. "Even now. So thanks for noticing."

The nurse beamed at her and said, "All of those things make it likely you'll go home sooner, rather than later or not at all. Keep up the good work, Countess," she said as she left the room.

Dottie's eyes clouded as she remembered Camilla, her running buddy, was dead. She pushed the grief from her head and turned to Mic. "What's going on? Did you get the guy that shot me and tried to kill you?"

Mic shook her head sadly. "No. Unfortunately not. But you know, Dottie, he was the same guy that tried to kill

Danielle in January in this very same hospital. The guy that poisoned her IV. Remember?"

"Yeah, I remember him. I'm pretty sure I shot him though. The tattoo guy, right?"

Mic nodded pleased nothing was wrong with Dottie's memory.

"And Angel, how is Angel?" she asked, as a look of fear darkened her face. "I think the guy stabbed him with his knife before I could get my shot off," she said as she tried to remember.

Mic smiled and touched her hand. "Angel's doing pretty well. He had surgery last night, just like you and he's doing good. We're gonna go and see him in a few minutes. Henry is waiting outside and he's driving us. Then I'm going to go join Slade over at the Carillon. The Feds think there'll be an attack at the art show today or at the ball field tonight."

Dottie shook her head. "It's coming back to me now." She looked up at Cookie and said, "Wasn't Angel missing part of yesterday? I can't get this straight in my mind. I vaguely remember you and me out looking for him, driving down Main Street in the dark. Did that really happen?"

"Yeah, it did." Cookie looked at Mic and continued, "Remember, Countess, Angel ran off late yesterday afternoon and we couldn't find him anywhere. We searched for him and so did Henry, but he wasn't about to be found.

Dottie lay back against her pillows and tried to remember. "Yes, yes, he came for me last night. He was scratching on my bedroom door. And that's when I knew Mic was in trouble." She paused for a second and added, "I think I fell on Angel. I seem to remember him jumping off the perp's chest and breaking my fall." She looked uncertain, "Is that true?"

Tears jumped into Michaela's eyes. "Yes, that's true. That's absolutely true," she said.

Dottie was quiet for a moment. "He saved me a broken hip and probably a concussion. Angel is unbelievable!" she said as she raised grateful eyes to Mic and Cookie. "Let me think about the story and I'll tell you more of it when I feel a little bit better." She gave both of her friends a weak smile and said, "I still feel rough. I think I want to take a nap, especially before Shorty gets back in here and pushes me around some more."

Cookie and Mic laughed and Mic bent down and gave Dottie a kiss on her cheek. Honestly, a gunshot wound, surgery, the ICU, and Dottie still smelled like Chanel No. 5, the scent that was part of all things Dottie. Michaela inhaled the fragrance of her and combed her untidy hair back from her perfectly oval face. She loved this uppity, ornery old lady. She was just the best.

"Cookie's going to put some of your things together to bring up this afternoon and I'll be back with her. We'll get your own nightgowns and cosmetics and if you feel better, we'll put your hair up. You'll feel a lot better when you have on your makeup and your hair fixed. More like yourself," Mic assured her.

Dottie stared up at Mic and nodded. "Okay, lower my bed so I can rest. And by the way, Michaela. You should take your own advice. You look like hell."

Mic stared at her and grinned, "That's all you're getting from me if you're gonna get ugly." She turned to Cookie and said, "Let's get out of here. She's gettin' mean and cross. Neither of us has time for that."

Dottie glared at Mic and looked over at Cookie and said crossly, "Give me a kiss, Cookie. You know I love you. And I want you to make all of my favorite foods for me when I get home."

Cookie rolled her eyes and said, "Yes, Countess, most certainly. Henry and I'll go to the grocery store on our way home. I promise when you get home everything will be perfect."

Dottie turned over and fell asleep in an instant. Mic and Cookie listened to her snore gently. Mic shrugged her shoulders and said, "Well, I'd say she's going to be okay."

"Yeah," Cookie said with a laugh. "I'm more worried about the hospital staff surviving."

Mic laughed. "They'll make it, they're pretty tough around here," she said with one last smile as they left the room.

"Angel is an incredible dog," Cookie said to Mic as they walked towards the car. "How many lives has he saved?"

Michaela smiled and said, "I don't know for sure, but a lot. When he's better, he'll save a lot more," she assured Cookie with a smile.

"No doubt, Michaela, no doubt," Cookie agreed gently.

Chapter 66

It was over almost before it began. Mic and Slade were walking, hand-in-hand under a large purple and gold umbrella. They looked like any couple out to enjoy an art show on a rainy Saturday. The sun had popped through the clouds. It was a few minutes past one in the afternoon. Mic had stopped at an artist tent to admire some pottery when they heard the first sounds of a disturbance. A loud moan rose from the crowd. Slade grabbed her arm and said, "Come on, something's happening," at the same moment their phones blew up with texts.

They ran quickly through the drizzle and mud, dodging people, baby carriages, tents and vendors until they saw the first bodies lying just outside the beer tent. They quickly moved into the tent. It was packed, wall-to-wall with people escaping the rain and waiting in line for beer. Mic looked to the right as another gasp escaped from the crowd. A middle-aged man fell to the ground. An older gentleman followed. A young woman looked on in horror. A few seconds later more people fell into each other. The crowd was so dense there was no space to hit the ground. It was impossible to tell how many people were down.

Michaela stood paralyzed as people staggered, lost their balance, and fell into the crowd. There were at least ten or twelve bodies lying in the mud near one side of the tent. Red solo cups littered the ground as people lost control and fell.

Beer saturated the ground and the air smelled of brew and hops. People screamed and cried. Shrieks of terror pierced Mic's ears and her heart until she wished she were deaf.

On the far side of the tent, no one had noticed or heard the cries from the crowd. Two beer trucks on the end served beer as quickly as possible. Suddenly, a big guy, probably over 200 pounds, fell over and his head rested on the serving counter of the beer truck. Moans of fear and madness erupted from the crowd. Another man staggered and fell. A woman followed him. A young child cried for her parents, both lay still on the ground. The child knelt next to them and tried to wake them up but couldn't. Mic quickly moved towards the child, pushing and elbowing her way through the crowd. She took the child by her hand and moved her to a safe area.

"Oh, my God, Slade. What kind of poison is this?" she cried as she looked around at the dead and dying. "It's killing them instantly."

Slade nodded. "It's the beer. It has to be the kegs. And possibly the air. They've been poisoned."

Slade edged along the side of the tent towards one of the huge trucks and motioned for the brewmaster to stop serving beer. "Your beer is bad, the beer is poisoned," he yelled and gestured frantically with his hands. "Stop serving. NOW."

One bartender gave Slade a dirty look and shook his fist while two others stared at him incoherently. Another motioned for clarification. It was impossible to hear. The screams and moans deafened any possibility of communication.

"Stop serving beer," Slade hollered and accepted a megaphone from a Richmond police officer. A second later, the loudspeaker came on and ordered the beer trucks to stop serving. By this time, the tent was littered with bodies. Anarchy and chaos prevailed. The survivors' moans and screams for help and cries from children added to the horror of the afternoon. At the far end of the tent, people continued to laugh, joke, and drink beer.

Uniformed police attempted to escort anyone who could walk outside. Police officers stripped off the side of the tent. Paramedics fought to get into the tent as people spilled to the outside as rescue vehicles and first responders attempted to enter.

Michaela watched from the periphery of the crowd and held the child against her. The fear was palpable. Bodies covered the muddy ground. She was shocked by the awfulness and terror of the scene. The beer tent had become a killing field and the screams of fear were horrific. Bedlam prevailed.

Slade was stunned. He waved frantically to Mic. He was trapped by the crowd and couldn't walk a foot in any direction, essentially a prisoner in his own body. The motion of the crowd carried him along. He was useless. Unable to help.

Finally, the tent was open on all sides. The hysterical crowd moved slowly, in an undulating fashion, outside of the tent into the dim spring afternoon. Pandemonium broke and the crowd ran as fast as they could. They trampled each other in the process. Mic watched helplessly as an older couple fell to the ground and were trampled to death by fleeing men, women, and children. The crowd was panic-stricken, their movements tentative and unsure. The screams and shrieks were loud, staccato sounds that deafened. Men, women and children broke ranks and ran like rabbits. Some scurried like rats back into the tent and looked for friends and family members. Added to the noise and turmoil was the sound of sirens and frightened, pathetic screams of children and the panicked sobs of survivors. The ground was littered with hundreds and hundreds of beer cups and bodies. The air smelled of fear, beer, and vomit and death. Michaela knew she was in hell.

For an instant, Mic wondered if tripping or falling to the wet earth could poison you. She clung to the child. She saw another toddler scream in the stroller as he watched his mother sob and hold his father's head.

Slade grabbed the woman to keep her from being trampled as Michaela pulled the stroller to a safe place. She still held on to the child she'd rescued from the beer tent earlier. The crowd was uneasy and angry. Hysteria and bedlam broke out. Several groups of people were fighting. It was ugly and moments away from a full-blown riot. Slade had called the Riot Tactical Unit.

Mic watched as the police Riot Tactical Unit approached. They were good and knew their stuff. The unit was mobile and adaptable to changes in any crowd situation. If the threat appeared behind or to one side of the unit, the line faced that direction and became the front of the unit. Each line of officers covered each other when the team moved or changed positions. When the unit was under direct attack, the team no longer moved together. Instead, one line moved while the other unit provided firepower or formed a physical screen with riot shields.

Mic felt easier as she watched the riot team take their formation. She tugged at Slade's wrist and said, "Look, they're gonna deploy a square formation with the command team in the center."

Slade nodded, "Yeah, it's bad and they're obviously predicting it'll get worse. They're not taking chances, and besides, we gotta get the rescue crews in there to see if we have survivors."

Mic shook her head and looked around. "Look, Slade, there are no survivors. No one is moving. They're all dead," she said, her voice final.

Slade watched the crowd as Mic watched the riot squad. She noticed a thin, skeletal man who sat on a bench and smiled into the crowd. He was the only person in sight who wasn't running, sobbing or screaming. She recognized him from the police artist's sketch. It was the man with the caved-in head from Busy Burger. The crazy guy who'd poisoned the school children.

She left the little girl in charge of the baby carriage and ran to Slade. She whispered in his ear and pointed her finger. "There he is. There's one of your poisoners. Sitting there on the bench, grinning like a Cheshire cat."

Slade followed her finger and barked into his phone. In a matter of moments the man was surrounded by six Richmond uniformed cops, guns drawn, as he sat on the bench chewing popcorn, watching the "show" as he described the death, murder, and mayhem that surrounded him.

He laughed an evil laugh and waved the police away as he held a vial of poison in his right hand. "Don't come any closer. If you do, I guarantee all of you will be dead in fifteen seconds," he promised as he leered at them.

Slade moved closer to the man. "Put the vial down," he said in a steady voice as he took a step closer. "If you don't put it down, I'll kill you," he threatened.

The man laughed a long, hollow maniacal laugh. "You think I'm worried about that? I just want to watch the show a few minutes longer. Then you can take me in, shoot me, or string me up on a tree. I don't care."

Slade was incensed by the man's laissez faire attitude and lack of respect for the dead and dying. "We've got five bullets aimed at your brain. Put the vial on the ground next to the bench."

The guy shrugged his shoulders, smiled and said, "It ain't gonna happen." He reached into his shirt pocket and popped something into his mouth. He gave Slade a maniacal smile and leered at the uniformed officers. A few second later, he slumped over onto the bench.

"What's goin' on? Did that SOB poison himself or something? Is he dead or is it a trap to throw the poison on us?" one of the uniformed officers asked excitedly.

Slade hesitated a second and looked for signs of chest movement. There was none. He moved next to Boris's body and said, "Yeah, he's dead. I guess he took his own poison." He turned his head in disgust and looked at his men. "What a chickenshit." He pulled a glove and evidence bag from his pocket and picked up the vial.

"Don't touch the body, Slade," one of his men warned. "For all we know the guy's radioactive. We need HAZMAT and biocontainment people in here."

"They're already here. In the beer tent," an officer yelled.

Slade grimaced and said, "Yeah, send them down here. This bastard looks a little yellow and may be glowing a bit." He looked over at the beer tent and saw the riot unit had made great gains in crowd control in just a few minutes. The crowd was quieter as hundreds of medical personnel gathered around to care for them.

Mic checked her watch. It was seventeen minutes after one. The massacre had lasted only seventeen minutes. She was shocked.

***

Snake watched the entire scene from a small grove of trees about fifty yards away. He turned to leave, to vanish in the chaos. He wondered how in the hell he was gonna get paid. Boris was dead and he had no idea who he'd been working for. Boris's death hadn't been part of the plan, at least not a part he'd been included in. He hoped his handlers would manage to find him and give him his money. He moved quietly near the lake, taking cover wherever he could. He wanted to cross to the other side, but someone grabbed him from behind and stuffed a rag over his face. *What the hell...* were the only words Snake uttered before his world went dark. He didn't see his captors and didn't know they communicated using hand signals. The major turned to one of his men and said, "Good catch, man. We'll turn the heat up on this asshole until we know everything he knows."

Chapter 67

Richmond, Virginia was under lockdown. The governor had mobilized the National Guard and a curfew remained in place. No one cared. The Old Dominion was in a state of shock over the deaths of seven hundred of its citizens out for a day of family fun at an art festival. Business and commerce had ceased to exist until the FBI and RPD completed their joint investigation. Downtown was a ghost town and the financial district was devoid of human life. The crackling energy of historic Shockoe Slip barely sparked. Michaela had reopened Biddy McPherson's bar, aware that people needed a place to decompress and put events into perspective. It was important to remember life as it had been a week before. More importantly, Richmond needed to move ahead and plan for the future. A long summer faced the city and Mic knew the spirit, zest and vitality of the Southern city would emerge again.

Mic remained at Dottie's Monument Avenue fortress. Her home, still a designated crime scene by the Richmond police, was scheduled for cleanup at the end of the week. She was happy to stay at Dottie's because she wanted to be close to Cookie and Henry to be sure they were coping with Dottie's illness and the changes in their lives. Also, with Angel finally home from the animal hospital, it was wonderful to know Cookie was available to check on him if she had to leave.

Michaela curled her legs up in an easy chair, cup of coffee in hand and looked onto Dottie's manicured terrace. It was a beautiful sunny day, a perfect day to be alive. The roses and lilacs were in full bloom. Everything was calm and peaceful. Dottie's XM radio was turned to a soft classical station. The scent of wisteria permeated the room and the glass panes in the French doors glistened in the sun. Mic closed her eyes for the first time in five days and didn't see death or feel terror. She breathed deeply, reached down and stroked Angel's ears. She was lucky, and she knew it. The people she loved were alive and getting well. Lots of others couldn't say that.

Her thoughts returned to the weekend. How could it be that only five days ago two maniacs had murdered over seven hundred men, women and children? They had changed lives and the image of Richmond forever. She shook her head as terror returned to the pit of her stomach. She looked down at Angel. He was resting comfortably. The vet had given him pain medicine and antibiotics and he was a little better each day. The dog had made a remarkable comeback, his leg was healing well and his kidneys seemed to be on the mend. Mic prayed his kidney function would return to normal. Angel was on a diet with limited protein so Cookie couldn't feed him prime rib for every meal like she wanted. Nevertheless, she'd managed to find him some incredible bones. Mic hoped he'd feel more like eating tomorrow.

Dottie's door chimes sounded in the center hall, the sound pure and celestial in the quiet home. Someone was at the door. She heard Henry's chair scrape the floor in the kitchen as he rose to check the security monitor in the butler's pantry.

He walked to the door and said, "Michaela, it's General Rothrock. You want me to get it?"

"No, Henry. I'll run and answer it. I'm sure he's checking on Dottie." Michaela rose from her seat and walked down the hall to the front door. General Stuart Rothrock stood on Dottie's front porch in full dress uniform.

"Good morning, Michaela. How are you?" the general asked.

Mic smiled at Stuart Rothrock. "Come in, General. This is a pleasant surprise. I was sitting in the garden room. I just returned from Angel's vet visit so he's back there with me having a short nap."

General Rothrock smiled. "Oh, that's wonderful, Michaela. I know how worried you were about him. He's a pretty incredible dog."

Mic smiled happily in said, "Incredible is only one word of dozens I can think of. How about some coffee? Cookie has fresh coffee in the kitchen and she just baked cinnamon buns."

The general smiled and said, "Aw, to be truthful, I can smell them. I wouldn't miss any food at the countess's home ever. Cookie is the best cook I know."

Mic nodded and ten minutes later, Michaela and the general were seated in Dottie's garden room overlooking the terrace. Angel remained on his pillow but dutifully thumped his tail to acknowledge the general's attention.

Mic and General Rothrock sipped their coffees in silence for a few moments. "How are you doing with this, Mic, all of the terror stuff?" he asked. "It has to be hard."

Mic nodded her head and said, "All right, I guess. It's still so vivid in my mind. Every time I close my eyes, I see people dying all around me and I hear their screams. I feel the chaos and the pandemonium of that day. I'm suffocated when I remember the crowd in the tent." She paused and met his eyes directly. "I'm sure it'll go away at some point."

The general nodded slowly. "It'll fade, but it will never go away. But it'll take some time. You need to take good care of yourself in the meantime. If you need something to help you sleep, you should check with your physician."

Mic nodded and said, "Yeah, I thought of that. Honestly, General, it's the worst thing I've experienced in my twenty years of law enforcement. I've never felt so useless and helpless in my entire life as I did a few days ago."

The general nodded again. "You've experienced a terror attack, firsthand. You'll get better, but you must take care of yourself and by that, I mean exercise, sleep, eat, have fun and realize the answers aren't at the bottom of a wine or whiskey bottle. Find something to believe in. That's exactly what we tell our soldiers. This isn't any different, trust me. It's the same." He paused and added, "PTSD can be experienced by anyone. The military doesn't have a monopoly on post-traumatic stress."

Michaela nodded. "Yeah. I know. Had you ever heard of the guy that took the suicide pill? Slade told me the FBI had determined he was the mastermind of the attack."

The general nodded. "Yeah. We've known about him for years. He was recruited to make poison for the Soviets before the fall of Communism. He worked for them as a young man fresh out of medical school. His name was Boris Koliensky and his nickname was 'The Dart' because he always made poison darts. He ran the Russians' chemical and biological warfare lab for years. He specialized in the development of chemical and biological weapons, primarily stealth poisons. A very competent and efficient killer."

"He was a doctor? I'm stunned," Mic said.

"Yeah. His dossier suggests he was quite brilliant. He also had a PhD in chemistry. Of course, all of his patients were the ones he killed injecting poison. He was reportedly a genius, but he was crazy, a diagnosed psychopath in fact."

Michaela nodded. "No question, General. He was insane. How're you coping?"

General Rothrock smiled. "I'm well, Michaela. I've about got my mother's estate settled, and as soon as her house is on the market, I'm heading back to Florida."

"That's good. I know you'll be glad to get back to your life." Mic munched a cinnamon bun and said, "It's only been a week since Camilla passed away. This last week seemed like forever."

"That it did," the general agreed. "Fortunately, like in most things, my mother made things easy for me." He paused and added, "She always did, you know."

Michaela smiled and touched his hand. "I'll tell you one thing, Dottie is gonna miss her. They were tight. They walked together, went to the gym, out to lunch. It'll be hard for Dottie, but we'll help her."

General Rothrock nodded. "I know. I was out at Wyndley Farm with the congressman and Kathryn yesterday afternoon. Kathryn promised to keep her eye on Dottie as well and will come to town more often to see her."

Michaela nodded. "That's great. Dottie will love that. She loves to spar with Congressman Lee and she adores Kathryn." She paused for a moment and continued, "What's Adam think about the terror attack here?"

Rothrock held his eyes with hers. "He's incensed, as you can imagine. Adam Patrick Lee has been the one consistent voice in Congress who has warned about Russia's duplicity and escalating power. He wasn't surprised at all. Angry, as you can well imagine."

Mic pondered this for a moment and asked, "Do you think your mother was simply caught up in the events at the Madison at random, or do you think she was targeted? You seem to have a history with the Russians."

General Rothrock laughed and contemplated his response. "I've thought a lot about it, and I'm fairly certain the attack on my mother was random. She happened to be at the wrong place... purely coincidental," he said as he locked eyes with her. "But the attack on Richmond, I'm not sure."

Mic looked at him steadily, "But... I know there's a 'but'. Are you giving me the official version? I can see it in your face, General."

The general picked up his coffee cup and took a sip as he contemplated his answer. "There's a 'but' Mic. There's always a 'but' you know."

Michaela nodded. "I know."

"I don't know why the Russians attacked Richmond, and we don't know why they sent as valuable an asset as Boris to Richmond to kill a few hundred people. There are dozens of other Russian killers who are younger and stronger who could have done that – assets who didn't have the value and skill sets of Boris. That's what puzzles and concerns us."

"Are there theories?"

"Yeah. Of course. There's always theories, lots of them. I'll present a couple this afternoon at the debriefing at the FBI building. You're coming, correct?"

Michaela nodded. "Yeah, Slade's picking me up. You do know, don't you, that the other guy was involved with a human trafficking case in Richmond earlier this year?"

Rothrock nodded. "Yeah, I know. The guy's a mercenary, a 'heavy for hire' as they say. We know who he is. He's a Russian national who's been living off and on in the US for years. He's a thug, an international assassin. But he's skilled, tough and evil. He always works for the highest bidder. He goes by 'Snake', last name is uncertain. He has dozens of aliases."

Mic smiled, "Not surprised to hear that. He has a snake tattoo on his hand. That's how I recognized him."

The general gave her a grave look and said, "I'm worried about you, Michaela, because he came for you and this is the second time you've beaten him, or at least bested him. It's personal for him. He'll come after you again and again. I want you to know that and be prepared. He's in the wind now, but he'll be back. It may be six months or longer, but he'll be back. Get another dog, upgrade your burglar alarm system. Increase your weapons. Hire a security consultant. Get married. Do whatever it takes, promise?"

Michaela gave him a tight smile. "I'll be as prepared as I always am. I already have the best residential security system available and the guy dismantled it like it was a child's toy. He's tough, but I promise you, General, I'll be on my toes and I will get a security consultant. I'll have the guy down at the RPD, Big Dawg McGraw - the officer that runs the surveillance – check on stuff for me. He's the best."

"That's all I can ask, Mic," General Rothrock said as he stood to leave. "Also check with Adam Lee. They've got state-of-the-art security at his farm now since the attack against him."

"Good idea, General. I'll do that," Mic promised.

"We're looking for him, there's an international manhunt and we'll find him. When he surfaces, we'll let you know."

Mic nodded and said sweetly, "Why, General Rothrock, I thought you were retired?"

The general flashed her a smile and said, "People like me never really retire. We simply fade away and resurface from time to time."

Michaela smiled as she walked the general to the door. She noticed the two men in suits waiting outside Dottie's mansion for him. "I'll see you later," she said as she pecked him on the cheek. *He's a good man. And he's nowhere close to retired. I'd bet Biddy McPherson's on that.*

Chapter 68

A few hours later Mic twitched in her seat in the conference room at FBI headquarters. She saw the people around the table were the same group who'd met a week ago after the poisonings at Busy Burger. She wondered if they felt as defeated and useless as she did. She looked around the room and was overcome by a sense of failure. She'd had enough terror discussion and wanted out of there. She dreamed of going down to Biddy's and tossing back a couple of Irish whiskeys. *But first, I'll go by and make sure Angel's okay and then check on Dottie. She was on a roll a couple of hours ago.* She listened to Special-Agent-in-Charge Burnley as he reviewed the case frame by frame. He showed slides of Boris's lab the police had finally located over on Porter Street. The slides were of lab equipment, cigarette butts, a bloody sofa, and a large fish tank with dozens and dozens of dissected fish. Mic tuned off her brain and looked out the window. Her attention returned as someone asked Peggy Grey a question.

Dr. Grey said, "Folks, we've identified the poison used on Saturday. As best we can tell, the killers injected the poison in lethal amounts into the hoses leading to the beer kegs contaminating the kegs and hoses with poison.

Slade asked, "But, why did so many people die? They were only serving beer for about fifteen minutes."

"That's true," Dr. Grey said, "but the level of toxins in the beer was lethal. Based on laboratory tests, we believe the kegs were initially poisoned on Friday evening and then additional poison was added on Saturday morning prior to the beer tent opening. So the beer was extremely toxic."

"Yeah, it was." Chief Herndon added, "The RVA brewery had at least twelve guys pulling the tap handles and they had eighteen taps on the truck. A couple of the other breweries had four to eight guys pouring. That's a lot of beer poured in a short time. Folks were lined up for the beer. Visualize eighteen plus men pouring beer as quickly as they can."

Burnley added. "That's true and a couple of the beer managers admitted to pre-pouring beer a couple minutes before one o'clock so the first round was already available. No waiting. Folks drank what was poured. So, in some respects, it could have been a lot worse."

Mic shook her head. She couldn't imagine worse.

A FBI agent added, "Yeah and remember, a couple of the small breweries were offering flights, just a couple of ounces of five or six beers so they were available in small two or three ounce cups. I saw lots of people sharing a flight of beer."

"Peggy, what was the poison? It must have been pretty lethal stuff to kill so many people so quickly," Mic commented.

Dr. Grey exchanged glances with at Dr. Duncan and he signaled her to go ahead. "Michaela, you're right. It was very lethal. In fact, the poison used last week is one of the most lethal poisons in the world. It was Tetrodotoxin and it comes from a fish, most commonly found in Asia."

"Ah," Slade said, "so that explains the fish tank."

Burnley was surprised. "A fish? A poisonous fish killed all of these people?"

Dr. Grey nodded. "Yes, specifically a puffer fish and a small blue octopus. The poison, Tetrodotoxin or TTX as it's called, is a potent neurotoxin that interferes with the movement of body fluids. It's particularly effective on nerve impulses and produces muscle paralysis almost immediately. This prevents the diaphragm from moving and the victims can't breathe so they die."

So you suffocate to death. Anger surged through Mic.

"But… how can it be so lethal? There were a lot of dead fish, but honestly, it was just one aquarium," Slade asked.

Peggy continued, "It is one of the most lethal poisons in the world. Tetrodotoxin is extremely potent and found mainly in the liver and sex organs of puffer fish, globefish, some amphibians and octopus. Human poisonings occur when the flesh and organs of the fish are improperly prepared and eaten."

"How much does it take to kill a man, or precisely, several hundred men?" asked Chief Herndon.

Peggy shook her head. "It doesn't take much. The blue-ringed octopus secretes the same tetrodotoxin as the puffer fish. Research suggests that less than an ounce of tetradotoxin can kill up to ten or twelve adult men. We speculate a similar dose for the pufferfish."

There was silence in the room. No one spoke around the table.

"To put it more in perspective, it takes very little to kill an adult. And there's no antidote. Injected, as little as 1-2 mg will cause death, making it one of the more lethal substances known to man. Consider that a drop of water is about 50 mg, so what that means is that 1/50th of a drop of water will kill you. Unbelievable, isn't it?" Dr. Grey added.

"So, it's more potent that cyanide?" Slade asked.

Peggy nodded. "Oh, yes. Much more potent. It's estimated that TTX is 1200 times more toxic than cyanide."

Slade shook his head.

"Man, that's some powerful stuff," one of the FBI agents said.

Dr. Duncan nodded. "Yeah, it is. Very lethal. Very hard to harvest, but Boris had the training, knowledge and expertise to do it. He used poisons to assassinate; in fact he developed poisons for stealth assassination."

Michaela racked her brain. She'd heard of puffer fish. "Isn't puffer fish considered a delicacy in Japan?"

Dr. Duncan nodded and said, "Yes, it is. It's called fugu. Many people have died from eating fugu, another term for puffer fish, usually about a hundred or so a year. Japanese chefs train for years to be qualified to prepare the fish. The first symptom of a toxic fish is numbness around the mouth that spreads and affects voluntary muscles. Then the person's respiratory center shuts down and he can't breathe. In fact, it is believed an assassination using TTX occurred in London just a year or so ago."

"So, why Richmond? Why did the Russian's attack Richmond?" Slade asked FBI Special Agent Burnley.

Burnley spoke up and said, "I'm going to defer to General Rothrock."

General Rothrock stood and spoke for the first time. "We're not sure. We do have several theories. One is they're angry at the RPDs crippling of the Bratva's East Coast human trafficking organization a few months ago and this attack was in retaliation."

"Bratva? That's Russia's organized crime syndicate. Not the government, right?" a man asked.

General Rothrock nodded and smiled. "Now, that's a good question. Even though each group pretends to dislike the other, the Russian government and Bratva are in bed together. "He paused and continued, "Another thought is that Boris had ties, possibly family ties, to the Bratva official, Dimitri Kazimir who was shot and killed by the Richmond police. There's a backstory that suggests Boris was an orphan but some speculate he was Dimitri's son. We haven't been able to validate that yet. It's possible Boris attacked Richmond in retaliation for Dimitri Kazimir's death, in essence, for killing his father."

Slade shook his head. He wasn't convinced. "Does that mean Boris acted alone?"

Rothrock shrugged his shoulders. "We don't know, Slade. It's possible, but we don't know. Boris was a valuable Russian asset. He'd created chemical and biological weapons for the Russian government for years. Why send an asset as valuable as Boris to kill a few hundred Americans? We are still investigating this. We've still got lots of unanswered questions."

"Any other theories, General?" Chief Herndon questioned."

Stuart Rothrock shook his head. There were other theories, but he wasn't able to share them due to national security. "Not really. Just that it was a terror attack. Perhaps to show us that if they can attack two hours from the Nation's capital, they can hit Washington, D.C." Rothrock paused for a second and added, "But make no mistake, the message is clear. It's not over. They'll be back."

Burnley interrupted and said, "We've got to remember that other U.S. cities have been attacked by terrorists without any reason other than the convenience and contacts of the terrorist. Look at San Bernardino and Orlando."

Herndon nodded. "What about the other guy? The one that got away? Do we know much about him?"

Burnley shook his head. "Snake. Not a lot. He's a mercenary and he's been around for years. He's a killer. We don't think he has ties to any one group, but he is a Russian national. We're looking for him," Rothrock replied in a matter-of-fact voice. "He'll turn up."

Michaela felt fear settle in her chest. She knew he was right. And Snake would come back for her. Perhaps Madame Toulescent had been correct all along, and she'd refused to listen. Boy she was dumb sometimes.

One Month later

It was a beautiful June day and Kathryn Lee, her granddaughter, Alex Destephano who was home from New Orleans, Dottie, Michaela, Margaret, and Margaret's granddaughter, Allison, sat with Cookie outside on Dottie's terrace feasting on shrimp salad, fresh asparagus, fresh-baked French bread and chilled white wine. The mood was festive.

Dottie was doing well and in great spirits. She was in physical therapy three times a week but found herself stronger and more agile each day. She looked over at the younger women and heard Alex invite Mic and Allison to Wyndley Farm to ride horses later in the week. Margaret and Kathryn were in deep conversation about the latest news of General Rothrock. Cookie looked at her and said, "A penny for your thoughts, Countess."

Dottie smiled and said, "I'm happy to be here today. I miss Camilla dreadfully, but I think she's with us today, right here at this dining table."

Cookie nodded and smiled as Kathryn Lee broke in and said, "Isn't that what life is, Dottie? None of us ever really goes away. We all simply become a part of each other. We pass our knowledge, wisdom, education, philosophies and so on to others through human contact. That's what life is." She nodded towards Michaela, Alex and Allison. "They'll be us in thirty or forty years. They'll be sitting around mourning the loss of someone and they'll realize, as we have, that the person is never really gone. They live in our hearts forever."

Dottie nodded as her eyes filled with tears. "Ah, Kathryn, that's so very true and I believe this is the first time I've ever realized that. Thank you." She turned to Michaela and said, "I want to go with you and Allison when you go to Wyndley Farm. Can we arrange that, Kathryn?" Dottie asked with a smile.

"Sure, you're always welcome. Will you be riding as well? I'm sure I have a horse you'd enjoy."

"Oh no, she can't ride," Mic blurted out.

Dottie raised her eyebrows and gave Mic the frostiest look she could muster. "Excuse me? Oh, yes I can ride." She turned to Kathryn and said, "Yep, of course I'm gonna ride. I always do," she said to Kathryn as she saw Mic open her mouth to object.

"Dottie, no way you're riding until you're stronger," Mic squeaked. "Over my dead body," she insisted.

"Then lie down and die because I'm going," Dottie insisted. "And, remember, Michaela, we're still partners so don't cut me out of any cases that come along," she cautioned. "I'm almost fit as a fiddle again and I have a big hospital bill to pay."

Mic shook her head and smiled, "We'll see, Dottie. No time soon, though."

Dottie protested in her uppity countess voice. "I'm going riding, and I'm solving crimes, starting next week." she said defiantly and said, "Remember, Michaela McPherson, I've saved your life *twice* this year."

Michaela grinned at everyone around the table and said, "Well, she's back and she's as big of a pain in the ass as ever," she announced.

"I'll drink to that," Cookie said as they raised their glasses up in a toast to Dottie.

Mic drank her wine. *Things were always about friends, life and love. We're all gonna be fine. Just fine. Life is good.*

The End

To Be Continued...

Want to read more about Mic, Dottie and Angel?

We hope you enjoyed reading book two in the Michaela McPherson Mystery Series, ***The Case of the Dead Dowager***.

Next up is book three, ***The Case of the Man Overboard***.

In Book three Mic, Dottie and hero dog Angel cruise the Mediterranean for a much-needed vacation. Michaela, Dottie and Angel take on Big Pharma when a research scientist takes a "tumble" overboard.

If you'd like to join my mailing list and receive updates on the latest news and releases visit www.JudithLucci.com

Have you read ***Shatter Proof***? It is the story of Dr. Sonia Amon, a Syrian-American physician and daughter of an ISIS terrorist who is constantly stalked and hunted by her father.

Made in United States
North Haven, CT
02 April 2025

67519166R00215